After cancer, then a stroke, losing 40 per cent of my brain, I then had a whole year of weird epilepsy. Attacks every two months on the same day with hallucinations, discovered a skill to write, even though that part of my brain is missing.

Interestingly, Charles Dickens, Agatha Christie and Lewis Carol had epilepsy.

Graduated in politics and philosophy at Hull University.

Have three children; one is at Manchester, studying drama ambition father-daughter Bafta for the same movie/screenplay.

My brain is like a pack of cards where each card is a memory I can access and generate a new story every day; in the last two years, have drafted 49 books across multiple genres.

My family, friends and NHS that helped when I was ill.

Andrew Charles

NATURE VS NURTURE

Diary of a Serial Killer

AUSTIN MACAULEY PUBLISHERS™

LONDON • CAMBRIDGE • NEW YORK • SHARJAH

A CIP catalogue record for this title is available from the British Library.

ISBN 9781035847204 (Paperback)
ISBN 9781035847211 (ePub e-book)

www.austinmacauley.com

First Published 2024
Austin Macauley Publishers Ltd®
1 Canada Square
Canary Wharf
London
E14 5AA

Prologue

A serial killer is someone that has killed more than three people in a repeated fashion and their characteristics are typically anti-social behaviour, psychopathic, narcissistic and paranoid and often very good at hiding these qualities from others.

Most famous UK killer, Jack the Ripper 1880s, real name unknown.
Most famous USA killer, Ted Bundy 1970s.
Most prolific UK killer Harold Shipman estimated 250 deaths.
Most prolific USA killer Charles Cullen estimated 400 deaths.
It is believed there may be 50 serial killers at large at any one time.
Rhona Smith wanted to set a record and not be caught. She was thinking 500.

Chapter 1

Paul and Emma's life appeared to be perfect for their friends. They had met while at Kingston University during their first term and had been besotted with each other after that meeting, often to the exclusion of their other friends. Interestingly, they did not meet at a university-arranged event but while they were shopping in the local shopping mall. The Bentall Centre Kingston; is a typical 4-storey shopping mall with a mixture of shops dominated by the principal shop Bentall's, which was established in 1867 by Frank Bentall and now opened as a shopping mall only the month before in 1992.

Having been a particularly wet and miserable December, the shops were busy, the first dry day in the last five. That Saturday was grey and overcast with a cold icy wind and the sun's absence was depressing. Paul's mood was low; he could do with some sunshine and hoped Christmas shopping would raise his spirits. It was just before the end of the term. He was leaving the menswear section of Bentall's having bought his father socks and pants for a Christmas present when an attractive blonde lady was busy with her mobile phone and not looking where she was going and walked into him.

"Oh, I am so sorry." Emma was embarrassed, her face flushed bright pink. The two 18-year-olds were giggling. With Paul being so much bigger, it was like Emma had walked into a wall but a flesh and bone wall but not as hard or painful.

"You can buy me a coffee if you like to make it up to me," said the male student. The young woman sheepishly looked away, avoiding eye contact. She did not want him to know she thought he was incredibly good-looking and reveal how much she would like the coffee date.

"Maybe I cannot afford to buy you a coffee," she said as Paul glanced at her Christmas shopping bags.

"Really?" he said.

"Yes, I am only a student and I need to be sensible of my loan money," she responded.

"OK, where are you studying then?"

"Kingston," she snapped back. Her response was quick she was still getting over the disappointment of missing out on a Russell group place by two grades. Her father had tried to appeal that Emma's mother had begun her treatment for breast cancer that final year during her exams, but although they were sympathetic, the institutions were full for her course.

"It is funny and a small world. What are you studying?" asked Paul.

"Art and design," was her reply.

"Well, must be destiny because I am doing architecture at Kingston. When did you start?"

"Just finished my first term."

"Me too. OK, let us get a coffee!" Paul looked her up and down and realised he was immediately physically attracted to the girl. "I want to know more about you and you can tell me what have you bought?" as Paul looked at her bags as they queued up to get a coffee, they both ordered lattés and before she had put her card in the machine the money had already gone from his account.

"Thank you!" *Very smooth*, she thought to herself. They grabbed their coffees and found a table. "I thought I was paying?" said the naturally blond young woman.

Chapter 2

Paul just shrugged his shoulders and gave a big, broad smile. His teeth were perfect and white; *they must be veneers,* she thought. "You have amazing teeth?"

"Just lucky I guess; but the home whitener kit I got helped and of course my face is still brown and hair bleached from the trip to the Caribbean just before the start of term, which is making them stand out," he paused. "I did not do so well in my A-level but my younger sister did wonderfully well in her G.C.S.E's and as a reward, they took us to St Lucia where we learnt to dive it was fantastic like being an underwater astronaut!"

"What, the Pitons? I have dived there, by the way!" Emma wiped her mouth with her napkin.

"Yes," said Paul.

Emma dropped some sweetener in her coffee and stirred it. "Looking at the volcanoes was interesting!" She peered into her bag.

"I have book tokens for my dad and a diary, lounging trousers for my younger sister, *Sega* games for my younger brother's Sony *mega drive* and new dressing gown and diary for my mum, although did treat myself to a new dress for the Christmas thing before end of term," said the attractive young woman.

"Are you going?"

"Of course, chance to meet hot women!" he began to laugh.

"Oh, we have the St Lucia connection; I Have a black tie from a cricket function last year, although may have bulked too much over the summer to fit My Jacket, have just enough time to shred before the ball hopefully for it to fit." Emma reached out and touched him on his chest.

"Wow, very firm!" They both laughed again.

Paul hung his coat over the back of his chair and then brought his right hand up to tough his right shoulder like a bodybuilder in posing pumping blood into the contracted bicep. Emma touched the firm, impressive muscle through the cotton material of his black *Star Wars* t-shirt. Emma took off her coat and flexed her biceps through her very worn white *Choose Life* T-shirt.

"OK, just as impressive. How often do you train?"

"Three times a week gym and twice a week on the water as I row and scull; it's my legs and bum that are really impressive." Her face reddened again as by boasting she had embarrassed herself.

"Maybe you can let me have a closer look purely for scientific purposes?" and they both started to giggle again.

Emma took a big mouthful of her drink then spoke, "Although it's actually the jaw muscles that in unison are the strongest in the body but with all the chatting, we probably don't need to worry about those."

"Sounds like your shopping has been productive. Where are you from?"

"I am a local girl so do not need to spend money on accommodation, Teddington." Emma took another sip of her coffee. "I just jump on the bus or train." She looked across at the hunky man. "It is my time to grill you. Where are you from?" as she bit into her cake, revealing the cream filling.

"Wandsworth and decided easy commute on the train don't need halls either. I only applied to London colleges because I am captain of a cricket team did not want to abandon the club as I run winter training and I also coach little ones on Sunday mornings. I have a mate that lives in Kingston so can crash at his from time to time; do not need halls either; especially if it is a late one." Paul winked.

"Show me your bags, then?" looking at the branded plastic carriers. Paul started to laugh as he opened them. As he laughed, Emma looked at his teeth; *it is amazing how attractive you can find someone just from their mouth*, she thought.

"It's a long running joke with my dad because they named me Paul." He reached into the carrier bag, revealed striped designer socks and put them on the wooden table.

"Socks are nice," said Emma. She looked puzzled as to what the joke was, as socks are often a present; she had bought her dad many times. Paul picked up on the expression on her face even though she did not voice her thoughts.

"Yes, but my surname is Smith, hence the joke. Also!" he put the socks back in his bag and placed a pack of five the *Star Wars* pants on the table. Emma began to giggle. "My dad loves anything sci-fi so either *Star Wars* or *Star Trek*; both my dad and I are into geeky sci-fi and I collect comics. I also got my mum a dressing gown and my younger sister a *Top Shop* gift card!"

"OK, so that's *Captain Kirk* and *Jean-Luc Picard* and *Jedi, Luke Skywalker*, that is not really my thing I am more a romance although have enjoyed the *Alien* movies and *Abyss* and adventure movies like *Indiana Jones*!" Emma said.

"OK, on that theme, what romance films?" he questioned and leant closer to her, showing genuine interest and drank some of his coffee.

"Well, I loved Roxanne the comedy with *Steve Martin* and *Daryl Hannah* but my favourite film of all time is *Jean De Florette* and the sequel *Manon De source*. They are French with subtitles but I am fluent, anyway." As she finished speaking, she smiled.

"Well, maybe you can invite me around to watch them sometime; although my French is only fair?" looking at the lovely girl.

"Oh, I do not own them!"

The muscular young man took her by the hand and spoke, "You finished your drink?"

"Yes!" the girl looked puzzled. He took her well-manicured hand and led her down the escalator, entering the famous music shop. While she was browsing.; he was at the till with two VHS tapes. She came up with her music tape *Now that's what I call music '23*.

After she finished her purchase, Paul wrote his name number and address on the *HMV* receipt for the two VHS movies. "Merry Christmas even if it is a few days early; if you're not doing anything, tomorrow come over to mine and we can watch together?"

The girl was still thinking. "Your quite sure of yourself that two VHS tapes can get you a date," replied the natural blonde girl.

It was clear these two young students were of like minds, both physically equal no one could claim anyone was punching above their weight. That meeting did not just raise his spirit for the day or week but for the rest of his life.

The Sunday was romantic and the emotion of the movies led to them having sex. "You are only the second boy I have slept with but it just felt right!" She went to get out of bed and started putting her clothes back on!

"You are amazing and, like I said, I needed to see your arse for scientific purposes only." Paul smiled and Emma approached and pretended to slap him by grabbing his face and slapping her own hand.

"You're a cheeky bastard. I must go but let us do dinner in the next few days, come over to mine in Teddington; I will cook; do you have a diary?"

"Yes, over on the table!" The black leather diary had the first two pages designated to contacts. She found a space and using a blue pen and wrote:

Emma Love of My Life.

Mobile: 0789 5678905

25 Hampton road, Teddington.

"OK, my house is a ten minutes' walk from the station. Let us say 730 Wednesday evening." They kissed and they both carried on, thinking about each other constantly for the next three days.

Paul was on the train from Wandsworth to Teddington, he pulled out his Nokia 101 from his denim jacket and dialled Emma's number. "Is that Emma, the love of my life?"

The girl at the other end of the phone was uncontrollably laughing. "Just at the station. See you in ten."

They both felt the powerful chemistry.

Chapter 3

He knew she was the one after they had made love. The physical connection was amazing. It was also the post coital conversations about life and their dreams and aspirations.

Emma had already told her mother I think I have just met the man I am going to spend the rest of my life with. Irene Rawlins was a retired history teacher and was secretary of the Teddington rowing club. Paul nervously knocked on the door of the imposing Victorian house. He walked past the Mercedes SUV parked in the well-lit drive. The large wooden blue door opened and the attractive lady that Paul had made love with three days before was looking great in her blue jeans and simple white blouse and black heels.

Wow, she really did have a great butt as he followed her into the house, he remembered how good that peach looked naked. The hall's floor was the original black-and-white tile and it echoed under the noise of Emma's heels clicking along. The walls on either side were covered in framed sporting photos of the family, with rowing pictures on one side and rugby and cricket pictures on the other side. Under each side of pictures were several small shelves with a collection of trophies.

Emma had warned him it was her chicken risotto but more importantly, her mum Irene and her dad Spencer were joining them as she wanted them to meet him already. A grey-haired, stocky middle-aged man and glamours woman appeared from behind the imposing staircase. "This is my dad Spencer and this is my mum Irene," the blonde wig and make-up hid the 6 months of chemo treatment. "Mum and dad, this is Paul."

He put out his hand and zoned in on her father, there was a very firm handshake and Paul spoke, "Pleased to meet you, sir!"

He immediately turned and was greeted with a kiss on the cheek from Irene which took Paul by surprise. "Let me show you through to the dining room," said Spencer.

Paul was interested in the trophies. "If you do not mind first?"

OK, those are three I won over the years at Henley and those two are Emma's and those three with Teddington rowing club. "Oh, so you row on the none tidal bit of the river above Teddington lock."

Irene's face revealed the impressive nature of his knowledge. "Do you row?" inquired Irene.

"No, my thing is cricket and skiing."

As the word cricket came out of Paul's mouth, you could tell Spencer wanted to join in the conversation. "At school, my friend rowed and explained it as, like you, Kingston grammar's boat house is located higher up the river."

"Kingston grammar, we have a future Olympian the headmaster told us in James Cracknel, he has just won a medal at the junior world championships," said Paul.

"Do you still row, Mrs Rawlins?" he continued.

"Yes, to keep fit, but Emma is the star now, just missed out on the England squad before left knee problems restricted her full potential." I see their trophies on the other side. "There are some from my rugby and cricket days!" said Spencer with a beaming sense of pride.

"What, sir?"

"Opening batsmen, son!"

"Are you still involved with the club?"

"Yes, I coach. I still play cricket in the fours now but playing days for rugby are gone."

"I coach and involved with Battersea Ironside Cricket Club so that is why I did not want to go university outside London."

"Can I take your coat?" said Irene.

"Yes, please!" Paul took his backpack off and out of.

It he revealed some flowers and quality French wine; the flowers he handed to Irene. "Wine for you, Mr Rawlins." He had impressed the future in-laws with his polite demeaner.

"Nothing for me?" said Emma, looking disappointed. As her parents walked into the other room, leaving them on their own. Paul reached into his back pocket of his black jeans and produced a large 135g bar of *Galaxy Caramel Chocolate.*

"Come here!" He took her face in his hands as he started to kiss her.

The kiss took her breath away and she felt his tongue in her mouth she felt weak. "Wow, let's go eat!" as she regained her composure.

"Where are the other two?"

She pointed upstairs. "My brother does not like chicken risotto so had something earlier and now in his room glued to mega drive you can meet him another time and my sister is on a sleepover."

Over dinner, they realised Paul had bowled his future father-in-law out as Paul was a good fast bowler. Having his debut in the adults at a young age. They were all tucking into the homemade crème brûlée when Spencer got up. "Give me 5!" and left the room. Spencer went up to his study and dug out the old score book. "There you go," and placed the tattered book on the table. "Spencer Rawlins 5 runs three dots, a lucky 4 and a one, bowled Paul Smith. I remember my teammates gave me grieve that a schoolboy with a clothes designer's name had clean bowled me although you did take 2 more wickets, I got the grief as Captain."

"The food was amazing and your mum and dad are cool. See you later fancy another movie day at mine, next weekend. I will go into *Blockbusters*?" This time, it was Emma that initiated the passionate snog. She waved at Paul as he turned left towards the station and out of sight.

Emma sighed with a content sense of happiness and although the first term had gone well, it was the first time her disappointment of not getting into Durham had left her thoughts. Emma returned to the kitchen to get her parents' feedback on the young man. Irene and Spencer were drinking coffee in the kitchen, sat around the large antique oak table. Irene had removed her wig, which upset Emma walked in to see her mum without hair. "It will grow back, darling. Well, what do you think?"

In unison, "He is fantastic, darling!"

Paul Stood up and gave his oldest a hug. "I give you my permission to marry him."

Chapter 4

The following Saturday, instead of going to watch Chelsea with his mates, Paul spent the day with Emma and they had a movie marathon comedy, drama and romance, *Wayne's world, A few good men and The bodyguard.* A Chinese, a bottle of wine and sex. As they both laid in Paul's bed, after their exertions. "I don't want to scare you but I love you!"

Paul smiled and looked at her in the eyes. "Me too."

They got engaged at the end of that first year at university and 6 months after graduating in a small ceremony at Richmond registry office and reception at Teddington Rugby Club where her father was still involved; Emma Rawlins became Emma Smith. The autumn wedding was a bit different being November. For their honeymoon, they decided to go skiing. Emma was keen to learn what was all the fuss about as Paul constantly went on about it. Their honeymoon was delayed to combine Christmas and New Year into the trip, making it magical.

Paul was a patient teacher being a coach and with Emma's leg strength and general sporting Prowse, she took to skiing like she was born to do it. Courcheval was perfect Emma showed off her GCSE French to the appreciation of the locals. On that trip, Paul bought her a mug with Courchevel on it and her hobby started.

Chapter 5

5 years later, with the end of the century approaching, they owned a big period house, with the distinctive half hexagon shape bay windows and wooden sashes associated with Edwardian houses. Paul's parents were older parents so they sold their large house and moved into a small apartment gifting him and his sister their estate before their death to avoid legitimately the substantial inheritance tax.

By the time they reached their 5th wedding anniversary, Paul's dad was dead and his mum Lavender now lived with them in a granny annex attached to the house. Being just off Wandsworth Common, both Paul and Emma ran around it or the Clapham common park run on a Saturday morning's only 5 minutes away. Their house was one of the few houses in the road not split into flats. They rewarded themselves for their hard work with amazing holidays, as their business had grown from strength to strength. Diving in the Maldives for their 5th anniversary and skied every winter in France.

With their hard work, Paul's skills as an architect and Emma specialising in interior design, combining both their skills was the key to their success. However, as their other friends began having children, it just compounded the heart ache behind the scenes. Emma hosted fabulous dinner parties, as she was an excellent cook.

They were hosting a dinner party to see in the new century. Emma stood next to the fridge, getting the deserts ready to take through to the dining room. Emma's red wine glass was half full and her eyes matched the colour of the alcohol. Julie, a big brunette that was a junior architect in Paul's office, entered carrying her wine glass. "Hi, I have been sent in about another bottle."

Emma wiped the tears from her cheeks and pointed to the wine fridge. "Whites at top and reds at bottom take one of each!" she sniffled.

"Oh, darling, are you OK?"

"Yes, fine." She avoided eye contact. "Paul wants us to continue trying for a baby but I keep losing them!"

"Oh, sorry, I didn't realise. Danny and I are thinking of getting married as we been talking about kids, especially as meeting your friends and what 5 kids between those two other couples?"

"Yes, it's 5," and Emma burst into tears again. Julie put her glass down and gave her a big bear hug. Their friends would talk about their kids. She watched full of melancholy as one of their friends waddled around Val d'isere, 6 months pregnant sitting in coffee shops one easter while her husband skied with the group. Emma had helped with the group's other kids on the trip and it focus her mind about next steps. She had miss carried three times.

Chapter 6

It was a pleasant Sunday morning in May with the large folding doors open onto their generous garden. Emma had been melancholy for the last two months and was staring into her black coffee, debating as to whether to add sugar; she had put on weight as she had not felt like going to the gym and could not remember the last time she was on the water and was almost slipping into depression. Work had been so busy Paul had not noticed the change in his wife's mental wellbeing.

Paul was just washing his breakfast bowl in the sink. "Oh, I am a numpty; I am washing my bowl in sparkling water." He was daydreaming and not switched the setting on the multifunction tap to hot water.

Emma was sat on a chrome and leather stool at the square island with the black granite worktop in the high-end designer kitchen looking out to the lovely garden. "Darling, why do you not put it straight into the dishwasher?"

"Because it was Muesli and it always ends up with some stuck without a pre-wash and surely that is the point of this flash tap, darling."

Emma took a deep breath. "I want a child desperately but maybe it is not meant to be!"

Her eyes reddened and the tears began to flow. Both Paul and Emma were into fitness and you could tell because he wrapped his strong muscular arms around his wife to comfort her. Emma reached for a *Kleenex* out of the box on the kitchen worktop and blew like the sound of a trumpet to clear her nose and wiped away the tears from her cheeks. "Honey, with the two rounds of IVF I have failed to carry a baby to term 5 times, I cannot cope physically and emotionally."

"But it only has to work once!" was Paul's response before realising the emotion of the moment. His statement was right but it lacked sensitivity.

"OK, I will make a deal with you; we try one more time after that we adopt." Paul took a sip of his tea and took two chocolate hobnobs out of the packet and handed one to his wife. With a mouth full of Hobnob, he began to speak again with some of this biscuit, landing on the worktop out of his mouth.

"If we adopt, can we find a child that looks a bit like one of us?" Emma nodded confirmation as she brought her white mug with a blue Palafore lift, Tinges branded cup to her lips. He picked up the cloth and wiped up the biscuit spit off the counter.

Paul had been collecting car parts for cars he was planning to restore. He had learnt car mechanics from his father plus his collection of 2000 Ad comics.

Paul's father Donald would get his son the *beano* kids comic but then the newsagent gave them the newly released comic in 1977 by accident.

This happened when Paul was three and Donald then read it and kept buying the science fiction comic from then and continued long after Paul no longer wanted to read the beano. As Paul got older, it was something they both read together. When his father Donald died, the collection was over 2100 issues. Emma collected mugs and had over 60 souvenir mugs from every French resort they had been to. They were both passionate people about each other; their work and hobbies. They so wanted to give this passion to in raising a child.

Chapter 7

6 months later, after the emotional conversation in the kitchen and the last failed IVF. They found themselves on a different path to getting a child.

Janice, a grey-haired lady in her sixties, had overseen this branch of Bernardo's for many years. She had dedicated her life to her job as her husband had died young when a faulty bit of scaffolding meant the young bricklayer had fallen to his death.

The sadness of losing her love had been compensated well by the insurance claim that proved the famous house builder was at fault and it would enable her to buy her council house and put her one child, her son and one granddaughter through private schools. She may have been from a humble background but Janice understood the importance of a good education. It had paid off her son and granddaughter both had successful lives in Hong Kong. It was the autumn of 2001 and had been a nice summer but they were still childless.

The Smith's paperwork had been filled and back ground checks carried out. They fitted the profile for good prospective parents. In the room were several children from ages 3 to 7. The room was a typical child's playroom. It was brightly decorated and numerous shelves with books and toys. The walls were covered in paintings done by the children. Two teachers were supervising. When Janice Stephenson opened the door, most of the children stopped what they were doing. The older children knew what it meant.

Many times, a child would leave with whoever entered the room and not return. Only two boys playing on a popular computer game did not turn around. Another little girl was doing a jigsaw puzzle of the little mermaid and a boy that was constructing a castle from Lego. There was a little blonde-haired girl in the corner with bright blue eyes. Paul spotted her immediately as she looked just like the pictures his mother-in-law Irene had shown him of Emma as a child.

They were both mesmerised by how cute the little girl looked. They had not been aware that the little three-year-old in pink dungarees and yellow socks was surrounded by dolls and action figures; all the toys were missing their heads.

Little Rhona spotted them looking at her and stopped what she was doing, got up and ran across the room. She started to hug Emma around the leg and sat on her *Nike* trainer.

The little girl looked up towards Paul and Emma. "Are you going to be my new mummy and daddy?" She gave a big smile, revealing the one baby tooth that had still not properly arrived.

The sentence melted Emma's heart she was the one.

"OK." Janice pulled Rhona off. "We will see, young lady. I need to speak to these lovely people first."

"Is there a problem?" questioned Paul. The little girl obeyed Janice but her reluctance to move from the clamp around Emma's leg was on her face and in her vice like grip with her skinny legs.

"Let us go to my office I will explain the circumstances of why she is up for adoption."

In Janice's office, she opened the metal filling cabinet and searched alphabetically until she got to Rhona's birth surname Nicolaescu. The office reminded Paul of the headmaster's room at school, apart from the poor quality of the desk; when he had been called to his room for communication and given the nod, he was getting the head boy position. The grey-haired woman pulled out the brown folder and opened the folder and placed it on the basic teacher's desk. It contained her birth certificate and information on her parents and her only other living relative and some newspaper cuttings. They did not think what Janice had shown them should make a difference but conceded they would meet up with Rhona's biological aunt Lilly first before the adoption was official.

Chapter 8

Paul and Emma were waiting at the *Starbucks*. "Do you know this company is from Seattle in the United States and is the most successful coffee company in the world now over 4000 stores and the name comes from the character the first mate in the classic novel Moby Dick." Emma looked her husband inquisitively as to why he had said that and squeezed his hand.

The King's Road shop in Chelsea and was the first store location for the United Kingdom. The now famous coffee shop was just 5 minutes away from their own shop. Paul and Emma felt it was better not having the meeting in the office with the other staff around. "What made you mention that bit of useless information now, you nerd?" as Emma leant over and gave her husband a kiss on the cheek.

"Just super nervous and my brain is all over the place!"

"Thinking of frazzled brain; if I had got those extra UCAS points, I would have gone to Durham and every chance we would not have met, fate is funny."

Paul had picked a table at the back to give a perfect view of the door. They were munching muffins and drinking lattes when the striking 5 feet 10 woman walked in with her natural blonde hair tied up in a tight bun. When Lilly had email over her picture, they thought she was winding them up. Paul was looking at the picture of the woman in her police uniform that he had printed off. Lilly played rugby in women's metropolitan police force team and could have been a professional, if her passion for crime had not taken her into the police.

Paul looked at the picture Lilly had emailed him. He turned to Emma. "That's her."

He walked from the back of the cafe. "Hi, Lilly Boswell."

"Paul Smith," as he thrust out his right hand.

She shook his hand but knew she knew Paul worked out and could take a firm handshake. She thought to herself, *it was nice to meet men that were physically her equal.*

"What can I get you?" asked Paul.

"Erm, a cappuccino, please," replied the imposing woman.

"Any cake?" he asked.

"OK, millionaires' shortbread. Please."

"Large Cappuccino and two Large Lattes and two millionaire shortbread please!"

"Name, please?" asked the barista.

"Paul," Paul ushered the women over the table.

As they approached, Emma got up. "Good afternoon, I am Emma, pleased to meet you."

The two ladies shook hands and Paul went back for the drinks. "More cake, darling," and Emma laughed and Paul patted his clearly flat stomach. The three of them sat down and started to talk. "I have to say I am sure this has been said many times?"

Before Paul could finish, Lilly started to speak, "Yes, I am the spitting image of *Charlize Theron*, the Hollywood actress; my boss joked I should write to her as a stunt double, being so strong and the physical resemblance!"

The three of them laughed and any tension from the meeting was broken.

"Also!" the tall lady began to speak and took a black-and-white picture of her mother, Rhona's biological Romanian grandmother, out of her black leather jacket pocket. As the Smiths looked at the picture, "Unfortunately my parents are dead, as are Rhona's fathers so she has no biological grandparents to visit!"

Clearly, if Rhona had either her aunt or grandmother's genes, she would grow up to be beautiful. "Let me start, what do you do and why do you want, little Rhona?"

Emma could tell Lilly cared for her niece. "We met at university I am an interior Designer and Paul is an architect and we own and run probably the most successful home renovating companies in London *DAY DREAM HOMES* with clients from Chelsea to Weybridge and our office is 5 minutes away, just next to Marks and Spencer."

Emma paused and Paul took over. "Above that success is our desire to have a family."

Lilly was quite sympathetic to Paul and Emma's miss carrying problem. Lilly took a deep breath and sighed. She reached out and took Emma's hand.

"Rhona's mum was my identical twin, Anna; when she died and I became her guardian, I knew I could not give her the right home as my career was going to be my priority and a 2-year-old was too much responsibility. I am not really the maternal type."

Lilly talked with them for another thirty minutes, explaining about the circumstances and about Anna and Gregor, Rhona's father. Lilly had only one request, could she visit and take her out now and again. They both agreed they would like that. Janice wished them well after they signed all the relevant paperwork and the three-year-old left with her new parents. Janice was particularly fond of Rhona above all her residents as she looked through her family photo album when Rhona left.

Janice asked, "I would love if you encouraged her to visit sometime." Although it was not until she was 16 when Rhona finally went back to visit the orphanage.

Chapter 9

Emma and Paul felt complete with this wonderful little thing. She was very precocious. demonstrating advanced abilities. Sometimes she would stay in her room more than they would want but as they thought it was understandable, she was adopted. Three different psychologists had all said nothing to worry about. There was a clue that the little girl was different when Rhona was 4. Emma's PA Magda spoke, "There is the headmistress on the phone, apparently there has been an incident."

"Can you find out what the problem is?" said Emma.

Magda spoke, "Mrs Smith is in a meeting; can I ask what it is regarding?"

The stern sounding headmistress of the nursery school spoke, "A goldfish has been killed; we have spoken to Gus and Rhona, they both say it was the other one that took the fish out of the tank and put it in the floor to die; we are disturbed as you can understand by the incident but have no evidence of which child did it."

After that incident, Paul and Emma watched Rhona closely but saw no evidence of anything wrong apart from some obsessive-compulsive disorder. Lilly visited her niece frequently and every now and again, Lilly, Emma and Rhona would go out together. Sometimes Paul would join them but felt like leaving them to make it a girl's day out. The latest psychologist they took her to see said that the staying in her room was maybe to do with being adopted a term called Adopted Children Syndrome and nothing else. Although did not appear to demonstrate all the characteristics associated with these conditions and not to worry.

As Paul and Emma sat in the psychologist's office of Donald Peterson. He had placed several puzzle tasks for Rhona to complete, including organising cards with different criteria as quick as possible and classic Mensa tests with sequences and number maths problems and spelling and word recognition. Her IQ was super high in the genius range. "I think the obsessive-compulsive disorder is just a by-product of her high IQ. They often go hand in hand," explained the psychologist.

Rhona bonded with her mum in cooking and learnt how to cook and would watch *The bake off and master chef* with her. Rhona's relationship with her father centred around his hobby for classic cars and comics and together they rebuilt an original 1970s Porsche 911 from three different cars, using parts from all of them. She liked the mechanic's overalls and understanding how things worked. Her ability to absorb information meant she could as easily make a French pavlova or strip and change cylinders in an engine.

Rhona also shared her adopted parent's passion for reading. Summer holidays with her parents dominated by Scuba diving/snorkelling and reading it was on one of these trips Rhona formed her idea why villains like to have secret lairs and she knew she would come back to Thailand in the future having visited the fictitious villain Scaramanga's hide out location just off the coast called *James Bond Island* because it was where they filmed for the *1970s James Bond* movie *Man with a Golden gun.*

Chapter 10

Rhona was obsessed with crime and serial killers; she must have watched everything on *Netflix* and *Amazon Prime* and read everything she could get her hands on about crime. She always wanted book tokens for presents. Her favourite fiction authors included *James Patterson* and *Martina Cole* and Classics Like *Agatha Christie. And Sir Arthur Conan Doyle.*

Her grandmothers Irene and Lavender both called her by pet name since a baby, as Rooney, Paul's mum Lavender also thought it was weird for her choice of books in her room. "Rooney darling," said her grandmother Lavender, "who's book is this.?"

"Those three on that shelf are *Mein Kampf,* the book that Adolf Hitler wrote and the two next to it by Karl Marx, *Das Capital* and the other one is the communist manifest written with joseph Engles," Rhona paused. "Thing is, granny, if you want to understand the human condition, you need to study political theories and religion."

Irene had taught history and political history so knew the books. "That is why the shelf above is the Bible and the Koran?" Lavender Smith asked. "Why not A *Harry Potter* darling? You also have lots about crime."

"I just love crime, granny and I do have an aunty that is in the police." Rhona noticed it was often the smallest details that led criminals to get caught. The darkness had been growing now for years. She was 16 when she realised her beauty was an asset and her mind was a powerful weapon. Rhona was tall and strong and had taken martial arts. It was easy to think she was not adopted because facially she looked like Emma and physically she resembled Paul.

They told Rhona she was adopted when she was 8 and they were both surprised how, as a matter of fact, she took the news like it was no big deal. "You're my mummy and daddy!" she said and that was the end of any further debate.

However, Rhona was intrigued by how she had come to be adopted but would find out in time. They had not explained the details of how she had become adopted, just that her mum and dad were not around.

Although Rhona could easily go onto do philosophy or politics degree because she had read so much even before she was 16. However, the future choice of pharmacological degree would give her better access to chemicals and drugs. She somehow knew she had a calling; a dark destiny to fulfil.

Chapter 11

Courchevel French Alps, December 2016

The Smith family were on a French Skiing holiday located in an up market fully serviced skiing chalet called Chalet Delight with 6 rooms with the ski in ski out on the main green run back into Courchevel 1850, the Bellecote. Emma and Paul were checking out the lounge that had a fresh vanilla smell in preparation for the guests. Rhona took their equipment to the boot room.

They looked around the main room chalet featured a large open plan lounge with a traditional fireplace at one end surrounded by a stone hearth and mantle with a stack of fresh logs, three large sofas facing all in different colours, a very eclectic mix that the designer thought worked very well in the colours she had picked for the room. The fire place and a large oak table with matching 12 chairs set around it.

The ceiling had large wooden beams supporting the floors above and a double glass door on the left that led to a decked balcony with built in jacuzzi. The wooden open stairs that lead up to bedrooms and another set that led down to the boot room, laundry and front door. A wooden door next to the stairs that gave access to the kitchen.

Rhona emerged from the boot room. "This looks nice."

"It should do, it's costing enough," said Paul.

"Darling, don't put a damper on things," and Emma and Paul hugged as they were just teasing each other. The only thing that Rhona liked from the balcony off the lounge was the view, not the built in jacuzzi. Rhona was happy to be covered in the blood of her victims but the idea of a jacuzzi disgusted her; the concept of soaking in other people's germs, dead skin from exfoliation that would clearly take place. Her interpretation was dead skin was just dead, whereas blood was the liquid of life.

Rhona went outside. "The view is great, but there is one of those horrible germs spreading hot tub things."

Paul laughed. "Well, we are here to ski not bath so not a problem, Rooney."

With 10 other guests and a private chef and two chalet girls, Georgina or Georgy as she was known and Ruby. As the Smith family had come by overnight Eurostar, they were the only people in the chalet on the first morning. The other guest coming by plane would not arrive until the afternoon when their transfer arrived. Paul had pre-booked their lift passes, they could take advantage of quieter slopes on the Saturday as most tourists would not have arrived. It was the third night of their stay when David, the chef, was feeling unwell.

"Can I help? I am a good cook," asked Rhona.

The food that Rhona produced was magnificent and the guests gave Rhona a round of applause. A small man started to talk, "I would like to give a toast to our stand-in chef, our fellow guest Rhona Smith."

There was a clinking of glasses and a cheer and a big sense of pride for Paul and Emma. Rhona could not have hoped for a better result. The small man he approached Rhona. "What do you do, young lady?"

"Just finishing my A-levels this summer, then university, applying for pharmacology."

"Well, I think you should train to be a chef as I would fund your restaurant, as finding talent and funding them is how I have made my money."

"I am flattered, Michael and I will give it thought even if not now but maybe for the future."

The next day, the Smith family got up early to maximise the slopes at their best as it was warm and the slopes were slushy in the afternoon. They just stopped for early lunch. Her father Paul was just trudging back, struggling in his ski boots with the blue plastic tray of food and her mother with the drinks. Rhona removed her Oakley helmet, Rhona needed everything to match.

Her sunglasses and watch were Gucci and her ski outfit was Prada and all her ski equipment was Head until that first day they arrived and her expensive head helmet had been broken; she had dropped it and it rolled into road. A stupid man had driven over it in his car. "Fucking twat," was the words she shouted. She tried not to dwell on it; the shop had ordered one in for her and she had rented the Oakley one in the meantime.

Chapter 12

She removed her goggles and gloves and put on her Gucci sunglasses to fully soak up the altitude sun. Rhona removed a travel size tooth paste like tube from her jacket pocket and squirted some greasy sun cream from it and rubbed it into her cheeks. She was about to put more lip balm on when she stopped herself, because they were about to eat. The strong sunlight and wind chill at altitude her cheeks and lips were felling sore.

Most of the establishment was laid out with rows of picnic style tables apart for the front row that did not have picnic tables but had deck chairs facing the direction of the sun with the material of the chairs in stripes of the colours of the French flag. *All I want for Christmas* started on the speakers giving the guests music to entertain them. Her mum and dad were in deep conversation about Christmas songs. Emma thought *White Christmas* by *Bing Crosby* was the best, whereas Paul was more contemporary and was torn between *Last Christmas* by *Wham* or the lesser known *E17 Stay another day*.

There were surrounded by other picnic tables, probably half full with other skiers that had the same idea of an early stop. The café was playing English/American music, even though it was a popular French radio station. Most of the records were of Christmas. The D.J. announced in French, "I hope you enjoyed my favourite Christmas song from the fabulous Queen of Christmas *Maria Kerry.*"

Rhona had been tapping her foot to the iconic song. Plus, people sitting in the stripped deck chairs equally enjoying the sun. Two people had got up from their chairs and started to dance, well it was 23 December. Her parents sat down. "What you chatting about?"

"Our favourite Christmas songs," said Emma.

"OK, I reckon *Fairy Tale of New York* by the Pogue's and *Kirsty MacColl,*" said Rhona.

"Good call. Although sad she died by being run over by a speedboat, but pushed her son out of the path of the boat, saving him," said her father.

Rhona thought for a moment before reaching out and touching her father on the hand.

"On the topic of protecting your child, is there anything I could do that you would not protect me from?" said Rhona.

"No!" But *what a strange question,* he thought but let it drop. Over the years, the three of them had interesting philosophical debates about the existence of god and the rights and wrongs about the death penalty. The latest debate was the right to identify as whatever you liked. Paul was not religious and did not believe in God, but did respect others' beliefs in a god but about the LGBT community, they had a trans man that was assistant to Emma, previously hired as Debbie but now called him Derek.

For Rhona, how you identified was not going to make any difference to her plans. How a person identified was irrelevant, as Rhona had developed her own criteria to be selected for her 500-death club. Paul started to eat his spaghetti bolognaise, he began to speak. Paul then changed the subject from music. "I reckon, this is the most exhilarating thing to do!"

"What about eating spaghetti, daddy?"

"No skiing, of course!" Emma had just finished a slurp of French onion soup and took a bite of the cheese topped garlic crouton. "Maybe, but a good roller coaster is up there," and smiled.

Rhona was thinking it was killing but she would add to the discussion. "What about parachuting or base-jumping?"

None of which any of them had tried. Paul said, "You know what, maybe the three of us should give parachuting a go well, at least the tandem stuff?" The women both looked at Paul.

Emma responded, "Sounds like a plan, I will investigate it."

Rhona that had a mouthful of sandwich so put her hand up and made the thumbs up gesture. *Andy Williams* came on through the cafe's speakers. *It's the most wonderful time of the year* when she dropped the university bomb. Rhona was studying psychology and biology and chemistry A-levels. And it was thought she would take a pharmacology degree. Instead, she announced she did not want to go but instead go to a catering college. As Rhona took a bite of her toasted cheese and ham sandwich, the cheese oozed out, her dad spoke, "I don't understand we thought you loved science and your teachers say you will be getting A-stars."

Her dad would have stormed off but in ski boots, not really have the same effect. Emma jumped in, "OK, you are a great cook but surely, you're too smart to just be a cook."

"Last night David said he would speak to his boss and is a job for me next season and that businessman said he would help me start a restaurant."

"How about you apply, get a place, then defer it and get a job cooking and see if you enjoy it enough and that keeps your options open," said the family negotiator, the role Emma had always played when Rhona had demonstrated some of her worse characteristics.

"Maybe, but not even taken my exams yet," replied Rhona.

"Darling, if someone with your IQ cannot get the results, what hope is there for the rest of your class?"

Her parents were effectively approving of her to be in the Alps all winter if she could get a job. The idea of working as a cook in the Alps would form a massive part of her strategy Her first killing spree would be in the Alps even though she had already killed in London. Rhona had dropped something in David's diet coke, making him feel sick so she could jump in and help cook as she had done the night before.

Chapter 13

Earlier in the Year in Central London

The Old Bell was a traditional pub and, like so many, it survived by serving good food. It was located near the hospital so many of its patrons were people that worked across the road in the large medical facility. Rhona considered it was a good place to pick up a doctor. Dating more than one person at a time makes you a player but for Rhona, Simon and Angela were assets and future victims.

Her first kill started when the over tired young doctor had met Rhona. Rhona was sitting at the bar looking more slutty than glamorous, as she was showing cleavage and legs. The 17-year-old had nursed three diet cokes and eaten two packets of salt and vinegar crisps. Although her fake identification in her pocket said Rebecca Stephenson, 18, she did not need the landlord to be a possible credible witness in the future of her existence by showing her ID may make him remember her more should he ever get interviewed so stuck with coke.

The middle-aged landlord had asked her twice, "Are you waiting for someone?"

He knew she was very attractive but he was very happily married so he was not chatting her up. He had said many times before to friends you can appreciate art without ripping it off the wall. Dominic was taken back by the young woman's answer, "Fate." She looked at her diamond encrusted watch.

"That's a nice watch!"

"Yes, a present for my father."

She was about to give up for the night when the man walked in. Royston, the handsome young doctor, entered the Old Bell. "Hi doctor, your usual?"

"Yes, please I now have two days off, thank god!"

He paid for the drink and sat down he could not help but look across at the amazing blonde sitting on the mahogany stool. The pub had been busier earlier but it was late now and only probably 5 people in the pub. She got up just as the barman was giving the doctor his beer and in heels was almost 6 foot and brushed passed him and he could not help but smell her perfume he was immediately intoxicated with her but that unique smell.

She checked herself in the mirror in the ladies and pulled up her skirt to check and adjusted her hold ups. More lip stick and gloss, perfect she thought as she looked at herself in the dirty mirror. He was wiping the froth of the beer from his beard with the back of his hand, well, more designer stubble than beard, when she came back from the toilet and sat next to him. He was taken aback by the brazen nature of this woman. She crossed her legs and she knew he could see the top of her thighs where her hold ups ended and her white flesh was revealed in her short faux leather skirt.

"Do you mind? Are you a doctor?"

"Yes. And I don't!" he stammered.

"What is your specialty, as I am thinking of doing a pharmacology degree?" She looked the tired man in the eye while licking her red, glossy lips. Rhona thought potentially a great target to capture.

The young doctor looked at the girl. "Can I ask you a couple of questions first how old are you?"

"18," she quickly answered, although in reality she was 17 and continued, "Why is that a problem? What are you, 26/27?

"Yes, spot on, I have not decided yet!"

"Great! So, you're a man rather than a boy." He composed himself as this woman's confidence. "What is your perfume, its unusual fragrance?" Although not that being surrounded by disinfectant and anaesthetic smells in the hospital helped for her fragrance to make an impact.

"It is called *the Flower Bomb* by Viktor &Rolf." She then showed him a picture of the bottle on her phone.

"Wow, it looks like a pink grenade, is it explosive like you?" Royston was trying his best to flirt. "You must be a model because you're tall and beautiful?"

The first doctor she had tried to seduce was gay and not been interested in her. "Can I ask your name?"

"Yes, it's Royston Barrington—Beer!"

"That is a mouthful and unusual," the doctor shrugged his shoulders. "Well, Royston is the passed down name as the first-born boy, whereas my younger brother is just Mark and my old sister Daisy, which was my grandma's name!"

"Is your father that Conservative member of parliament and minister for the environment?"

Royston was not shy by nature but her knowledge put him at a disadvantage. Rhona suddenly realised she had made him think he was on the back foot. Hopefully, he would gain his composure because she wanted him to think he had chatted her up. He swallowed and regained his self-confidence. "Can I buy you a drink and what is your name?"

The landlord had gone to the cellar so she was happy to give her name out of his earshot. "Yes, please diet coke and its Rebecca Stephenson!" as Rhona put out her hand, "Please to meet you."

The landlord came back and Rhona had another coke. She wanted to start the killing and needed access to certain drugs, so adding a doctor to her list of relationships, to use his prescription capability. She was aware of common poisons contained in normal plants that you could grow in your garden but her requirements were more specific. She had done her research, there was a list of relatively innocuous drugs that could be combined or use for different purposes.

She had an estate agent. The beautiful black estate agent had been easy to seduce. Angela had found her the warehouses, more accurately lock-up garages, that she needed. Finding out she was gay was a bonus; they general would spend an evening watching Netflix and snogging and general pleasuring each other, Rhona always cooked for them at Angela's flat.

She explained to each of her lovers that revising for her A-levels was the perfect excuse for an inability to spend lots of time with them; although with her superior brain, Rhona needed no time revising as all the information she needed for her exams was locked up in her brain, ready to splash all over her exam papers. When she sat her exams, she finished writing and put her pen down at least 30 minutes before everyone else. Her third relationship was a project manager in the building until she was fully up and running, a body or two might end up in foundations, like a sixty's gangster.

Chapter 14

After exchanging numbers from that first meeting in the pub and some light banter. Rhona knew finding out what someone was currently watching on TV was a good starter to understand their personality. He liked to binge watch on his days off. His two-favourite series, like the rest of the world, had been *Peaky Blinders* and *Game of Thrones*. Interesting, he hated medical dramas and even comedy ones like *Scrubs* or *Green Wing*.

They agreed to meet up for the next date. Rhona was happy to go out for dinner; the next date they agreed in Chinatown in London and they would go Dutch as it was a convenient location for both. However, Royston wanted to impress her and insisted he would pay and by pulling some strings, using his father's name, he was able to get into the *Ivy* in Covent Garden. Rhona had to admit she did enjoy the food and took the opportunity to have caviar for the first time in her life.

"I enjoyed that; I have to say I have had saltier things in my mouth than that!" and winked.

Paul got embarrassed and tried to change the subject. "OK, I am looking forward to my steak!"

The ambiance was good, but she had wanted a less high-profile location. But as they were not celebrities, there was no reason for anyone to remember them having been there. Royston hailed a black cab and they were on their way to his for coffee.

As they rode in the taxi, Rhona thought to herself, *if he knew the underwear she was wearing, he would realise he was getting sex tonight*. She had prepared because she had a toothbrush and make-up wipes in her bag for staying over and regular granny or harvest festival pants, as she called them, because they gather it all in to sleep in. She always carried condoms.

Chapter 15

They entered the lobby of Royston's flat. "How do you afford such a central London location?"

Rhona noticed the security camera in the lobby and immediately put her hand up to cover her face and look down as they walked to the lift. There was a concierge desk but nobody was there. "Family money, although this flat is owned by my father!"

She got out of the lift and the doctor led her by the hand to his apartment. Wow, what an amazing apartment! It was like a showroom, a smaller version of her flat but in a more prestigious location. A large open plan room with L-shaped kitchen breakfast bar in white quartz and shiny gloss units then a white dining table to match the kitchen, then in the middle of the room a large designer L-shaped sofa from an exclusive Chelsea shop, Rhona liked the symmetry of the shape of sofa and kitchen.

The sofa was positioned to maximise the TV and fire, both of which were built into the wall, then between the sofa and TV was a glass coffee table with 5 magazines perfectly arranged so you could see the title of each magazine. The magazines represented a mixture of the current bestselling publications. Under the massive built in TV was a polished metal slit 2 metres wide by 20 cm high. That was the fireplace. The layout was exactly how she would organise the room. Rhona picked up the lighter and lit the bio fuel fire.

"Do you mind?" asked Rhona.

"No, it's great, the effect." The flames began to fill the polished metal slit.

"How big is the TV?"

"75 inch but, of course, as soon as I had that built in, they brought out a larger model onto the market."

"Would you like a coffee?" as he turned on his *Nespresso* machine.

"Do you have decaffeinated coffee as I need some sleep as I have an early start with my revising planned: How many bedrooms does this flat have?" as

Rhona looked around, taking in the choice of art and decoration as she was pirouetting on a heel.

"Two, with two bathrooms, plus a balcony and an allocated parking space and a resident's gym plus, as you probably noticed as we came in, a concierge service."

"OK, cool. Can I go out and see?"

"Yes, but it's a bit dark!" he could see Rhonda slide open the glass door.

"Is that Lords Cricket Ground?" inquired the blonde as she poked her head back in from outside. Even though it was late, the noise of being in the heart of London from cars and buses carried up on the air. Close to the door was a set of binoculars on a side table. Rhona picked them up.

"For watching the cricket!" said Royston.

Rhona laughed. "You sure it's not for perving on other people?"

"Yes, my dad is a massive cricket fan." Having taken in the view, she decided it was a bit chilly in the night air in her skimpy black dress, so came back in and slid the door shut.

"My dad played a lot of crickets when he was younger so got to watch him play and went to see some 20/20 games with him at the Oval in south London mainly," said Royston.

Rhona was going to mention that her father and grandfather were big cricket players and fans when she clicked back into focus, she was Rebecca Stephenson, not Rhona Smith. Rhona sat at the coffee table, looking through the selection of magazines. *Top Gear, The Economist Science Focus* and *Time*. Plus, *The Week;* Rhona began to read it so it was a selection of recent news stories, she thought *she may have to subscribe to that one.* "So, what is with the magazines?"

"It's good to be informed."

"I have been meaning to ask, why did you become a doctor?"

"Because of my uncle has a practice on Harley street and my father said to me with such an expensive education, you need to show it paid off."

"What school was that?"

"Chigwell in Essex!"

"Well, talking about education, from your diction, you must be a good school, perhaps a grammar or privately educated?" asked the doctor.

For the Rebecca Stephenson persona, she had picked her mum's old school because her mum had filled her with so much knowledge. For her date of birth, she had switched the date as if her birthday was the way it read in the USA. So,

Rhona Smith's birthday on the 5 September becomes 9 May for Rebecca Stephenson. "Yes, Lady Eleanor Hollis in Hampton Middlesex, which is a good private school," as Royston was pouring out her coffee.

"Do you want milk?"

"Yes, please a splash."

"So, my father said to go into city like him or go work with my uncle, which is going to be the plan after I have done a few years in the National Health Service; Longer term, my father would like me to consider politics!"

"OK, I have drunk my coffee. As this is our second date, do you want sex?"

Royston nearly choked on his coffee. "Oh my god, yes, you are so hot! But we literally just chatted for a little while in the pub last time." Before he had put theirs cups in the dishwasher and had turned away from her, she was stood in her bra, thong suspenders, stocking and heels. "Wow!" Her dress and bra were on the floor and her arms were crossed covering her chest, just.

"Take me to bed then, big boy!" As he came over, she jumped into his arms and let her heels fall from her feet before they had reached the bedroom. They clicked sexually.

Royston was lying on his back recovering from the exertions with his hands behind his head, feeling good about his performance as he was sure he was not going to be able to do a good job with her looking so amazing. Rhona was sat up on his groin with her expensive French seamed stockings and suspender belt still on but her thong was the other side of the room. With her heels, bra and dress still in the other room. "You have amazing boobs."

Rhona then pressed her boobs against his chest and kissed him on the forehead. "Well, if we are talking about physical features, you have the perfect size penis!" Rhona had embarrassed the confident doctor again. She then rose back up and dragged her finger along his chest as she did. "You have a pretty good body and good stamina!"

She left her finger lingering on his sweaty chest. I have always wondered about the design of the human body and the heart being so vulnerable as she poked his chest with her finger? "There are several flaws in the design of the human body but that is not considered one, as you have the sternum and rib cage to protect the organ; to damage the heart, you would need to penetrate just here between these ribs here!"

Royston indicated the sweat spot with his index finger. Rhona's knowledge of anatomy was as good as Royston with the amount of literature she had read but this was all part of building up the anticipation for her this kind of conversation she knew she would not always get the opportunity to have relationships or conversations with all her victims.

Rhona got up. "Do you have a robe?"

"Yes, borrow mine in the ensuite." Rhona put on the expensive navy-blue *Ralph Lauren* cotton robe. She grabbed her handbag that she had left on the breakfast bar and took out the facial wipes to remove make-up. She had put the toothbrush in as she planned this would happen. Rhona began to brush her teeth; she came back into the bedroom with white foam around her mouth.

"I have a question, have you ever cheated?"

"Yes, a couple of times obviously with this as he pointed to his good-looking face and physique woman often are attracted to me and I cannot say no but I think your different to any girl I have ever met." Rhona thought for a minute, she certainly was and Royston was very conceited and was going to be her first victim. She spat out the toothpaste and rinsed her mouth in the sink in the ensuite. "Where are you going?"

"I am going to have a snoop to get a better read on you!" She began looking through his desk. "What are these?"

Royston leant out of bed to put his head around the door.

"They are prescription pads; when I do my rounds or see an outpatient's if they need medication, the name goes here and either the patient or nurse takes it to the hospital pharmacy to get drugs."

Rhona opened his wardrobe and took out a hanger and hung up her dress. "Do you have a spare t-shirt I can sleep-in in that draw?" She pulled out a grey university of Oxford t-shirt. She put on her big pants. "Love the pants," as he started to laugh.

Chapter 16

They had both slept soundly in Royston's king-size luxury bed. The sun was shining through the window as the blinds had been left open. Before breakfast, Rhona had another look in the daylight at the great view of the home of cricket.

Royston was just handing Rhona her tea as she tucked into Weetabix, there was a buzz at the video entry phone. Paul had put a t-shirt and tracksuit on so Rhona could use his robe for breakfast. Paul had considered getting a second robe but thought it might make girls think he always have overnight companions, which of course he did, although it was logical to have a second robe as there was a spare bedroom. He thought it was easier to just have one. "OK, come up." The video phone cleared. "Sorry, my brother is popping in for a minute."

Paul went to His desk. Rhona watched her lover write Methadone on the prescription and his brother's name on the form and signed it and teared it off. The slightly worse for wear younger version of Royston entered wearing torn jeans but not the trendy deliberate ones, these were more from someone you would think was sleeping rough and a dirty jacket. He grabbed the piece of paper from his brother. Mark noticed the robe wearing woman. "New one," said Mark.

Rhona thought for a minute, it would be more memorable to introduce herself or not. "Hi, I am Becky," as she shook Mark's clammy hand.

He had run down his drugs and was desperate. "You should have seen me last week," said Royston, annoyed at his brother.

"Nice to meet you!" said Rhona. He was gone as fast as he had arrived.

"Sorry about that, Mark got himself into trouble and addicted to heroin and I have been helping him get off. And Methadone is a heroin substitute."

"He looks like you, although a little worse for wear."

"Yes, tried to get him to stay in another place dad owns but he prefers some dump in Lewisham."

Chapter 17

Rhona arrived back to her other flat and the two *Amazon* packages for Rebecca Stephenson were in her mailbox. She grabbed them. She poured herself some squash and opened a packet of honey coated cashews. She ripped open the cardboard packing as she removed the items. Then carefully tied her hair up and clipped into place and put the wig on her head.

Rhona stood in front of the full-length mirror; *Jessica Chastain,* eat your heart out or who is the girl that was in *Game of Thrones,* oh yes, *Sophie Turner,* perfect. Opening the other package, she took a handful of nuts and slipped on the blue tunic that was two sizes too big and the push bra that was three cup sizes bigger fully packed out to create the illusion. The busty red head nurse was unrecognisable from Rhona. The fake nurse would spend a week getting as many prescriptions as she could risk before the doctor was noticed as being missing.

Rhona was naturally right-handed but had spent hours learning to do everything left-handed, including writing to give her options. Because Simon was right-handed, she factored that in her planning in for Royston's future demise.

Chapter 18

Having mastered his signature over the next few months, it was time. Whenever they went back for sex, Rhona chose Rebeca Stephenson's flat because of the concierge and cameras at his flat. It was a shame that Royston was going to be her virginity kill because, in many ways, he was a perfect match with his fastidious nature and she found him physically attractive.

She had been dating the young doctor for several months. Her anticipation was growing to her first kill, like children cannot wait to open their presents on Christmas morning, but dark and sinister. Royston thought the sex was amazing and his anticipation matched Rhona's for the hot sex. She was the most amazing woman he had ever been with and there had been a lot. Rhona was able to juggle her three lovers with the excuse of revising, for Royston that was made easier because of his shifts. The other thing was Rhona loved sex too and Royston was a great lover.

She had wondered if initially was his understanding of anatomy that made him so good but it was his ego; he wanted Rhona to tell him she had cum, otherwise he never wanted to leave; she had lied at least twice as sometimes her thoughts of taking his life preoccupied her so she couldn't climax. She would soon discover killing would give her a small orgasm. It was a slight dilemma but it had been too many weeks and was a moment she had been dreaming about as long as she could remember.

She had cooked him his favourite dinner as a last supper with candles around the table and poured him wine while she pretended to drink the fine red wine; she did not want alcohol to cloud this night. She cleared away the plates, putting them in the dishwasher and then turned and planted to put a big kiss on him and then turned the light on in her bedroom. Get comfy and then she put out the candles on the dining table with her fingers. Giving a burning sensation on her fingertips, which she enjoyed. "I want to try something new tonight. Can I tie you up?" asked Rhona.

"OK!" he said; she dropped her pink silk robe, revealing the black Agent Provocateur underwear, push-up bra, thong suspenders and nylon stockings. She dangled the handcuffs in front of his face and he had drunk a few beers so was willing to let her put on the cuffs behind his head. I will get the wine and she left the room and turned up the music. Rhona enjoyed the irony of the song she had picked as the distinctive voice of the Canadian's Oscar winning song. *Every night in my dreams, I see you, I feel you. That is how I know you go on.*

Clearly, his heart would not be going on with the 6 inches of steel in it, the music would have covered his screams if he had been able to scream but she was too fast. He saw the shiny, expensive Japanese kitchen knife as she walked back into the room. He realised in a few seconds he had just made the worse mistake of his young life. "Sorry honey, you're just number one," as she plunged the knife deep into his chest with her right hand.

As the knife was entering his chest, the doctor knew such an injury was death and began to cry before his brain shut down from shock and pain.

The sharp blade had hit the sweat spot between ribs, avoiding the sternum. The precision matched that of the soon to be dead young surgeons' ability with a scalpel. The blood was everywhere Rhona was drenched in blood, the muscle of life was now just offal, it squirted her face in red liquid as its parting gesture; she wiped it out of her eyes before it stopped, she rubbed it all over face and ran her bloody fingers through her hair, the exhilaration from taking life was unbelievable.

The doctor knew he was dead even before his body had caught up with the blood loss to the brain and he passed out. The buzz she felt as she watched the life drain from his brown eyes was unbelievable. Unlike her lover Simon, his condoms were thrown away, whereas her other lovers used condoms would be essential, she had collected a significant amount of semen from his used condoms and they sat in her freezer in her real flat.

Although habitually she scratched both her male lovers back again, it was only Simon's she would go to the bathroom and carefully collect the skin cells from under her nails. A scratch on a lover's back was sufficient to capture samples. Even though this flat and the prescriptions were under false names, its details that get you caught and she had several strategies and options for future events. She spent the next two days cleaning the whole flat of any possible DNA.

She boiled her sheets; she needed a more practical kill room. She could turn the spare room into one but when her aunt gave her the account information and fully understood the scale of inheritance, her plan was altered and a bat cave/kill room could be created. She looked down at the dead body lying on the bed, she picked him up and placed him at the far end of the bath and cutting his femoral to allow remaining blood to drain from his body.

The white acrylic shower bath now had a red path, she climbed in and pulled the screen to her end of the shower bath and stood in with the body; she was still wearing her underwear but her stockings were equally blood drenched. These could be washed but she needed cheaper brand, not this expensive designer underwear. Most of the blood had gone.

She unclipped her stockings and took off her bra, tossing them on the tiled bathroom floor. She stepped out of the bath, turned off the shower but turned on the bath tap so the blood continued to drain from the dead body. She walked across the bathroom floor to look in the mirror and wiped the condensation away from the mirror. Her face washed now and make-up and blood-free. She looked at the beautiful blue-eyed angel. Could you tell she was a ruthless killer, I think not. The virgin killer smiled in the mirror to reveal her perfect white teeth, thanks to expensive dentistry.

She put on her robe after she placed the towel back on the rail and left the bathroom and calmly picked up her green cased iPhone and dialled. Her long blonde hair was still wrapped up in a white cotton towel and she poured herself a whisky and placed two chunks of ice in the glass. The ice cubes clinked against the fine cut crystal tumbler.

She opened a draw from the antique bureau and shuffled in the draw removing her favourite *Mount Blanc* pen and noted the details of her first ever kill in her pink diary. I think it will be 6 to7 years if all went well to complete this grand endeavour. She necked the alcohol and poured another one. "Wow, I am a killer!" And sipped and savoured the fine single malt red looking fluid for the second drink. She sighed, time to call Simon.

Chapter 19

"Simon darling, can I borrow your pickup on Monday while my car is in the shop? If I stay at yours tomorrow and take it, then?"

"Of course, my darling Becks, would I refuse you anything!"

With Royston in the bathtub, Rhona used his *Samsung* phone to call his boss. "Hi, is that Doctor Farooqi? This is Royston's girlfriend; he is totally sick, reckon he has flu, letting him sleep, I would assume he will be off all week."

"Thank you for letting me know, tell him to get better and not to rush back until he is 100 per cent," replied the senior consultant.

Simon had told her the foundations were being poured on Tuesday morning. She knew the building site had closed-circuit television but no security guards. She had a black hoody covering her head. Royston's emaciated body had sat in her bathtub since Saturday night, although she had hung him over the bathtub, so was fully drained of blood, reducing his weight and wrapped up in black plastic and grey gaffer tape. She lifted the plastic wrapped body. The plastic plus the concrete should protect Royston's phone, should that be the way she needed to go.

The corpse was hung over her shoulder. The rigour morticed body made it a bit harder as it was quite stiff. As she made her way down the corridor towards the lift, she was a bit wobbly and nervous because she had a body on her shoulder that she was totally responsible for. She pressed the button and entered the lift. The flat was on the third floor and the car park was -1, although the legend next to the button just said car park.

The car park had automatic lights so was pitch black apart for the far side that had escape stairs to the street and the car ramp up to access where the yellow from the high-pressure sodium street lighting was penetrating the dark as she stepped out of the lift it was like she was some god to quote the bible from Genesis said out loud, "Let there be light," and the fluorescent lights came on as she stepped out of the lift with the sensors from the lights above picking up her movement.

It made her chuckle to herself every time she did that. She knew, of course, there was no correlation between her words and lights working. She lifted the body up and carefully placed it into the back of the pickup. She pressed the fob and the gate to the underground car park opened. People saw Rhona's beauty and often did not notice her physical strength or intellect. It was Monday and according to the green illumination, the clock on the dashboard, said it was 2 AM when she arrived at the site.

She lifted the body of Royston out of the back of the black pickup and dropped the body shaped plastic bag into the deep trench. She heard the thud of the dead surgeon hit the ground. It was a very dark night, thick clouds so no stars or moon. There was not a breath of wind. She could not even smell anything, it was like someone had removed all her external senses. She could feel her heart pounding in her chest, the adrenalin was coursing through her veins.

The only light was her small torch. She got a metal ladder that creaked as she climbed down into the trench and covered the body a bit with the sandy soil. She did not need someone to discover it before it was covered with a ready mix. She felt a shiver, it was not the cold night air but the excitement of what she was doing. The keyring for the truck also had the key to unlock the site office.

The site office had the plans for the 60 flat apartment development. Using plans to calculate the exact position of the body and there was a project plan stuck to the wall plus on Simon's desk a kettle with biscuit tin and box of PG tips and jar half used of Nescafe gold also in the metal cabin was a small fridge just for the site manager.

The site workers had their own facilities in the metal container next to this one. On the side table, she pressed the eject button with her black gloved fingers and replaced the disc with a new one. Any evidence of a figure arriving in a black pickup at just after two am was now in her pocket and she put a new disc in the recorder. The footage would just be missing from 6 PM to 3 AM. She calculated the discs were only checked when there had been a problem or something gone missing on site, no one would notice the switch.

She relocked the metal site office and headed to the main gate and relocked the combination lock (the number was on a note written and stuck on the other side of the sun visor) for the gate of the building site and drove back to Rebecca Stephenson's flat. She parked the black Ford Ranger in the underground car park in the space two along with her Blue Kia Picanto. Flat 5 in the building was rented under the name Ms Stephenson and owned by some offshore account in the Cayman Islands and flat 3 two doors down were owned by Rhona Smith.

Both flats were identical, two bedrooms with a large double and a small double and open plan living space and two bathrooms, one with two doors. So, acting as an ensuite to the larger bedroom. When Rhona had taken her friends Belinda and Rose to see her flat, they were blown away. Especially as both girls would get a chance to live there in the future.

Rhona had learnt everything about lying and the tells that people give when they lie. She had practised in the mirror and had hours of footage until she was confident, she could make people think she was telling the truth when she was lying or equally make someone think she was lying when she was telling the truth.

Chapter 20

In the morning she left the underground carpark with an amazing sense of achievement. She picked up Simon in his truck. "Are you OK? You seem a bit fidgety this morning?" and kissed her on the cheek.

"Can we get coffee, just need some caffeine, did not sleep well, just think I am fascinated, never seen a concrete truck before doing its job." She looked away. She had watched many times before with some of her parent's developments and it was an inspiration of hiding bodies before the more practical, less risky freezer plan.

Originally, her idea was to have an *Indiana Jones* treasure map with the locations of all the bodies with names, time of kills but that would change with her inheritance. "I have coffee in my site office?"

Rhona made a face of disapproval as she arrived at the drive through. "My treat."

They arrived to site, just before the first concrete truck arrived. They both watched, sipping their coffees. Sitting on a pallet of bricks in morning sun with a Rhona wearing a yellow hard hat and the black one for Simon, showing his status as the qualified site manager. He knew he was not as academically intelligent as his younger partner, although he was proud of his construction diploma.

It was fortunate that Simon had big feet so he could lend Rhona some of his spare safety boots. Simon had taken a rug he had in the site office to make the pile of bricks comfier. "Are you comfortable enough?"

"Yes, fine!"

Most of the staff on site frequently wound Simon up on a Friday in the pub after work, how he was the luckiest bastard alive with how good-looking his girlfriend was. Two of these, Carlton, a Jamaican born carpenter and Rufus, a bricklayer from Swansea. The sun was just breaking through the clouds and a beam of light appeared to hit the trench as the splashing of the ready mix filled the base for the construction. The barrel turned with the sound of the truck's engine and the smell of diesel on the air.

She thought to herself, it was like a bizarre funeral service that only she was party to. The light made her think that if she was religious, then you could interpret the beam of light shining on the trench as Royston's soul going to heaven but Rhona had no interest in such religious nonsense. Humans are natural born killers and only modern society stops us from doing it. Too many wars, too many other killers prove that. She would become the ultimate apex predator.

Her brain flipped from that heavy philosophical argument of the rights and wrongs of taking life, she was in favour of the death penalty but only for murder, otherwise rapists had no deterrent for not killing their victims. Although hoped in the future, rapists and paedophiles would end up on her table if she could access the relevant information to locate them.

She was trying to think what would be the most fitting piece of music for this funeral service with one guest. She let that thought simmer in her brain as the strong coffee kicked in. She had asked for an extra shot that morning and then turned to Simon. "It must be quite satisfying watching the project develop," and began to smile.

She had measured the exact location of Royston's body by studying the site plan of the future apartment block but thought again it was dark, maybe she should check. "So, where do the apartments start?"

He pointed. She was correct in what she had entered in her pink diary. She had left enough clues that it meant Simon could be implicated as a rival lover if required or Royston's body buried under several tonnes of concrete or he would be just one of thousands of adults that just disappear every year in the United Kingdom.

She decided the piece of music was Shubert's *Ave Maria*. The piece of music composed in 1825 has made appearances all over modern popular culture in numerous TV and movies, including the latest version of *Batman* with *Robert Pattinson* as the lead. After the fifth and final truck had deposited its load, Simon turned to Rhona. "Where do you want dropping off and am I seeing you?"

"Yes and the tube is fine, darling. I am making chicken curry."

She would hit the hospital with numerous prescriptions before anyone realised the doctor was missing.

Chapter 21

"OK, see you later, Becks; you need to be quick jumping out at the lights."

Rhona entered the tube as she put her sunglasses in her bag. Hampstead underground, one of the deepest in London. She pressed her fake Rebecca Stephenson bank card to the reader and the barriers opened, there was only a woman she figured with two children under 4 waiting for the lift to come up. One child was sat in a push chair while the other was moaning. She began reading the adverts on the inside of the lift and it was for Chicago, the show that Simon had taken her to see.

Rhona was thinking how important Simon's role could be in the bigger picture. He was certainly a charming man and she had begun seeing him only three weeks before Royston and now Royston was buried in the foundations of one of Simon Brown's projects. Hampstead to Waterloo, which was normally her route back, but she was going to get off and go shopping for some vintage clothes at Camden.

Only three stops away on the northern line but thinking about other stuff, the doors were closing as she jumped up. "Fuck!" Tube doors closed. "I will get off Euston and come back."

Speaking to herself out loud, the girl opposite was laughing from behind the *Metro* newspaper. "The amount of times I have done that."

It annoyed Rhona for an instant but then lightened the mood. "It's so fucking annoying," looking towards the fellow passenger with a sarcastic expression. The other girl lowered her paper and smiled back.

She was just checking out a dress in a shop as she remembered going through profile after profile on the dating site, then bingo occupation construction site manager. The 32-year-old was a bit overweight, too many beers and he could not believe the attractive young woman had reached out to him. The fake info for Rebecca Stephenson had been deleted after she had met him, she immediately cancelled her profile and took down any social media related content. It was a risk, as this was potentially traceable.

She needed Rebecca Stephenson. As well as buying a dress, she got Simon a shirt. He was the perfect boyfriend and unknowing accomplice. She also preferred sex with men over women and now Royston was covered in concrete. She got a top for Angela and a gift, each for Belinda and Rose. Having so much money made life that much easier. She knew her friends liked jewellery and had got them something to celebrate this momentous day even if she could not tell them the reason for the gifts. "You are just the greatest friends!"

Rhona dropped her Camden shopping off at home before getting changed.

The attractive busty red headed character had gone to Royston's flat with his keys to enter his apartment and took the prescription pad, his phone and passport and car key for his car that was in the underground car park from the desk draw. She had deleted all pictures from his phone and the cloud that featured her, which took her an hour. She then made her way back to her home to change into the nurse tunic and flat white shoes and hunched over to make herself appear shorter. Then headed directly to the hospital and making her way to the dispensary and every day, she collected medicines with the correctly signed paperwork. Each day was a different fictitious patient.

Having got all the drugs she needed on the final day, she stayed with the big boobs and red wig and headed back to Royston's. It had been a productive week.

Chapter 22

Rhona now went straight to the carpark of Royston's apartment block. She had been able to access the car park by the emergency exit. The flash black Aston Martin with number plate DB 11 ROY in its allocated space. The car like the flat was family money, as Royston could not afford on a junior doctor's salary.

Wearing the red wig, Rhona pulled out of the underground car park as she was not sure what the camera would capture from leaving the car park. Within 5 minutes, she was on the Finchley road; the satellite navigation in the Aston said 45 minutes to the airport, straight up the M1. The sound of the finely tuned engine was making her want to speed but she stayed focused. She selected *Ride Like The Wind* by Christopher Cross from her music collection. The lyrics seemed appropriate; she had created her own driving playlist. 80s and 90s music was her preferred era of music.

If the police were on their game, they would find the car from the ANPR. The powerful classic British sports car made a seductive roar from the magnificent, more powerful 5.2 litre V12 engine, it would have been tempting to exceed the speed limits. Rhona was very much a petrol head but she did not need for her grand plan to be upset to something as silly as being pulled over for driving in her missing boyfriend's car wearing a wig. Her dad had allowed to take the 1970 Porsche 911 out once before they agreed it was too valuable to have on the road.

She arrived in Luton without a problem and followed the signs for long-term parking. In the car park, she got out of the luxury car and looked around to check no one was about and took out her overnight bag out of the boot and put her wig in the holder and changed her jacket. Thoroughly wiped down her seat and steering wheel and then put the used wipes and gloves in the overnight bag. She removed the special tape and pressed it against the key parts of the car. Walked across to bus stop K and waited for the bus to the terminal. She didn't have to wait long for the train back to London. Hopefully, the deception that he had run off with Rebecca was complete.

The Luton misdirection had not been a plan until she overheard him talking to his sister on the phone.

"My whole life has been about what dad wants for me but you know what, I love this girl so much if she asked me to run away with me, I would drop everything and go." As Royston put the phone down on his sister, he did not realise his girlfriend had heard his conversation. Rhona was supposed to be listening to music on her AirPods but had listened to his conversation.

Lots of misdirection was all about stretching police resources to the maximum as she recalled with a lunch with her mum and aunt. "Lilly, you seem more stressed than usual."

Lilly finished her mouthful of pizza and wiped her mouth with her napkin. "We do not have the resources, I have two murder manslaughter cases I am helping to prefer for court and tomorrow, I must interview the two suspects for that young Croydon kid that was knifed last week."

"Do you think it was racially motivated?"

"Oh, yes!" said Lilly.

Chapter 23

Harry, the senior police officer, came into see Paula Patel, in charge of missing persons.

"We have a problem, I am under pressure from the commissioner whose best friend's son Royston has gone missing, please prioritise this case!" Paula had never known her boss to get so animated about anything before so she knew it must be important.

They began to investigate it, with interviews with his three closest friends at the hospital. They all said he had mentioned he was seeing a girl he had met at the pub near the hospital. His friends said none of them had met this elusive girl that he confirmed he was falling in love with and Jin, the young Korean doctor, said, "He told me he would drop everything and go off with her."

Paula thanked Mark, Royston's brother, for coming to them but it had been a disappointing interview. All Daisy, Mark and Royston's older sister could confirm via phone interview was that her brother was saying he was falling in love and was even prepared to drop everything for her, which, off the record, was strange because he had been such a player. So, all the testimony was saying he had run off. Paula understood how love could do that she felt just as strongly about her husband and child and even though she loved her job if she had to make a choice, there would not be.

Mark explained he had met the latest girlfriend for 5 minutes to borrow something from his brother. He did not want to tell the police about his problem. All he could remember was her name was Becks that is what his brother called her and she was tall, blond and good-looking but all his brother's girlfriends could fit into that description, he generally preferred blonds as a type.

Interviews with landlord Dominic that the doctor often met girls in the pub and confirmed that Royston had been a regular but after a girl he had met, he could only recall him with colleagues in his pub once.

Chapter 24

It was then the job of a junior officer Dipesh Chakrabarty to go through hours of security footage from Royston's building. He had gone back 12 months showing him entering the building and, on several occasions, he was accompanied in entering with many different women over the last 12 months.

Dipesh came to see Paula. "I need to show you something. He brought 22 girls home, all but three were white blonde, one was black and one was a brunette but we have one that is like the landlord's description of being very tall but unusually!" he paused and Dipesh picked up the remote and zoomed in on the footage. "We cannot see her face but you can see she deliberately put up her hand to conceal her face from the camera and looks the other way as they walk past the concierge desk!"

"Wow, game changer, even if it not helps in identification, it is incredibly suspicious. Can you talk to IT and see if there is any way we can make the picture clearer? One thing we do know is the woman was 18-24, tall and blonde and did not want to be seen."

Chapter 25

Harry's Office

Paula entered. "How you getting on?"

He gestured with his hand. "Please take a seat, Paula. What have we found out so far?"

"Not much. Apparently, Royston was helping his brother get off his heroin addiction, so he was a weak witness. Mark did comment that his brother was besotted with this girl." Harry nodded. "We have a diary from his work desk and it highlights a plan to meet his brother every week to help him with his drug problem; the planned dates with Rebecca but no surname. I have emailed my report but have printed it all for you," dropping a brown folder on his desk.

"To summarise, his phone is off and missing, his apartment is empty, no passport, which is strange, which makes me wonder if he has just run off with his girlfriend."

"Why do you conclude that?"

"We talked to a work college who said he had met the girl in the pub and he was besotted with her as tallies with his siblings' statements. Having interviewed the landlord, he gave us an approximate description of the girl. Tall, attractive blonde does not narrow things down much unfortunately, that is where we reach a dead end."

Harry spoke, "Unfortunately, I have been told I have to give the father the news that we think he has run off with some girl. It is a big world."

"Between you and me, we have footage of a woman hiding her face but it is such a weak lead, sir, of anything being wrong."

"I agree. I don't want that information to leave the department."

Royston's father would hire private detectives to see what they could find. But first, the influential Conservative member of parliament and junior minister was convinced after three weeks he was being held against his will. "I will not except he would have gone without saying something," insisted Royston Senior.

Chapter 26

The 9 o'clock news came on the television as Angela and Rhona were eating their Chinese take away. "Are you eating that last spring roll?" said Angela.

"No, go for it. I thought the black bean was too salty," said Rhona.

The news reader explained the headlines, which included the emotional appeal from the Conservative member of parliament for Epping and outspoken Junior Minister for the Environment. The burly man stood at a podium with cameras flashing. Stood next to him were two police officers, both in uniform. Paula Patel looking pale faced and Harry Binder brown with the last trip from golfing in the Algarve. Before the member of parliament even opened his mouth, you could tell he was not happy with frowns and flushed cheeks.

He looked down at a pre-prepared speech. "If my son has left on his own volition, then can he please contact us to let us know you are OK; alternatively, it is my belief someone is holding Royston, my wonderful son, a successful young doctor against his will," he paused to sip some water from a glass that Paula passed him. "To this end, here is his picture I am putting up a reward of 10,000 pounds for any useful information that can be provided. The email and telephone are below."

Harry then took over talking, "Please only contact us with genuine useful information as we are already pursing multiple lines of inquiry."

Royston's mother had been sat behind the podium and could not bring herself to speak, they were already been through enough with her son Mark. Angela turned the TV off. "You could tell that he genuinely cares for his son. Do you have time for a play before you go?" as Angela began to kiss Rhona.

Chapter 27

Paula said to her team, "I want to go over everything again; I want to know what, if anything, is missing from Royston's apartment and office at the hospital?"

Doctor Farooqui confirmed that Royston's prescription pad was missing from his work desk, although the police should check his flat as lots of his charges took those home with them to plan a week ahead and organise what meds they would be needing. The concierge confirmed that he had not seen Royston's car in the car park for a while but had seen someone take it from the car park on the camera.

They went back through the video from the lobby and the camera on the entrance to the car park, although the occupants of the car could not be seen. That day, a red head entered the building and the car left the building. Rhona had been seen going in wearing the red wig to get the fob for the car park and leave the block twenty minutes later before entering the car park via the emergency exit. Despite all her planning, she had forgotten the car park gate fob and had to make one last visit to his apartment; it was probably because this was an amendment to her original plan.

"It's Smithy, the car is here, boss; we are just getting forensics going over the car now. It's clean apart for Royston's prints and know later for any DNA." Rhona had used a special tape to capture his finger prints after he was dead and apply them back on after wiping the car down.

"We have had a break, it now looks like the car was left at Luton on the day the car left the car park," Paula explained to her boss.

The young officer that had been going through the video footage on the day car left summarised for his boss.

"We have ten women and 15 men enter the building none match Royston or the description we have of his girlfriend but we now have this red head that has entered twice in the last few weeks but not appeared in previous 12 months. She enters the building the day the car leaves but is seen leaving again 20 minutes later, so apparently nothing to do with anything, but according the concierge, there is an access stair that the residents keys operate and it is possible that they entered by the access stair to get a car that does not currently have a working camera, it was broken three weeks ago and not been repaired yet."

Paula wondered what this all meant. The broken exit camera was Rhona's handy work. "So, boss, with passport missing, a suitcase and some clothes and his car at Luton. Every chance he has just run off with this girl."

Even though she was telling her boss this, something said some bits did not add up redhead and prescription pads and hiding face, but just wrote them in her own private journal. "OK, I will let the minister know and contact Interpol to see if he pops up."

Harry was trying to remember that politician that faked his own death, then it came to him, John Stonehouse and whether it was something like that.

Chapter 28

Rhona opened her MacBook. Her cool new flat was organised like something out of a magazine with everything just where it needed to be. Rhona maybe a cuckoo but her adopted parents had brought her up with love and she had not wanted for anything. Rhona had been spoilt in every way, from emotional demonstrations of physical affection with a kiss goodnight or bed-time story to toys and then as a teenager, it was clothes and the latest mobile phone or other electronic devices.

With her outstanding GCSE results, her parents had taken her to Westfield's. Emma gushed as Rhona tried on new ski outfits and the pink Prada one was purchased and her father Paul revealed the Gucci watch. The biggest surprise was the massive deposit down for a luxury apartment in a new development and paying the mortgage to give her independence and hoped the encouragement to stay in London for her degree.

Being under 18, the property was in trust for their daughter. She picked the development because of underground parking and the ability to buy two adjacent flats and she looked at the results confirming her brilliance, three A-stars. University College London maybe one of the best universities in the world, but they were willing to wait for Ms Smith and give her the deferred place. She met up with her friends. Belinda was going to come and visit over Christmas after she broke up from her first term.

Rhona had organised her a bedsit in Courchevel for her for free. Belinda did not know how she did it. She was grateful for the free accommodation at Rhona's new flat for her first year at university.

It was a fun summer 2017 after getting results but time for Rose and Rhona and to head to Thailand. Rose left two weeks before as Rhona wanted to oversee the construction of her Batcave first. Belinda to get a head start with the course books for the start of term. Rhona had been back in the country from her trip to Thailand for a few weeks before to head to France again for her winter job in her gap year.

Chapter 29

Rhona had been back from Thailand only a week and Rose had landed in Sydney as part of her year travelling thanks to the financial help from Rhona. The extra 20 thousand pounds that Rose received for the trip was explained as a small lottery win.

Rhona was putting her purchases from the duty-free shop away when her gate come up on the board. It was British airways flight BAW362 the 13.00 to Lyon Airport. The sign indicated 15-minute walk time from her location. On other occasions, her family often travelled via Genevie as flight time is the same but transfer from airport to resort is quicker to parts of the French Alps. She was wearing her crystal turquoise ski jacket inside the terminal, which meant she was warm so was only wearing a white Gucci t-shirt underneath.

The t-shirt she was wearing just emphasised with her bra, her beautiful upper body strong shapely shoulders and arms but still soft bosom. She put her chocolate and perfume in her backpack with her black cased *iPhone* and *iPad* and put her air pods back in her ears. Rhona was listening to the current mix of pop music. She arrived at gate 24. Wow, lots of people waiting. She noticed David and Georgy from last year. Ruby, the other chalet girl she knew from last year, was going from Birmingham as she was a black country girl.

Ruby's plane was scheduled to land thirty minutes before them so she would have to wait on the coach for the other people to arrive. David was dealing with Georgina; she was panicking as she was not able to find her boarding card. They were too distracted and did not notice her slip into the room for passengers about to board and sit down. Seeing them triggered her to check.

Yes, it was in her blue jeans with her credit card she had just used for the chocolate and perfume and in her jacket was her new dark blue appearing almost black British passport and boarding card. She would either be called first or last as she was in row 5 and window seat. It was the start of the ski season, Meribel was due to kick off until the first week of December and today was 26 November and just as Rhona was taking her seat.

Rhona was clicking her seat belt and putting her phone into plane mode. Dave passed her. "Hi," he said and raised his hand to give her hi-five, she reciprocated and hands clapped together. "Talk to you when we get off as I get too nervous on planes," and David walked down the aisle to his seat.

At the same time, the passengers were boarding, a ceremony was about to begin in Paris, France.

A middle-aged, quite glamorous lady got on the plane and sat next to her. Oh my god, it's *Marion Cotillard.* Rhona was star truck by the glamorous lady. In French, "Hi, sorry to embarrass you, but can I say I am so grateful your sat next to me and not on some private jet with a lady of your status."

"Well, a private jet is not good for the environment," the actress responded.

"I know, it's *la vie en rose,* you won the Oscar but you just happen to be in two of my favourite films," Rhona continued.

The lady switched to English, "OK, your French is good and what films are those?"

"*Inception* and the *Dark Knight Rises* and liked you as *Lady Macbeth,* how come you are on this plane?"

"I was shopping in London and now I am meeting a friend in Val d'isere for some early skiing before all the tourists turn up," as the glamorous Oscar winner smiled.

"Enjoy your holiday, I will leave you in peace."

The annual awards ceremony of the Gendarmerie National in Paris was taking place. Rhona's plane was just flying over Paris at 30 thousand feet above. "Hello everyone, this is your captain we have great visibility and if you look out your window, you should be able to see Paris below. We should be arriving in Lyon in 90 minutes, as we have perfect conditions."

Rhona checked her diamond encrusted designer watch, it was 1.30 PM.

Chapter 30

Gendarmerie National Awards and Lunch Majestic *Hotel, Champs-Élysées*, 1 PM.

The ceremony is like the Oscars for the French police in the glamourous room with its real antique crystal chandeliers resembling *Phantom of the Opera*. The room had twenty round tables set with beautiful silver wear. On each table were vases with freshly cut roses and crisp white linen that covered the tables completely so the legs of the table were invisible. The carpets had been freshly cleaned so the room had a glorious smell of roses; the wooden chairs were painted gold.

The room could equally be the grand ballroom in the *Palace of Versailles*, the home of the French monarchy before they became a republic after the French revolution when *Louis xvi* and his wife *Marie Antoinette* were imprisoned in 1792. The revolution had started because of food shortages. Sometimes simple things can bring down the powerful. The most famous thing to have survived is this the quote from Antionette "let them eat cake" slang, you do not care, please yourself.

Sharon was quite nervous as she was sat at a front table which was normally meant winning. She had won an award three years ago as best newcomer but had been completely unprepared and floundered when accepting the award; she had remembered to thank her boss and the amazing training and working with great colleagues. This time she had an acceptance speech ready along similar lines but with more personal touches, as she knew her colleagues better. The 26-year woman had had a great year at work plus she had fallen in love with her boss's secretary Maria.

Maria was a Greek Cypriot girl whose parents had moved to France when she was a young girl.

Cyprus is one of many islands that is split into more than one country.

The head of the French police returned to the podium and began to speak French. "It is my pleasure to announce the most astounding officer of the year, with her third award of the afternoon for the most successful crime solving ability in recent years on the *Credit Suisse Bank* robbery, bringing three people to justice when there were no suspects or how the money was stolen. I give you Sharon Dubois."

The short woman approached the stage. What she lacked in stature, she made up in personality and intellectual capability.

There was a massive round of applause as the young French Indian/Kenyan woman approached the stage. Lots of people shook the young woman's hand, she well-deserved the recognition. A woman approached her.

"Can I write an article as I think it would be inspirational for other women, considering the police as an option for a career?" the journalist persuaded Sharon, the generally private person, to agree to the expose. This was part of why she ended up in the Alps a few months later.

Within the next 4 months, Sharon and Rhona would be in a room together.

Chapter 31

The 44-year-old balding Professor Samuel Rothstein, a tweed wearing academic, teaching the psychology of crime but had developed a specialty on unusual weapons that killers use. His expertise meant he had become a regular consultant too many police forces around the world. The FBI had used him to help with a killer from Utah USA, the American state that is dominated by the rocky mountains and although it has skiing, in the winter with its lack of rainfall, puts it as the second driest state of the States.

The killer was slitting people's carotid artery with a sharpened icicle. Although it was three and a half years ago when this the professor had had helped catch Santiago, the samurai killer. This caught the headlines around the world. Santiago was beheading tourists in Barcelona, Spain, with a samurai sword. It was the perfect nature of the cuts that led them to conclude it was that weapon. The Spanish police were able to narrow suspects down to two collectors of Japanese memorabilia. The deranged killer thought he was reincarnated from an ancient death demon. It was this notoriety that finally got the man's well-deserved tenure. Tenure being a job for life.

Georgetown University Washington DC USA

It was 9:30 eastern standard time and professor Sam Rothstein was parking his vintage red corvette car in the university car park. His car needed a wash, he would get a student to do it. His first lecture was not until 10 30. Today's topic was "The unusual weapons murders pick" for his freshman students.

Copies of this book were required for the first semester. Rothstein loved three things; firstly, teaching and research, then his car. He had no room or desire for a relationship or even vanities, he dressed the way he thought a professor should dress with khaki slacks, brown brogue shoes and tweed jacket. In winter, he would have a matching hat and scarf and leather gloves. He kept healthy by long walks and excellent diet.

Over the years, the charismatic man had several opportunities with various women but his work was always the priority, plus his psychological fear of loss prevented a meaningful romantic connection.

Chapter 32

Both Wealthy and fashion-conscious men and woman will take more than one ski outfit for skiing holidays, to the complaints of their partners, about bringing too much luggage. Rhona's second blue outfit had nothing to do with either of those things and it was nothing to the length of her stay. Her pink outfit, which her parents had bought for her, made her stand out too much. The new blue colour choice was more to being unmemorable and a useful storage device. She also had her turquoise staff jacket.

She had learnt a lot from the first glorious kill. The blood splatter had made her realise kills in the Alps had to be different, otherwise she would get caught. The London murders would be easier at Rebecca Stephenson's flat or the newly built Batcave/kill room. Genes were not the only thing Rhona had inherited from her Romanian grandmother but a sizeable amount of money, most of which she could not touch until she was 30.

Her aunt had informed her of this information when she was 16 and a letter from her mum but she was not allowed to give her until she was 21. She could not tell her adopted parents, which Rhona thought was strange. Lilly informed that her great grandfather owned a large oil company in Romania before he sold it and moved the family to England.

Rhona had adapted her blue ski outfit by carefully removing the insulation that had been in the blue jacket and trousers, allowing her to hide some essential items. She had acquired 15 sets of forensic overalls and some heavy-duty cable ties to act as perfect plastic handcuffs from the internet. In a make-up bag was a specially modified suntan bottle containing essential fluid and plastic container that had some hair and skin in it she had collected discreetly from Simon. She had created a secret compartment in her wheeled suitcase. The information of her inheritance meant she could change phase one of her plans. A plastic syringe and a pack of disposable gloves were part of her tool kit.

Chapter 33

Lilly had been outstanding both academically and in sport. She is one of the few women in the world that can run the 100 metres in under 12 seconds. She pounded the tread mill regularly and often intimidated the men with the weight she could lift, but her strength was deceptive.

Her drive was unbelievable and had graduated top of her class with a first-class honours degree in psychology from Loughborough University and then applied to the metropolitan police force for the fast-track scheme. Lilly appeared to have no friends either from school or university and no social media presence. At the point she became guardian of Rhona, she had been given the role of chief profiler with the murder squad. If she was asked out for a drink, she always made excuses. So far, no one had picked up on her unusual lack of social life.

Lilly had chosen Rugby Union over athletics because of its physical nature. Lilly played on the wing because of her speed. Lilly Boswell have been prescribed with the drug Olanzapine for the diagnosis of being bipolar (extreme mood swings) at university. The drug had cured her problems.

Chapter 34

As Rhona headed down the stairs from the plane, she was patted on the back. At the bottom of the stairs, she turned.

"I hope you enjoy this," said David and stood next to him was Georgy, who had also worked in the chalet her and her parents had holidayed at last year. "Obviously, you will be in a different chalet to us. The season does not officially start until next week so we normally have a bit of a pub crawl starting at *Jack's bar*," said David.

"But I thought you were in Courchevel last year."

"Yes, it is a reshuffle so the three of us from that chalet have moved to Meribel," said David.

Rupert said, "Hello, let me welcome you back to France."

When Rupert had interviewed Rhona for the job in July, he had forgotten how attractive she was but as her resort manager, he knew that was a no-go area but maybe in the future when she went off to university. "Did you see who got escorted off the plane first?"

"Rupert, you should have mentioned you wanted to be an actor," said Rhona.

"It's fine, I am happy with what I am doing I get to ski; I have a great bunch of staff." He rubbed his chin to think.

"What about the lady that was sitting next to you?"

"Yes. She had got straight into a blacked-out range rover and driven off the tarmac straight to the VIP lounge to wait for her luggage."

Chapter 35

July, a few months earlier in the offices of TUI Rupert, had 5 vacancies for Crystal ski in Troi Valles and two for Ibiza; his summer manager's job.

Rupert looked up from the pile of CVs on his desk, he needed two chefs and three chalet staff. Nearly all the candidates were students on gap years or first job after graduating. One CV stood out for two reasons; firstly, it came with a personal recommendation from his best chef David. David had graduated from catering college in Richmond upon Thames, top of his class and was hoping to eventually own his own restaurant.

"This girl is the most gifted untrained chef I have ever seen and works well under pressure." It was a glowing reference. Rupert continued to read her CV. She spoke French, which he thought was good for dealing with suppliers and one less job for him to worry about, but it was the education connection that also interested him. The secretary was organising all the interviews for all the winter season managers, both skiing and winter sun destinations like the Caribbean and Far East and Egypt.

Lucy buzzed. "Your 3 o'clock interview is here."

The incredibly attractive tall blonde woman walked in. "Please take a seat, Ms Smith. Can I get you a drink?"

"Water please."

"Racheal, can I have a tea and water for Ms Smith?"

"I was looking through your CV, so it says you're trying to decide if you go to a catering college or go to University College London." Rupert leant across his desk at the beautiful blonde and could smell her perfume.

"With a place at one of the most prestigious universities in the world, there is no decision?" Rhona answered her Twickenham prep attendee. "I want to see if cooking for a living is a possible option, plus I love skiing and speak French."

"Honestly, with the reference from Dave Collins, even if I only get you for one season, it's worth it for us." He looked at the beautiful blonde. "I have one question do you remember me?"

Of course, she did but she mulled it over for a minute. "You were the head boy at Twickenham prep school."

The mixed prep school they had both gone to but Rupert was 5 years older so not aware of her when he was at school. "Where did you go after prep school?" she asked.

"Hampton boys then did a degree in acting but with no jobs, I decided to give this a go then got promoted and like you speak good French, I am sure we will be good friends," he continued. "By the way, you will get a Crystal ski jacket but as a chef you're not expected to take part in transfers because the Troi Valles gets complicated with both train people and airport arrivals."

"Oh yes, my family and I have done both."

"OK, ask Racheal to show you next door and try on and take a jacket with you."

Rupert stood up from his desk and thrust out his hand. "Welcome *to Crystal Holidays.*"

They shook hands and Rhona left the room and was shown to the rail as she tried on a turquoise coloured jacket. Good fit and the assistant Racheal passed her bag to carry it home in. Rupert still had four interviews but would struggle to get the girl out of his head through the rest of the day.

Chapter 36

Rupert Carmichael could be described as a posh boy. His family lived on the Wentworth Estate in Surrey because his parents were obsessive golfers and his father was chairman of a well-known bank. Rupert was in the skiing team at the privilege private school Hampton School, Hampton Middlesex. Then an acting degree at St. Marys in Twickenham, but after two years from graduating, all he had to show for it was three extras' roles.

Rupert was good at skiing and being charming and his maths kept the resort books in order. He had done one season before university. His dad used some favours and after another season at 25, he was the resort manager. Rupert was good-looking with his tall, well-built frame and his curly blond hair that he kept long on top but shaved the back and sides. He would sometimes put his hair up in a topknot.

Chapter 37

As it was her first season, Rhona was given one of the smaller chalets with fewer people but unfortunately that meant the staff accommodation was smaller. At the French airport were three coaches in the car park going to different resorts for crystal. Drivers had the doors open standing to load luggage underneath. She saw the one that said crystal Troi Valles and climbed aboard, having left her suitcase for the guy to load and she placed her skis on the rack. She found a free seat midway down the coach next to the window and put her boot bag/hand luggage on the shelf above.

With the sun shining on that side of the coach, it felt warm so Rhona removed her jacket and put on her glasses back on. The coach made its way from Lyon airport to the resort; she was looking at the French countryside with its beautiful autumn colours but she was imagining if these fields were covered in blood like 520 miles north of their location just over 100 years ago the battle of the Somme where 300000 people had been killed during that ill-fated battle in the first World War.

Her thoughts and comments on the battle during her GCSE essay had disturbed her history teacher so much he had reported it to the headmaster who shrugged it off as Rhona just trying to tease the weak man with the comments. This incident almost made Michael Pearson Rhona's first victim when she had followed him home. She was like a spy ducking behind trees and cars as he walked home. Her history teacher was one of three teachers that thought Rhona was strange; the other teachers at her school just saw her as a superstar.

The headmaster's comments summed it up. "Rhona, genius level IQ means some members of my staff will find her difficult to deal with," her history teacher had given her essay a F before the headmaster an ex-history teacher himself remarked and gave it an A. Mr Pearson was now in her diary for a potential future kill.

The essay was called **The history of war, A State Manifesto for Murder**.

The purpose of war is allegedly to resolve conflicts when political methods fail. Or secondly, it's god's way to reduce the population from getting out of control because apart from men going off to get killed; the birth rate falls because men are off fighting. It is estimated the death toll to war in history is between 150 million and 1 billion. Or finally, is it as humans are apex predators? We like to kill either directly or indirectly as the generals did in the comfort and no danger to themselves. We are maybe just naturally programmed to kill, as history has shown and are naturally evil.

Man is born of sin, **Romans 7. 14 and John 3.3**, *although the concept of original sin does not exist in the Muslim religion.*

Humans are killers, our ancestors had learnt to make weapons to ensure we were top of the food chain and in some tribes in the world cannibalism was still practised. She was going to be the greatest of all time; although many serial killers also eat their victim's human flesh did not appeal, she would stick with *Nando's* or *Five Guys.*

As she watched the countryside go by, she was listening to *Adagio for strings,* one of Rhona's favourite pieces of music. It was used for Franklin Delano Roosevelt's funeral and after JFK's assassination, it also features prominence in one of the best movies about the Vietnam war, Platoon. Rhona had often thought she should go on who wants to be a millionaire because of her knowledge but she was driving in another direction her ability to recall information was part of her gifts.

Chapter 38

She was deep in thought when a red head girl pointed to the empty seat next to her. She started talking.

"I can't hear you, one second." Rhona removed her air pods. "Hi, can I help?" said Rhona.

"Rupert has just told me we are going to be at chalet Visage and roommates. I thought would be good to get to know each other." The girl plonked herself into the empty seat.

"My name is Sophie, I do the cleaning and waitressing, also help with any cooking you need," the loquacious girl continued as she spoke. She was very expressive using her hands and face and spoke with her distinctive home town accent. "I am from Hull," without pronouncing the H. "I did a season before going to *Hull University* to do a business degree and then got a job in marketing with *Smith and Nephews* the medical manufacturing company based in Hull then I realised I had not really been outside this city apart from a ski season, an exchange week in Paris and holiday in Ibiza. What do you do?"

Finally, the girl came up for air. Rhona explained, "My decision is to do a gap year because I love cooking and do not want my academic prowess to determine what I do in life. I figure a season cooking before doing my degree gives me more life experience, a bit like why you are here." As she lowered her head, avoiding eye contact.

There were other members of staff to greet them, showing them to each of the chalets.

They arrived at their chalet. Rhona left her bags on the floor as she carried her boots, skis and poles into the empty boot room so she could pick the perfect spot near the heater to dry equipment out. Picking up her bags headed down the corridor towards the room.

"Sophie, what room are we in?" shouted Rhona.

"Room 6," replied the young redhead. The door was open and Sophie had started putting her stuff in the double wardrobe on the left. "I waited. Which bed you want, top or bottom?"

"Top, please," replied Rhona. The bunk beds gave the room more floor space as it was a relatively small room with the small window opposite the door with one side of the window only just above the ground snow as the chalet was on a slope. The room was small but it did have its own bathroom.

As the girls were putting their toiletries in the bathroom cupboard, Sophie noticed something. "Sorry to ask something that is probably embarrassing but why do you have a huge box of Tena ladies? I thought it was only a problem like my mum that has had babies."

"I have been diagnosed with a small bladder which causes leaks!" The truth was that Rhona needed to catch her DNA in post kill excitement.

Their pine clad room was boring so the girls went out for the afternoon in their crystal jackets to find stuff to decorate the walls and hoped as staff locals would give them better deals. The first shop Rhona was not sure if the bits and pieces being reduced were the staff thing or that he found the two young women attractive. "Andre was flirting," said Sophie. "We got 20 per cent off and I think that will look cool on the wall."

It was a green hoodie with white lettering saying Meribel on it. "Yes and use the Troi valley mug for my toothbrush."

When they got back to the room, Rhona opened the window to the room to see if it was possible for someone to get out if required. Yes, it was. That was important, as may be required. "What you doing?" said Sophie.

"I get claustrophobic just want to know I can get out in an emergency!"

It was the first night out with 24 members of staff plus Rupert. "What can I get you, Rhona?"

"Just diet coke please." Tonight she wanted to make notes on her phone about all the bars and the staff from the different chalets. They had gone from bar to bar she had noted emergency exits and toilets. She had timed the walk times from different locations and again entered the information on her phone.

After being out with the other staff that first night, she lay in her bunk and opened her diary she read to herself. The notes said strike quickly before the police could understand what was going on and react and confuse them with the motives. She put her diary away and slept soundly.

Chapter 39

The beautiful blonde predator sat at the restaurant watching skiers make their way down the *agile red run*. She took a bite of her pastry and pulled out the German's passport memento, number two she had killed him yesterday she looked at it, Hans Becker from Dusseldorf now dead age 38.

Rhona's chalet was empty of guests the first week of the season so she had time to get started and give Sophie and her boyfriend Glen some ski lessons; with an empty chalet, her future fiancé Glen had come over for a few days' lessons. He had been able to stay in a spare room. As a goodwill gesture from Rupert. Rupert had explained they had 15 spare rooms in three chalets and was willing to reserve them for staff to bring family and friends over but they had to get to resort on their own steam. Such gestures made him the highest rated manager in the company. For the few days Glen was in the resort, Rhona had their room on her own as Sophie slept with Glen in his room.

24 hours before, it was a lovely sunny December although cold and the slopes on the shady side of the mountain had been icy at first but as the sun had risen, the slopes were now perfect. This time of season, no school holidays meant no kids and families, lots of adults only. From her vantage point at the restaurant/cafe, she was looking for men skiing on their own. She observed the average skier in his red jacket. It made her think of him being a fox in a traditional English hunt. He was making his way down the run for his fifth time. She quickly finished her Orangina and threw the empty bottle into the bin.

She then clicked her head boots into her bindings and off she went she was 100 metres behind but her superior ability she carved down the slope, transferring weight from one ski to another looking like a professional before timing her turn perfectly to crash into him. She had quickly caught him up and would cut across him. Right of way is always the lower skier on the slope as you should always be looking down to what is in front. Boom! They both tumbled as their skis caught each other.

"Oh my god, I am so sorry," shouted Rhona.

"Are you OK, Fraulein?" said the man in his thick German accent. One of his skis had come off as his bindings were lose. Rhona being such a good skier, her bindings were set to the maximum. She helped him get his ski back on.

"Can I make it up to you, buy you a drink later? Do you know Jack's bar?" she said.

"Ja, yes, I mean," said the German, who thought he had luckily struck gold, having the collision with a beautiful young woman.

Chapter 40

Jacks bar 8:30 pm. A new jazz band was just starting its set in the dimly lit atmospheric establishment. Perfect for a secret rendezvous. Somebody was vaping near her and she could smell the sweetness, it was a berry one of some kind, when she saw him. Hans came in. It was now clearly snowing as he brushed it off his shoulders and hat.

He could not see the beautiful English girl. She was dressed all in black, which made her look good but it was more to be ninja like for later. Black boots, black leggings, a short black skirt and jumper and in her bag was a woolly hat. She spotted him straight away but she had been staring at the door for an hour like a security camera with one purpose. The successful businessman with his belly hanging over his jeans was used to get women because of his wealth but today's accident was going to be the most fortunate way he was going to get laid, he thought.

The bar had many people enjoying their après-ski. "What is your poison?" said Rhona and giggled to herself at the Freudian slip.

"Bitte," said Hans. "What can I get you?"

"Grolsch, please."

"Barman, two Grolsch, please."

They sat in the corner listening to the jazz as explained he was a property developer and was in the Alps to check out a site for a hotel and he could show her the plans if she was interested. The philanderer thought he had just given a reason to get this woman back to his room and Rhona was thinking the same. "Let us get a beer to go and you can show me the plans, big boy," and gave him a kiss.

Hans was immediately aroused by her touch. For Rhona, she felt nothing. Her ability to totally compartmentalise was one of her strengths. The air outside felt quite cold compared to the warmth of the bar. The stars were out and it felt cold as Rhona took deep breaths and cold cleansed her lungs of the smelly berry vape. Hans took her hand as they crunched through the freshly falling snow. He started speaking German instinctively before switching quickly to English. "It's only a 5-minute walk."

Rhona's face was quite flushed from her body reacting to the coldness, it was late and Hans took off a glove so he could enter the code to the chalet door and they entered unseen to his room on the second floor. His accommodation smelt of sweaty man and had two pairs of boxer shorts left on the floor as he laid the plans on the bed and tried to get rid of the sweaty underpants.

Rhona opened the door to the balcony that went all the way around the chalet balcony connecting all the rooms. At the far end she noticed a snow drift was under the balcony, that was perfect. The temperature difference between the room and the outside was striking. Will you excuse me, frauline and the German went to the toilet.

She added three drops of a clear chemical with a pipet from another small bottle from her bag to his beer, broke off a large icicle and left it outside. "let us kiss," she said. As they kissed, "Oh my god, sorry, I feel very woozy."

She pulled a knife, which she had taken from her chalet kitchen earlier, from her jacket and pressed it against his throat and he noticed his hands had been tied with cable ties. She could have been a pickpocket, like a character in *Oliver Twist* with her skills.

Give me your pin number, otherwise I will kill you. A hand towel was shoved in his mouth. He mumbled the number as the slightly chubby German businessman brow had beads of sweat. The first time in his life he was scared and was just increasing the hormones Rhona's body was getting a flush in her arteries, the cocktail, endorphins associated with exercise and oxytocin and dopamine with orgasms.

Next thing, she grabbed the ice and pillow and sliced his throat with her right hand and covered his face with the pillow to catch the blood. The cheap pillow was quickly soaked through. She cut the cable ties off with the knife and placed them, along with her knife, back in her coat.

She watched the last few seconds of life drift from his eyes. She grabbed his brown leather wallet from the floor; it had fallen out of his pocket and the passport from the draw she messed up the room and using the other pillow quietly broke the window from the outside. She dropped the icicle on the floor for it to melt. Making her way along the balcony before jumping off into the drift below.

Chapter 41

It had just started to snow again, hiding her tracks. That was disappointing, she wanted tracks to show an intruder from outside. As she trudged away from the chalet, she kept looking around, making sure no one had seen her. But all in black, staying close to the buildings, she was hard to see here even if you were trying to find her.

The snow was falling again and the amazing 6-pointed ice structures were cool on her hot, flushed cheeks. She brushed the snow from her face, got out the small make-up mirror she was hidden behind a building. She carefully applied the make-up and attached the other parts to her disguise.

She got back to her room super late but as Sophie was with Glen, in her empty room, no one to notice the time of her return. There was the first cash point. After the second one said balance zero, she wiped the make-up off and head back to her room. Rhona understood the rush from adrenaline hitting the blood stream from skiing and rollercoasters but this new cocktail from her dark activity could not be matched.

Chapter 42

It was 10 AM the next morning and guests were just having breakfast when they heard the high-pitched screams of Melissa, the young chalet girl from three floors above. She found the corpse of Hans and a blood-soaked pillow. The carpet in the room was sticky from all the blood The local police were on site within 45 minutes. Their initial thoughts were it was a robbery gone wrong. With no passport, official identification would take longer. Forensics confirmed later out of the 6 litres of blood that should have been in his body that the carpet probably had four of that.

The Moustached police chief had an idea. "Let us check the footage from local ATMs to see if there had been anyone using them in the middle of the night. Even though we do not yet know the account details yet."

An hour after the killing, she found a cash point with a camera and began to empty out his bank; within an hour, she had 3000 euros in her jacket. The police were excited; it looked like they had video of someone taking money out of cash points at 2 AM in the village. It was a dark Mediterranean-looking skinned man with thick black hair and beard. Both of which were now in Rhona's jacket.

Chapter 43

She would target a middle-aged couple from Middlesbrough staying in her chalet. There was a buzz in the village about people being vigilant as someone had been robbed and murdered. Victor and Mary were in their mid-fifties and had ordered extra wine with dinner and Rhona had been able to add her drugs into the bottle. She had spoken to them a few times and found out enough about them that she knew they fitted her code when they were young.

She knew they were in room 7. She had taken the pass key earlier in the evening. As they were saying goodnight, as they were feeling tired, she slipped out of the dining room before them. They entered their bedroom and a balaclava figure grabbed Mary and had her with the knife. "Stay very quiet, otherwise I will kill your wife. Put this on."

Victor put his shaking hands through the cable ties. Victor was not sure if he could stay awake as the drugs were kicking in. "Tell me your pin," said Rhona.

"5678," he mumbled.

Rhona shoved the hand towel in Mary's mouth as she sliced victor's throat with the icicle. Victor was spluttering with the blood in his throat then Rhona flipped Mary onto the bed next to her husband who was bleeding out as she sliced her throat, death is quite quick with a cut to the carotid artery as it provides blood to the brain.

Once she was happy, they were both dead; she grabbed money bank cards and passports and again broke the window from outside. With no overnight snow forecast, she again had to go from the window to prove someone had entered from outside but it was the fourth floor and no drift to jump into, she had to climb down the drainpipe. It was her day off and her plan was to ski over to Courchevel and get cash from there, as the police were all over Meribel. She did not really need the cash but it was just the power that she could take it. She had left footprints to a nearby building, then after that they disappeared.

She figured while they were still thinking they were looking for a robber, they would not be so thorough about DNA; also, these were local police that

87

generally dealt with minor misdemeanours from tourist, etc., not major crime. She had not used her suits but after the next one, she would have to. A German businessman and an English couple had nothing in common, they were just unlucky but when the next victim was in another village with only cash stolen and passport and 6 mils of semen on their bodies that would change their focus.

Rhona had found out that one of the chalet girls from one of the other chalets was gay; now she just had to seduce her. The fake compartment in her suitcase had three passports inside. The police had stuck a picture around the village they wanted to interview, it was a picture taken from the video capture from the cashpoint.

Her make-up and false beard had made the culprit look like a Mediterranean man in his thirties, not a 20-year blonde. She took one of the fliers, the picture was of low quality but she took out her green cased phone and compared it to pictures of Simon, her project manager boyfriend. Heavy foundation had replicated his natural Italian heritage's skin colour. With practice, she had even been able to replicate the small scar he had on his left cheek.

Chapter 44

Belinda's accommodation and trip had been organised before Rupert said about the free rooms. Also, Belinda did not want to miss any of her first term and thought Christmas would be more fun. Belinda's flight to Lyon was cheap and her accommodation was free; she knew the taxi was going to be expensive. To her surprise, there was a girl in a Crystal ski jacket with her name on a board. Belinda approached the girl. "Hi, I am Belinda Robinson but I am not with crystal."

"I know you're Rhona's friend, right?" and shook her hand, "our boss Rupert," she paused and winked at the girl. "I think he has a thing for her so it has been arranged we will drop you off with the 6 other passengers we have in that valley." Sophie showed her to her seat, then sat down next to her. "I do not know if Rhona mentioned but I am her roommate and she is teaching me to be a better skier. She is amazing."

Belinda nodded and smiled. "Yes, she really is."

Belinda dialled, "Wow Rhona, thanks for this.!"

"OK, get yourself settled, pass extra and then we could meet for a coffee as probably by the time get sorted, not worth skiing today," said Rhona.

Belinda, like Rhona, was a good enough skier to have her own equipment but maybe she could just drop her skis off to be sharpened overnight.

Rebecca Stephenson had booked Belinda into the apartment block in the summer after the girls had met that afternoon when they had made their pre-university plans. "Hi Francois, can you make a booking for me? It is for a friend of a friend?"

"Done, room 15 done," said the mature French man.

Chapter 45

It was Christmas week and Rhona had made Christmas themed meals.

Rhona's mobile rang. "OK, I finish breakfast at ten, then we can ski; if you want to head over here, there is a café next to the bottom of the agile run next to the Pas Du Lac bubble lift. See you there about ten."

On the Wednesday, when the chalet staff get the day off and patrons go out for food, it was an opportunity for Sophie, Belinda and Rhona to ski together. "OK girls, I think Sophie is ready for a day of red runs rather than blues and greens and then I am buying everybody lunch."

During lunch, Rhona quizzed her friend about life at Uni and what societies she had signed up to and any new friends she had made. Rhona would use her connections to help later.

After lunch, the girls split up, leaving Sophie on the easier blues to practise technique, whereas Belinda and Rhona took the Saulire cable and enjoyed the view as it made its way up the mountain. They got out. Rhona's adrenalin was already flowing as they made their way along a track before they reached the steep bit at 85 per cent maximum gradient. Not for the fainthearted, The Grand Couloir is so difficult several people have died or injured trying to ski it.

After Christmas was over and Rhona said her goodbyes to her friend, it was time to get back on the plan. Adrenaline from skiing was not the cocktail she was addicted to.

Chapter 46

Kylie was a gay chalet girl at the chalet Mistral. "Hi Kylie, I am Rhona. We have not spoken before." Rhona paused to go in to kiss the girl on the cheek. "Sophie was telling me about you and sorry to hear you have just broken up with your partner!"

Kylie was 24 and had been doing holiday seasons for 4 years with her girlfriend Joanna. They did Torremolinos in the summer. The heavily tattooed blonde loved Joanna but Joanna's career had ended their relationship, Joanna never enjoyed the cold or skiing and was offered a resort managers role in the Canaries at the party town of Playa De las Americanas which meant being there all year as it is a prime location for winter sun.

This decision for Joanna would mean Kylie realised Joanna put her job above her and did not want to be with someone where work was so important, as Kylie was spiritual. One of the reasons, she liked being in the mountains was your closer to God because of the altitude. Rhona would exploit Kylie for being vulnerable. For Rhona, believing in god did not protect you. Kylie had not exclusively been with the woman, she also had a brief one-night stand with Peter, her tattooists and body piercer in Camden.

What was also striking about Kylie was her make-up and hair. She routinely changed the colour of her hair and the colour of her eye shadow, which she made them look the same. When Rhona met her, it was a vibrant blue not unlike the images of *Cleopatra,* the ancient Egyptian queen, decorated her eyes and similarly sadly deceased singer *Amy Winehouse* or *Stefani Joanne Angelina Germanotta* or *Lady Gaga* as she *is* better known with the exaggerated black lines lengthen the width of her eyes.

Another Week went by and to the police's relief, the busy Christmas period went by with no incident. She was desperate to kill but she had to stay strong to stick to her plan.

Chapter 47

It was New Year's Eve and her other phone was ringing, Simon was desperate. "Rebecca darling, why can't I visit you?"

"Let's talk later," she hung up. Then another FaceTime on her black cased *iPhone,* it was her parents wishing her happy new year. She told them the news she was enjoying the experience but would be taking her university place next year.

"Oh, that's great darling!" Her other phone began to ring she answered bur realised she hadn't put her phone down to her parents.

She hung upon her parents and picked up the green cased phone. "Hi darling, I miss you! So it's all arranged, a week in January at the Hotel Tignes le Lac 2100, just you and me."

Angela was a loose end that needed to be tied up. She put her phones down, turned off and hid the green cased phone back inside her carved out copy of *Da Vinci code. Dan browns* great novel featuring his protagonist *professor Langdon.* She had got the idea from watching Stephen king's Shawshank *Redemption* where *Tim Robbin's* character *Andy Dufrane* hides his rock hammer inside a copy of the bible and using Velcro to keep the book closed with the hidden phone inside on her shelf behind her head.

The small room that Sophie shared, Rhona was on the top bunk with a small shelf and both had lamps to read by with flexible arms. At the far end of the room was a radiator and a window that on the left side was at ground level and about two feet above on the other side of the window because of the slope outside. Like most chalets were pine cladded and boring, only the hoodie on the wall between the wardrobe and bathroom door provided any interest.

With two girls sharing, the room had a smell of Chanel number 5 and Flower bomb. Both Rhona and her alto ego Rebecca shared the same perfume. There was no need to make some things more complicated than they needed to be. Opposite to the beds was a double wardrobe, next to that was an ensuite shower room/toilet. On top of her fake book was her lockable diary, it was pink. She had two, one was full of general young person thoughts with pin code 1234 and another one that looked identical with code 0666, this was generally kept in her secret compartment. She left the room.

There was Sophie. "Happy new year, darling!" as they went outside with the fireworks going off. "Have a great year roomy."

She watched the fireworks but not with the melancholy that many people feel at New Year although they pretend to be happy; she was generally excited about the summer ahead. A yellow streak of light with a screaming noise raced into the night sky before exploding into a million different colours. Thank you, Chinese, for these approx. 3000 years for fireworks and then refined into gun powder equally the weapons of war. The black powder that propels a bullet. She loved irony. Like the people have heard of the Nobel Prize, including for peace but it comes from Alfred Noble in 1895 that invented dynamite. Another weapon of destruction.

Back in London
New Year's Eve

Emma took a sip of her champagne. "See, darling, told you she would rethink things and not to worry." Paul smiled and gave his wife a big kiss. Paul loved his daughter but was amazed how in tune Emma was despite not being biologically related. It just showed how nurture was important and Emma had spent more time at home with their daughter.

The reason for different colour cases on her mobiles is so it would allow her to quickly realise which phone was what and the two diaries if anyone ever noticed her with it and wanted to see what she wrote she could show them. The next morning, 1 January, she opened the paperback and took out the green cased phone and dialled. "How is your head?"

"A bit sore."

"OK, I have a surprise. I have booked a week for us end of January." Simon was very happy. The ice slayer had started then in the summer both the beheader and the embassy killer would begin as the construction of the Batcave/kill room for body storage was ready.

Chapter 48

Sophie Rawlinson was the oldest of three children, with a sister and brother. They had all been born at Hull Royal Infirmary in Kingston upon Hull. They had family holidays every summer in a static caravan in Filey, the coastal town in east Yorkshire popular for its lovely beach. Apart from Filey, she had done a week in Paris as exchange student with girl Renee as an option for her French GCSE.

Renee and her family went skiing every winter to the trois Valles and it had peaked Sophie's interest in skiing. Sophie's father, a humble man but regional manager for a supermarket group, meant Sophie's mum could stay at home with the kids. Both Jonathan and Elizabeth were super proud when their daughter graduated with honours with her business degree from Hull University and pleased when she landed the job at Smith and Nephew so she would not be leaving the town.

When Sophie and her school friends had finished their A-levels, they had all gone to Ibiza, San Antonia and partied hard. Sophie had also invited her French friend. It was the second time Sophie had had sex. It was that holiday that meant she also deferred her place to do a ski season and maybe learn to ski. After working for the medical manufacturer for two years, she handed in her notice and Rupert was happy to welcome her back in the fold.

"How long have you been skiing?" asked Sophie.

"Since five," replied Rhona.

"Your boots and ski look good. Are they a good brand?" asked Sophie, who had no idea.

"They are Head as worn by Lindsey Vonn!"

"Who is that?"

"What! You have never heard of arguably the greatest female skier of all time, the lady from Missouri USA won more medals than anyone on the tour, but the general press was more interested in the fact she had a short fling with Tiger woods."

"Oh, I know who Tiger woods is, the great American black golfer," replied Sophie. "Anyway, you're so good. Could you teach me to be better? At the moment, all I can do is snow plough turns."

Rhona agreed she liked the red-haired roommate. Sophie was older than Rhona. Sophie's boyfriend Glen had got together at 16 and after a year, they agreed they were both too young and should play the field.

Chapter 49

It was a cold January, three weeks since the last robbery and murder and Charles Robert, the head of the local police, thought it may have been a crazy tourist that had gone home and certainly, that is what he hoped. He still had unsolved killings but he would have time and not so much pressure.

The skies were blue in the sun and felt great as Sophie and Rhona were approaching the ski lift sliding forward as the two people in front slid onto the conveyor matt. Now it was their turn, they got into position as the chair came behind them. Rhona put her hand behind her as this lift was fast and had a habit of hitting you in the back of legs painfully hard. They were away, Rhona waited for her friend to get herself organised before pulling the barrier down.

"I love lifts, fun little rides that begin to build your anticipation," said Rhona.

You could see in her roommate's face she did not agree as she squeezed tighter onto her poles. "No, I hate them. I always think I am going to drop something that I cannot retrieve."

Rhona wanted to reassure her. "But this lift only goes over the slope, so as long as you see where it lands, not a problem."

"It would be annoying if I dropped a pole," said the girl from Hull.

Because it was cold, Rhona had her pink outfit on, as the blue one meant she had to wear two sets of thermals, which was uncomfortable.

Rhona skied down first to the café as Sophie waited for Rhona to emerge from inside the restaurant. Sophie stood at the top. She put her hot chocolate onto the table as she signalled for her to come with her pole and watched Sophie. It was either her teaching or Sophie's natural talent but she was getting good since she had started, she would outski her boyfriend, Glen.

Rhona was sat on a picnic table with her head goggles on her, now new head helmet on the table. She had only copped with having the Oakley helmet a few days before she had to replaced it the previous season. She adjusted her sunglasses to put on more sunblock, although cold, the sun was strong as the sky was bright blue. Her left hand had a glove on as her right applied the lotion. She had been listening to Mozart and thinking about when she was 16, when Sophie was now completing the run and making her way over.

Rhona pulled out her headphones and the wires dangled out the front of her jacket.

"What do you think?" inquired the red head, revealing her platted pony tail as she took off her helmet and put on her headband. Rhona, however, was wearing a pink woolly hat with pigtails on either side.

"You're great. Look at the lines, you're better than your boyfriend!" Sophie looked back up the red slope, she could see her trail and smiles with pride. "Your carving just needs to practise and have confidence to increase your speed."

"Shall we go inside as it's cold?" inquired Sophie.

"No! It's cold but the sun is shining, no wind and lovely fresh air. Also, the forecast for the next few days is white out tomorrow and snowing the rest of the week, so good to be outside while we can and next week, we have a full chalet of guests."

Sophie nodded in understanding. "OK, what would you like?"

"Just some chips, bread roll and mayonnaise and salt and pepper and Orangina to drink, please."

"I am turning you into a northerner having a chip butty!" said Sophie and giggled as Sophie disappeared to join the lunch queue, knocking the remaining snow off her boots before entering the building. Although Rhona was quiet and kept to herself, Sophie really liked her, it made her mysterious. Rhona had made it very easy how to go from the v-shaped snow plough to lift the ski with no weight on it to go next to the other ski and parallel turn.

Rhona had brought two sets of headphones, her AirPods and wired ones to ski with. She did not want to risk losing a white AirPod in the snow. She knew skiing with headphones was dangerous but she was confident that her superior skills meant it was a lower risk than being caught at her grand plan. She had a skiing playlist with her favourite piece was the music from the ski sequence from the James Bond movie on *Her Majesty's Secret Service,* the John Barry music associated with bond movies.

Chapter 50

The young woman from Humberside was totally unaware that Rhona was now officially a serial killer, having killed 4 people. Sophie, having a one-night stand in Ibiza, made her a potential target for her roommate as she fitted her criteria. Sophie and Glen had lost their virginity to each other but agreed they should split up and play the field as they were only 16 but after they had both had one-night stands, each of them reached out to the other and they had got back together as they now believed there was no one else for each of them. Glen was a qualified personnel trainer and, after a few years, was now a manager of a popular gym in Hull.

When the girls had been laying in their beds one night chatting about their sexual experiences Rhona had written her name in her diary before crossing it out and adding it to the safe list on page 1. Adding Sophie taking her list to eight people she would not harm no matter what. While Sophie was getting the food, Rhona went back to her reminiscence.

The girl from Hull with her natural red colour hair reminded her of the two red-haired children that had been part of the reason her history teacher had not been her first victim. She could still picture the house with the climbing purple hydrangea that rambled its way over the arch of the doorway partial blocking the front ground floor bay window before stopping just below the upstairs bay window above and a woman leaning out the window that Rhona assumed was Mr Pearson's wife, she shouted out to him, "Hello, darling."

The house had a well-stocked plant border and a manicured lawn. Two children ran out of their front door of the 1930s semidetached house shouting "daddy". The first a little girl about the age Rhona was when she had been handed over to the orphanage and the other little boy about the age Rhona had been when she joined Paul and Emma. Seeing that was enough for her to regain her composure.

She realised planning was the key and spent the next two years trying to cover every detail. She had been 16. It was also the day she had made her way to visit the orphanage for the first time since she had left. Sophie came back with drinks and food. "There you go." and Rhona tried to hand Sophie some euros. "Don't be silly. This is my treat because of the lessons."

Chapter 51

She was 17 when she came across a book by an American professor. His books she kept in the secret compartment in her room next to the television. The first book was about unusual weapons that murderers have used and knew she needed to have some like that as a calling card.

That winter, she used her hose on the shed roof and was able to make several icicles and with practice could sharpen the ice with a knife so it would cut flesh. She practised cutting into joints of ham from Sainsburys with the ice. Plunging them into a chest would not work as ice too slippery to get a grip but both the femoral artery in the leg and the carotid artery in the neck are vulnerable. The carotid is fast as it feeds the brain the femoral in the leg is good for draining the body of blood.

So, she created **a diary/handbook of a serial killer.**
With several points:
Point 1: Unusual Weapon: icicle/knife beheading/removing limbs.
Point 2: Memento: passports/driving licences/heads and hands.
Point 3: Location: The French Alps/London other.
Point 4: How to be in the Alps: Ski instructor, Chalet girl, Cook.
Her book had over 30 points. She considered herself well prepared but be flexible and be prepared for the unknown.

Rhona was a loner but she liked her roommate and Sophie had just joined the list of people that were untouchable.

Isaac Asimov, the great sci-fi writer, came up with three rules of robotics as follows:

1. A robot cannot harm a human or by its inaction allow a human to be harmed.
2. A robot shall follow any order unless it contradicts rule 1 or 3.
3. A robot cannot harm itself.

Rhona had developed her own rules for killing:

1. Any one of low moral standing was a possible victim. Unless they had children under ten. Low morals like one-night stands or being disrespectable to others, bigoted or racist rapist, murderer, sex offender, paedophile.
2. Everyone else was safe unless Rhona's life or plan could be in jeopardy by them staying alive.
3. Even people with low morals could still be safe if she wanted them to be.
4. Others could be included on the list if she chose like Michael Pearson.

It was not a perfect code, was more guide lines.

Chapter 52

Nathan Rothstein was brought up in a middle-class family in Baltimore in the United States. His father was a successful accountant and his childhood was perfect until he was 12 and his older brother Samuel, 13. When the most horrific thing happened. A man with m16 machine gun entered the school and gunned down 8 teachers and 30 children; Nathan had been in the toilets when he was aware of the noise of the shots and, instinctively, he hid in the janitor's cupboard.

Samuel ran into the toilets. "Are you in here, Nate?"

The brothers were two out of four survivors and one of those had life-changing injuries and was left in a wheelchair.

"Yes!" was the faint response from the small cupboard.

For the next eight hours before the police were able to enter and subdue to killer as they hid, terrified in the cupboard. The police were searching the building, a young officer heard crying from the cupboard. Despite years of counselling, both were never the same and still would wake up sweating every now and then.

It had made Samuel interested in killers but stopped him being intimate as he feared loss, four of his best friends had died that day and he could not put himself in that position if he ever got close to someone to then lose them. He took three tablets every day that kept anxiety attacks at bay but he was still damaged by that childhood incident. He had even done lectures on dealing with being a victim and sufferer of Post Traumatic Stress Disorder.

His younger brother had taken his own life at 21 with a planned overdose. The professor was a leading figure for gun control and had spoken at numerous rallies as what had happened to him was all the often. "Many of you here are victims or know someone. There have been 380 shootings in schools since 1999, effecting more than 350 people. When will this end?"

The crowd cheered as the professor got choked up.

Chapter 53

Michael Pearson was not the only potential future victim in her diary from her school days.

A young man called Chas, as everyone called him, he was 21 and she was 16; she had defeated him in a regional final of a chess competition. They dated for three weeks and they had sex and then he never called her again, she was devastated.

From his point of view, he felt he was too old but he should have probably called her and explained because that decision had him on the list. She was only 16 but for her, she was angry. It had helped to form her kill guide lines of her moral code. Having lost her virginity to him, if she ever discover his whereabout he would go to the top of her list. He had become a recluse from society and decided to abandon the modern world, living off grid with his wife and children using wind power and solar panels. Rhona had been frustrated to not be able to track him by social media.

Chapter 54

Kylie was sat at the bar, drinking a craft beer and very noticeable with her tattooed arms and nose and ear piercings. Her amazing make-up, her exaggerated eye shadow and matching hair colour in a burgundy red. "Can I buy you a drink?" asked Rhona.

"Yes, please a bud."

"Your hair and eye shadow were blue before!"

"Yes, I change every month!"

"Can you keep a secret?" asked Rhona.

"Yes, of course!"

"When did you realise about your sexuality?"

"I knew early on."

Rhona shuffled closer. "Well, I think I am maybe not straight and I am a bit nervous and have never been with a girl and wondered if you might be up for it?"

Over the coming weeks, Rhona had found out that Kylie had been quite promiscuous. Kylie would be a game changer but not for the reason she would have guessed. Her plan was to leave her body in the snow, as she was petite. Kylie was a good snowboarder and, like Rhona, had her own equipment and had the board personalised with a design with flowers and butterflies.

"Butterflies represent metamorphosis," said Kylie.

Rhona was aware of the significance but let the girl have her moment.

Chapter 55

Ski Holiday Previous Season Courchevel 1850, December 2016

Rhona was excited as she put another spoon of muesli like cereal in her mouth. It was not Alpen, her favourite brand; it was out of a glass jar, so who knew who manufactured the mixture of oats and raisins and nuts. "Who makes the Muesli?" asked Rhona.

David said, "It just came in a big bag from the supplier's marked MUESLI, sorry."

She had a Pain Au Chocolate and a mug of breakfast tea. There were only two other people in the room they were waiting for an order, David making them something bespoke. She was still in her comfy trousers' slippers and a fleece top. She finished her cereal, took a swig of tea and ripped a mouthful of the French pastry as if that was her last meal, then carried over her bowl and mug to the side and Georgy the chalet girl thanked her for bringing her used items back. She headed back up the stairs to get changed.

Rhona was just coming down the chalet stair in her blue jeans, timberland boots, headscarf and pink jacket. "Are you not having breakfast?" shouted out Paul.

"I did earlier. Have a nice day, catch up later!"

"OK, darling," said Paul.

Emma gave her daughter a hug. "Enjoy shopping."

They had given her Christmas money early so she could buy her own present, too many tantrums over the years let her get her own stuff. Emma and Paul finished their breakfast and headed to the boot room. It was an unseasonably warm morning and outside was slushy. Rhona did not need the headscarf to keep her head warm but it did make her look good with her blonde braids. The French estate agent explained Francois Matter would be at the café that was situated below his apartment block and was owned by him but not the café itself, the cafe rented the premises from him.

The block called le home Courchevel *1850* was 30 apartments, mainly bedsits and it was that had interested her. Bedsits meant lots of single occupancy during the season. The block had been built in the 1980s and was a concrete construction with a wooden facade. This allowed more rooms to be fitted into a smaller area but still looked like a traditional building. The office had a small one-bedroom apartment attached to it. This café was more popular with locals than tourists.

As well as reading everything about crime and serial killers' forensic science techniques, she was a master strategist. She had won chess and draughts competitions and won the mind lab Olympics. The risk club at school had banned her participation because she was too good. Acquiring the apartment block was like her favourite chess opening, the Kings Gambit, which allows the most powerful piece, the queen, early access. Rhona saw herself as the queen in this analogy.

The 68-year French man was sat at the café with his expresso and croissant; he saw the lovely lady in a pink jacket. As she crossed the road as a car drove by and splashed Rhona's legs with the slush from its tyres driving through the melted snow. Francois got up from his table and stood up and ran across the road and blocked the car and bashed on the bonnet of the small fiat and started shouting abuse in French at the man.

Francois was bashing the bonnet. "You just splashed that woman, you're an arsehole. Be more careful!"

The young man leant out the window. "She should have not stepped out until I had passed." The young man saw how attractive the woman was and got out of his car. "Sorry, I am so sorry."

"It is OK. What's your name?" Rhona asked, he gave his name as Peter and then the young man drove off in his yellow car. Rhona was not sure if splashing her leg constitute a reason for your death but in the future, she would go out the way to see if he had done stuff that did.

"I am so sorry about my fellow countryman."

"It is OK; it was very gallant. Are you Francois?"

"Yes, I am. Your French is very good. Pleased to meet you." They shook hands and Francois ushered her to the café. "What would you like?"

"A crepe with chocolate and cappuccino. Thank you." They sat down at the very French café. It had four tables outside, another four inside with a small bar and little kitchen and toilet. She figured he had been waiting at least 45 minutes based on the number of cigarette butts in the ashtray. Everyone was smoking real cigarettes rather than vaping. *Very French*, she thought. "Can I ask why you're selling?"

"It is a good business you get the money from 30 flats plus rent from the tenant of the café, but my heart is not in it since my wife died last year." He wiped a tear from his eye. "My wife Madeleine inherited money and massive passion for skiing; thing is, I am from Marseille and my true love is to sail and I do not really like the cold." He coughed and lit up another cigarette. "Do you mind?" Rhona shook her head to indicate it was fine. "Also, would like to visit my daughter in Melbourne and my grandson and I can do that if I sell up. Why are you interested in this?

"Like your wife, I have inherited money and love skiing and the fact you're willing to stay on for another season to manage it."

"Let me take you through to the office and show you some of the amenities." He opened another door. "There is also a garage and large store with electricity and there is a communal laundry room and boot room." Francois opened an apartment that was a rear view from a road with a fire escape that connected a lot of the apartments. *That would be useful,* she thought. *You could move from apartment to apartment without being seen.*

They entered his small office. On his desk was the PC and a picture of his late wife. "Was that Madeline?"

Francois started to sniffle. The other picture was clearly his daughter and son-in-law and grandson. The picture was from the Australian city with an iconic Yarra pedestrian river bridge in the background. On the wall was a picture of a yacht. "Francois, is that your boat?"

"Yes, she is called Mistral, my 11-metre-long pride and joy and at the end of next season, I am heading to Melbourne with a friend who is helping me."

"Can you book me and my boyfriend for next January?" He turned on the computer and typed in the password: Napoleon 007.

"Why that?" she asked.

"Well, our dog was called Napoleon and I am a massive bond fan."

"OK, where is the dog?"

"He was my wife's dog and he just refused to eat after my wife died. The vet tried everything but, in the end, we had to put him down," François sighed. "You could see there is only sadness now for me here."

Now Rhona understood.

Rebecca Stephenson and Simon Brown. Booked in. "There you go."

She quickly saw it was a popular week for single men. *Perfect*, she thought.

"The money will be coming from an offshore account. I have your solicitor's details. Let me give you a deposit." She handed him cash counting out the 5000 euros and he printed off Rebecca a receipt and Rhona left. In her chess analogy, Simon Brown would be her pawn sacrifice.

Chapter 56

Rhona was saying goodbye to Francois. "Nice doing business with you." At the moment, she had concluded her business.

Paul and Emma stood looking down the mountain. They were at the top of the Chanrossa Black run. The wind was whipping snow at that altitude and it felt colder. "How are you feeling about what Rhona said yesterday?"

"I was half expecting her to turn around and say she wanted to be a mechanic in a garage."

"We spent ages talking through her A-levels and we thought she would pick maths and physics and do engineering because of the hobby with cars, but she was adamant she wanted to learn about drugs."

"Do not worry, darling, I reckon one season working as a chef and she will change her mind, racing you down, big guy."

Emma was gone down the slope in front of him. Paul was heavier so was faster, so let Emma have a 20 second head start. By the time Rhona had spent 3,000 euros in the designer shops, her parents had made it down to La Tania; she walked back to the chalet smiling in the sun with all her bags, feeling great like Julia Roberts character *Vivian* in *Pretty Woman* with all her bags. She had a present for her mum and another for her dad. But more importantly, she now owned property in the French Alps.

Chapter 57

Rhona had skied all over the French Alps because her mum was fluent in French. They had preferred the Troi Valles because it is the biggest ski area in the world and you can get there by train as well as flying. One season, they had driven the whole way but had decided it was not worth having done it once. By getting the overnight train, it would mean two extra days of skiing. Rhona preferred Tignes for skiing and the next valley Val d'isere for its upmarket feel.

The French estate agent could not find her anything that matched what she was looking for in the middle valley of Meribel. So Courchevel it was. By Rhona being based in the Troi Valles and a working out of Meribel being the middle of the three, it was perfect for her to kill in all three.

She needed some time off in January before the half term holidays and Rupert was willing to let her. Rhona had snogged Kylie but nothing more than that. It was time to get into the next phase. The first week of January, Rebecca Stephenson had a weekend booked in Alps d'Heuz. While there, Rhona was able to kill two more men, with throats cut with ice and 6mil of semen squirted over their bodies using the syringe to represent an ejaculation. Then Rhona got a local train to Les Des Alps where she had killed again with ice and semen deposited.

Chapter 58

From there, she made her way to meet Angela in Tignes. As far as the hotel knew, the only person staying in the room 107 at Tignes 2100 Tignes le lac was Angela Goldsmith. Angela's artery was slit like the others. Rhona had pressed the syringe full of semen on her body, squirted over her chest like the others victims. Rhona was watching her lover die, feeling confused.

"What is happening?" said Angela.

"It's OK, it will be over soon."

It was her first victim she had not wanted to suffer she had sedated her before slitting her throat. Watching her die from the plastic chair in the room was like playing a computer game *Mortal Kombat* where the bars representing the life force were going down with each combatant's blow, although in this case as each ml of blood squirted onto the carpet of the room.

As Rhona contemplated as to whether her resolve was waning already, she began to reminisce when she had first met the girl with the longest nails and eyelashes; she had ever seen with her delicious big booty. As the last signs of life drifted away, Rhona took Angela's hand and began to speak to her.

Chapter 59

As she held Angela's hand, she began to remember back. Rhona entered the estate agent.

"Hello, I wonder if you could help?" said a small receptionist.

"I saw online you may have some commercial property I might be interested in."

Then a tall, skinny white man came up to me. "I am Mark, the branch manager, but it's my colleague, Angela, that has just stepped out will be back in a few minutes. You can sit here." he pointed to a seat. I remember, must have waited only a couple of minutes, before a busty black beauty entered carrying a range of sandwiches from subway and trying to juggle several drinks. I got up, not wanting to disturb.

I remember saying, "I would come back," and you said, "No, I will eat while you show me, if you do not mind."

"My father and I rebuild classic cars, so need space to do this and store cars and parts."

"Interesting then the property you have looked at online then is not your best option because you're paying a premium for good footfall from traders or the public; instead, I have a better option, a selection of rundown garage/lock ups."

Although the cost did not matter, being a less used location did suit better.

"If you have time, I can take you there now."

I remember getting into the little green mini with you and that fantastic smell of coca butter moisturiser you used.

"So, there are 6 available out of 8 but potentially buy 2 next to each other and get builder to knock the wall down between them."

"That was such an inspirational idea."

We went back to the office and signed a contract; we went out for a drink later to celebrate.

"I remember you just decided to kiss me and was embarrassed in case you had got your radar off."

No, you're right, I am bicurious. The truth was Rhona was pansexual. She could find anyone sexually attractive.

"Goodbye, my love, you helped me more than you know in this great enterprise. OK, I need to go now."

Angela was dead.

Chapter 60

Rhona left the room and went out of the hotel unnoticed and into town and took a cab over the dam to Val d'isere. During the journey, she was wiping her eyes; that was the first victim she had got emotional about but that was probably why Angela had been kept alive longer and not disposed of back in the United Kingdom. She got out of the car and stepped into the snow outside the bar.

"Can you pick me up next morning at 8 AM?" she said in French.

The French cab driver was happy she was giving him a fist full of notes; more than the standard fare to guarantee the morning pickup. The day before Angela arrived, she had sized up another victim and arranged to meet that night. The public knew the murders were just in the trio valley. The Alps d'Heuz and deux Alps victims were yet to be found. This confident rugby playing accountant was cocksure of himself until he saw her come out of his bathroom wearing the forensic overalls and felt strangely weak and could not focus from the poison, she had given him.

She kicked him into the solar plexus and it stunned him slash, the ice had severed his carotid. As he fell to his knees, he grabbed at his neck as the red rich liquid poured through his fingers. He felt weaker. He began to cry realising he was nearly dead. "Sorry, Elliot, you should have thought about your moral standards."

Another one done bringing her total in the Alps to 8. She would leave early, get the taxi to station via Tignes to pick up her bags and stuff and then train from Bourg St Mouritz and be back in Moutiers station to meet Simon from his Eurostar. Rebecca would get the keys from Francois without Simon knowing she was the new owner.

Simon skied one day with Rebecca before coming over with flu-like symptoms and spending the rest of the week in bed in an out of consciousness. The Alps d'Heuz killing had generated a response from the French government. Some information had leaked onto social media, ski bookings were down so if the killer was not caught in the next couple of weeks, they would shut the Alps down a month early. Their first response was to issue a press release that French police had the matter under control and would send their star detective to the region.

Chapter 61

Sharon was excited to be getting on the private plane as she waited to be shown aboard, she knew environmentally speaking it was wrong. She was leaving from Charles de Gaulle. It was the first time she had been on a private jet. The plane was an Embraer Legacy 450 and the seats were amazing. Sharon was looking through the case notes that she had printed off. The Steward approached. "Can I get you anything?"

"Sparkling water, please."

The killer was three possible people. She scribbled on her pad. A French local, tourist or a seasonal worker. Why are all the victims' tourists? The first three victim crime scenes were different from the next ones. She examined the photographs. The wounds on the neck were unusual, not clean cuts. They were slightly uneven, but there was an expert that could confirm if she was right with her theory.

85% per cent of the tourists to the region are British so it could be useful to get someone from the United Kingdom to assist her. "Boss, is there any chance I can get these two experts to join me in the Alps?" said Sharon.

He agreed this could be organised as she texted him their names before she had got on the plane.

Chapter 62

Sharon's mother was born in Kenya from Indian descent and had met and fallen in love with Claude, a French businessman, who regularly visited Kenya on business. His interests centred on tea and coffee, being Kenya's biggest exports, Aluna was 24 when she left with him back to France, quickly married and after 18 months Sharon was born in Paris. Because of his wealth, Aluna was able to bring her parents to France. With her father's money, Sharon was privately educated and inherited her father's intelligence. Aluna had chosen the name Sharon, as it can mean princess. Sharon was quite spiritual and all her tattoos were of spiritual significance. Her spirituality came from her mother, Aluna.

Sharon had been incredibly lucky to have been surrounded by multiple generations of family and wealth and privilege but it was the balance of Aluna's parents' poor background that gave her insight at a young age of your surroundings into your perspective of the world. Sharon's problem-solving ability developed when she was young, she mastered crossword puzzles and sudoku with ease. She also had her IQ tested and was high 181. She had wanted to be a detective as long as she could remember and read every fictional and real crime story she could get her hands on.

She had read about a lady at the end of the 19th century in New York called Grace Humiston and was dubbed Mrs Sherlock Holmes because of her detective skills little did the teenage Sharon Dubois know that she would be given the title of the greatest living detective by the time she was 36. Her notoriety would grow after the next case when she meets Professor Rothstein and four years later, he recommends her to the FBI to help with a kidnapping case.

Sharon's piercings were not strictly in keeping with the look of senior officers but most were not visible and her long hair covered the multiple ear ones. Her nose one was quite subtle. She had a massive tattoo on her back it was a butterfly, the symbol of her faith in god and freedom to be gay and the transformation to the loving woman she wanted to be.

Chapter 63

The chubby handlebar moustache head of police Charles Robert for the region was waiting for her as the door opened to the private jet. The sun was blinding as she climbed down the stairs and put on her jacket and felt the wind on her, causing her to shiver.

It was quite chilly, so zipped up her padded jacket. There were several things Rhona and Sharon had in common. Intelligence, privileged education and a keen interest in fashion and a great sense of style united the future adversaries. The only time Rhona dressed poorly was for the character. For Rebecca Stephenson, Rhona had decided Marks and Spencer was a suitable look.

The French Sleuth put her *Ray-Ban* sunglasses on as she climbed down the stairs. Her leather laptop case with her computer, notes and photos draped over her shoulder.

She could tell the French policeman waxed his moustache because of the strong smell of sandalwood of the bestselling brand he clearly used.

They shook hands. "We are allowed any resources we need, so I have called in two foreign experts to help."

"Yes, they have already arrived. We were lucky they had both just finished a crime talk in Berlin so got here quickly on the train."

"That's fantastic. How long will it take to get to the resort?"

"Not long," said the police chief as he put his foot down on the accelerator. Another strength of Sharon was to use other expertise to help her. She was not burdened with an ego to get in the way, getting the correct answers was what drove her.

Chapter 64

Having gone through the computer and while Simon was drugged up, Rhona had followed the four different men and, across four nights, had killed them all. Their bodies would not be discovered until Saturday morning on change over ~~the~~ day.

On the Friday night Rhona had given Simon extra sedative, so Simon would not notice she was not back until the following morning and had killed in Val Thoren and slipped out in the morning and head back to where she had left her skis and made her way back via two lifts and three runs to get back to Courchevel, making sure no one noticed her pass through Meribel to get back to the apartments in 1850 that she owned. She helped Simon to the taxi.

"I am so sorry, darling, for being sick and spoiling the week."

"It is OK, love, nothing you can do about being ill."

As Rhona was making her way back to Meribel, as maids/chalet girls for both the apartments de Courchevel and chalet in Val Thoren, the five victims were found and Rupert was welcoming Rhona back from her break. Rupert had been given the nod that looks like the season may end a month early. Rhona knew maybe one more. She was at thirteen in the Alps plus London took her up to fourteen could she get one more. She had done the groundwork, number fifteen was ready.

"Sophie darling, can you stay out tonight as I am asking Kylie over," asked Rhona.

Chapter 65

Charles Robert, the only son of a local baker. Joining the police gave Charles a chance to stay local but gain respect in the community; now at 35 with a wife and two children, this was the first ever murder and he did feel out of his depth and was stressed, his assistant and nephew Joubert had persuaded his boss to contact Paris and get Sharon Dubois whom he had read about.

Charles said to Sharon, "We have had 5 more, just discovered but interestingly, first time we have had more than one killing in the same building."

The young Sergeant Joubert corrected his boss, "We had the couple. I mean, this is four different individuals in four apartments apparently unconnected."

"We need to get over and find information on the victims," said Sharon. Joubert immediately headed over to Courchevel.

"So, the killer is raising the stakes."

It was time for Sharon to talk to her foreign experts and get their thoughts. Sharon was sat in a conference room that was 5 metres by 10 metres long, a wall of glass on the left-hand side with windows all the right with blinds to block out the late evening sun. One end of the room was a double door and then in front was a long table with 6 faux leather chairs on each side, plus one on each end.

When Sharon had entered the room earlier in the day, it stank of soured milk. She noticed in the room was a mould on a paper coffee cup in the bin. She got Charles back in the room. "I take it last time this room was used someone spilt a latte?"

"Yes, that was me," said the chief.

30 minutes later, a small Spanish lady was working magic on the carpet with a wet and dry vacuum cleaner. The sour smell was just about gone and Sharon could now think again. Sharon was sat at the far end behind her laptop with paperwork all over the desk. On the wall behind her was a pin board and a white wipe off board. The pin board had the pictures of the 8 victims so far. Sharon had placed stickers on the wall where she would place the new 5 victims' photographs.

A young officer came into the room he had just printed off the pictures of the new victims, the police in those resorts had taken pictures and had been emailed. The white board had several questions, motive, any connections between victims. As her two guests came in, Sharon stood up and gestured for them to sit both on the left. They could read the information she gave them at the same time rather than wasting paper on making extra copies. Sharon was a big environmentalist, always trying to reduce her carbon footprint but understood taking the jet was a necessity sometimes. In fact, got to the office in Paris by cycling.

Chapter 66

Sharon spoke, "Have you guys been introduced to each other?"

"Yes!" replied the American. "Mr Robert did that earlier while his assistant has been keeping us topped up with coffee and croissant."

"What is your initial thoughts?" said Sharon.

"Yes, you have a serial killer that is learning their craft. The ice is to represent their power, whereas a knife would be easier."

"You think it's ice, then?"

"Yes, the discoloration as the ice burnt the flesh first and the uneven nature!" He opened his book that had pictures from the work of the Utah killer. "See the similarities?"

Sharon looked at the pictures with real interest. "Do you agree?" as Sharon looked to the British expert.

"Yes, this is someone with a significant god complex."

"OK, why the robberies then the semen and bank cards are left?" the female expert spoke.

"I agree we have a serial killer, not as the police initially thought a robbery gone wrong and the ice being a weapon of opportunity when they were interrupted during the robbery," the Expert paused. "The semen is our killer is now getting aroused by their achievements and he does not care that he is gifting us his DNA."

Sharon interrupted the British expert, "OK, so why the robberies then stop taking the bank cards?"

The Brittan answered, "I guess they are thinking, may as well take the money as they were there but once they realised after seeing the fliers that taking the bank cards could help the police catch them, with the bank cards being traceable; that's when only cash was taken."

Sharon had another theory but was not willing to share yet. "OK, why only tourists?"

"Probably because they are more vulnerable, as they do not know the place as well." Both the experts thought. "I would think we will find either the perpetrator is either strong enough to overpower their victims or autopsy would show drugs in their system to incapacitate them."

The profile that the British expected was as follows, "A male between 20s to 30s, mature enough to stay calm and intelligent to not get caught, although leaving a DNA sample by getting over excited was a mistake. But unless their DNA was on file already, they would still be untraceable."

Chapter 67

"It's been shown that most serial killers come from abusive homes, so you may want to go back from your arrests of locals over the last 30 years of abusive parents and any children that had to be taken into care. Serial killers are generally made," concluded the British expert as the British expert was running through the psychological evidence over the years to support the theory to Sharon.

The American jumped up from the table. "The killer was right-handed!" It startled the Parisian and the Londoner. "You can see from the start of the cut the angle," he pointed to several photographs.

"Are you sure as that immediately narrows the search by 50 per cent?"

"90 per cent as it would take a lot of self-control not to use your natural hand and I assume you would agree serial killers are quite emotionally driven," as he turned to look at the British consultant. "And unlikely to have the self-control to use the wrong hand," the British expert spoke.

"The other thing about serial killers is they often swing between remaining elusive and wanting to be caught to bask in their achievements, it is a strange paradox of their mental condition."

Chapter 68

The apartment block in Courchevel was cordoned off with police tape and two police cars were parked outside. The bodies had already been removed. Sergeant Joubert got out of his police car and a young police officer came over. "Do we have the owner?"

"No sir, but we do have the manager and the previous owner, Francois Matter. He can explain, sir," said the young officer.

Francois explained about Rebecca staying and buying but was on her way home to England but did have her number to get permission to access the computer. Rhona's green cased phone rang, it was the office number from the chalet. She was expecting the call.

"How can I help?"

"I am inspector Joubert and you're probably aware of the problems we have been having. I am sorry to say you have also had four victims in your apartments, we need access to the computer to look up the details of the victims."

Joubert typed in the password and printed off the information on the victims. Rhona had decided not to change the password on the computer yet, as Francois was still there. Three English men from different UK cities and an Australian living in London.

Joubert had been part of the French Olympic ski team before he ruptured his left kneecap and his uncle Charles Robert had given him an opportunity for another career. He was able to get through to Rebecca, so he thought and she explained her buying but that her main job was working for HSBC in Hong Kong and was getting on a plane from Heathrow in the next few hours so would be uncontactable for the next few hours if they had any other questions. Rhona put down the phone to the French policeman.

Rhona had based her character on the real Ms Stephenson, she had learnt about when she was 16. Cloning Rebecca with the knowledge she had been given had been easy. The real physical resemblance was the additional factor that swung it. Back to her chess analogy, Rhona had set up pieces for the endgame.

Sharon's theory about the killer was about to get some additional credibility when later that evening when the killer made a big mistake.

Rhona was convinced she had planned for every eventuality Sharon had studied magicians and the art of misdirection and she thought that was what was happening now.

Chapter 69

Kylie was fully made up. She had gone with green hair and matching green eye shadow. She was going to show Rhona how beautiful sex was between two women tonight. For Rhona, number fifteen and her third woman victim. Rhona got a text: Will *be with you in five minutes.*

That was the cue; she opened the window, broke off numerous icicles that hung just outside, including the one she had worked on and put them in the kitchen sink. She loaded the syringe from the sun tan bottle approximately 6 milli-litres and placed it back in the secret compartment. There was a knock at the door.

"Come in, darling," said Rhona and gave a quick kiss.

Rhona handed Kylie a bottle of bud. Kylie took a big swig from the bottle of the American beer. Rhona thought, one minute, let the drugs kick in. "I am feeling nervous, probably need the toilet."

She slipped into the toilet to put on her overalls. She had left them in the bathroom in preparation with her gloves.

What Rhona did not know was that Kylie had suffered from epilepsy since a child and took medication every morning and night. Stress or certain light effects could still bring it on, although largely the medication stopped the seizures. She had only had one in ten years when her and Joanna, her ex, had gone to a club when the strobe lighting had triggered an attack and Joanna had put her fingers in Kylie's mouth to stop her from swallowing her tongue effectively saving her life until the ambulance arrived and administered her with Diazepam to stop the seizure.

What Rhona did not realise was the medication Kylie was taking counteracted the drugs Rhona had given. When Rhona came out in her suit, seeing her totally alert, she thought, *Fuck, I have messed up.*

Kylie glanced down and saw the shard of ice and started screaming. Rhona acted quickly, used one of her martial arts moves and pinned her to the bed and her screaming was muffled but not before the now active police patrol through the village had heard the noise. They were banging at the main door. The extra officers had been drafted in from several nearby towns.

The police officer Hugo said to his colleague, "It is screaming, it's coming from there," as the smaller French officer pointed to the chalet. In there, they ran to the nearby chalet, the bigger officer Rene tried the door, it was locked. He stepped back and ran at the door, it burst off the frame and he and door collapsed onto the floor with a huge cracking noise of the smashed and splintered door frame blocking his fellow officer from entering the lower levels of the chalet, giving Rhona extra time.

The small officer helped his colleague up and remove the broken door to allow access. It would only be a few minutes before they worked out which room. She turned Kylie over, looked at the shocked expression on her face and particularly her scared eyes and with her gloved hand pressed her mouth shut and slashed her throat. Although shaking and sweating indicated the fear, that was the look in the eyes. The last thing that went through Kylie's mind was one girlfriend had saved her life and another had ended it.

There were six rooms on this floor, the police were trying each of them. Rhona had seconds, she opened her window, ripped off the suit and stuffed the gloves in her suitcase and slashed her own arm with the ice and started to scream. It was not hard to scream as the pain from her arm with the deep cut was real. The police pushed opened the door. And Rhona pointed to the window and started to cry.

The police man grabbed a hand towel from the bathroom and wrapped it around Rhona's bleeding forearm. It quickly turned from white to red with the deep gash. The police escorted her to the medical centre and the doctor had been woken up to meet them there. He gave her an injection and Rhona watched as her now numb arm with the local anaesthetic received stiches.

As the needle penetrated the skin, pulling the medical thread through the hole to the new hole opposite and as he pulled, the flaps of skin came together, sealing the deep gash. It required seven stiches to close the wound. The process made her think of when she went to have eyebrows done using eyebrow threading. One pulling together with string, one ripping out with string.

Chapter 70

Sharon and her two guests were still discussing the case and it was considering time for a late dinner when Charles, the head of police, slammed open the double doors. The three of them were shocked at the French man entering the room with such force. "We have another victim but our first survivor."

As Rhona was brought in by Sergeant Joubert, another officer was bringing a remote control. The officer pressed the record button on the camera in the corner of the room and the light went on the machine and the recording of Rhona's interview started. Rhona knew the bearded American, his photo is on the inside cover of all his books. Rhona had read all the talented professor's published work.

She looked at the professor from the states, he had been air brushed for the book photo as he looked much older in person. The shock was the British woman that came across the room and gave her a big hug. "Yes, I was so scared," she sniffled.

Feeling her aching stitched arm as the anaesthetic was now wearing off. Lilly explained that this was her niece Rhona Smith that worked as a chef in one of the chalets on her gap year. Sharon spoke, "It's funny how life is full of small coincidences."

Sharon believed that apparent coincidences were just information that led us to make decisions without us being aware of it. An example of this was that Sharon bumped into a university friend during a Christmas holiday on a beach in Goa, the old Portuguese colony, before becoming part of India. A popular tourist destination, Southwest coast, 584 km south of Mumbai.

Sharon's university friend normally went to Thailand every year for Christmas. It appeared to be a random coincidence but in fact, Sharon going on about looking forward to staying at Baga beach in Goa had influenced her university friend subconsciously to change her plans. Sharon has a picture on her phone with her friend posing next to a cow on the beach. The cow being a sacred animal to Hindus. She had the cow tattooed on her calf, being a Hindu herself.

Sharon said she was 50 per cent vegetarian because she like chicken curry. The photo was a reminder, do not trust coincidence and never take things at face value.

Rhona sat down and Joubert came back in with a glass with ice and a bottle of Orangina, he opened it for her with the distinctive sound hiss of opening carbonated drinks and poured the contents into the glass. She picked up the glass and her hand was shaking. She started to drink. "What's that smell?"

"Sorry about that, we tried to get that out."

Had she been caught? Did they realise or would protocol one save her? All her suits were laced with Simon's DNA for this exact scenario. Rhona started to talk in English, "So, it is a bit embarrassing, I am bi curious and tonight was going to be my first time; I got back to the room 5 minutes before Kylie when I was making the room nice when a man came out of the bathroom in overalls and he was about to lunge at me when Kylie entered the room and he swung round and cut her throat, she fell to the bed. I started to scream, I grabbed at the suit and he tried to escape and caught my arm as he jumped out the window."

She finally stopped for a deep breath.

"Why did he not overpower you?" Sharon was bombarding the witness. Charles stepped in, "Remember, Ms Dubois, this young lady is our witness and just survived a horrific attack."

"It is OK. I used a taekwondo move on him."

"It's very important you give us the best description you can."

At that point, Charles laid out six pictures in front of her, much to Sharon's frustration, although he was in charge and she was just there to help. The six pictures Joubert had printed off, five known robbers that were no longer in prison, plus the flier. Rhona pretended that she needed time, then grabbed the one that looked like Simon.

"Did you get a good look at him?" Sharon asked.

Rhona gave a perfect description of the man they had on the ATM video. "Do you feel safe going back to the chalet; we are collecting DNA from your room but your stuff has been taken to a spare room with your roommates. And a police officer will be on guard all night."

Sharon had one last thing she wanted the girl to do. "Can you sign me your name?"

The members of the room were confused. Rhona knew exactly what the French detective was on about. She picked up the pen with her right hand and

130

saw out the corner of her eye the French detective smile before she transferred it to her left and did a perfect signature with her left hand.

"Wow, my arm aches." *Round one to me*, Rhona thought to herself.

Lilly looked her niece in the eye. *Was it possible?* she thought to herself.

Chapter 71

ALPS Closed as SERIAL KILLER STIKES; FRENCH POLICE BAFFLED BY ICE Slasher!

The British newspaper had given the young French officer Hugo 5000 euros for the scoop on some details. He knew it was wrong but he and his wife were saving for a house and it was too good an opportunity. He explained one English girl had survived an attack, although was not willing to give her name. Also, the murders were being committed using an icicle as a weapon.

That was it. With the killing of Kylie, the French Alps were closed and extra planes and trains were being laid on to get people home. Ideally, Rhona wanted more victims by the ice slasher from this first winter season but otherwise it had been a successful start. She had made one mistake but her planning had protected her.

It was good. Seeing her aunt even if initially it was a shock but this was her field of expertise.

That French detective looked super smart, she would see what she could find about her. She found the article online and it was clear she was an adversary to be reckoned with. She clearly suspected something, otherwise the signature thing was too random.

Sophie said she would keep in touch and she had a summer job in Ibiza under Rupert again, as she did not want to join the corporate world. "I will try to organise coming over to visit in the summer with my friend Belinda."

"I would like that."

It was strange, Rhona had been generally anti-social in her life, but suddenly she was widening the group. But her killing was her job and this was separate. Rhona's plan was because Kylie was small, she was going to carry her and she would be the first victim to be found outside. Yet another different variant, as she would be the first non-tourist and found outside. She imagined they would think she had just stumbled across the killer by accident.

Chapter 72

La Flambee Restaurant Meribel 8 PM

Sharon was sat at the table waiting for her guest, the next day dinner at the pizzeria in Meribel called La Flambee as Rhona was on a train back to London. The DNA results were in. Sharon and Lily would discuss it over dinner. "Good evening," said the tall British woman and then continued, "Are we waiting for the American to join us?"

"No," Sharon said firmly.

Lilly had picked up a gay vibe from Sharon and just wondered. "Just to clear the air, you are a very attractive woman but I do not swing that way."

"Very perceptive but I am in a relationship with a lovely lady," said Sharon.

"So, why is it just the two of us?" questioned Ms Boswell.

Sharon began her rehearsed idea. "We have the DNA from the room, it matches Sophie, Rhona and Kylie as we would expect and one other and this matches the DNA from the other victims and the DNA from semen."

"So, all the evidence points towards a Mediterranean-looking man. But what if this is all misdirection?" Sharon paused as she took a sip of her water. "The killer stole the bank cards to make the police think they were looking for a robber, knowing the ATM would capture their image but as a hypothesis that, in fact, the killer is the exact opposite," said the Parisian Detective.

Sharon let that sit in Lilly's brain for a minute before she hit her with it. "Tell me about your niece, the only survivor?"

"She is a black belt in martial arts, incredibly smart and has an offer to study at UCL."

"I would like to arrange for me to have school reports and a list of all her teachers to interview, plus interviews with her parents!"

Lilly took a deep intake of breath and coughed. "Do you seriously suspect my niece, who I have known all my life, is a serial killer?" She took a deep breath. "Is that why you asked her to sign her name?"

The French woman nodded in the affirmative. Ms Lilly Boswell knew she would have to arrange this; her boss has made it clear, they had to fully cooperate. But she adored her niece. Whatever she had done, she wanted to protect her.

Chapter 73

Harry Binder, Lilly's boss, was from a family of police officers, both his grandfather and father. His father was only recently retired as head of the metropolitan police. Harry had a high performing siblings; his older sister Louise was a solicitor, had her own firm and his older brother Charlie was a big record producer. Harry had been unplanned pregnancy and you could say a Christmas gift as he was born on boxing day. Harry's parents lived in the affluent Mill Hill, not that far from Hendon College where Harry had done his 13 weeks training. Harry worked extra hard to prove he deserved every promotion. He was now in his early forties and chief inspector.

He had formed a good team with Lilly Boswell, his hot shot profiler and Raymond Forrester, his murder squad lead and Mrs Paula Patel, who was back after maternity leave to head up missing persons/family liaisons. The amalgamated role for budget cuts.

Chapter 74

19 months later, The Old Bailey London. The most Famous UK Court for high-profile cases.

The case was being held in court number one. This grand room has a high ceiling supported by four hefty wooden beams. Four portraits lie towards the corners. The Duke of Wellington's is considerably larger than the others. It is an impressive room.

When the police had announced they had charged someone with the 25 murders, the press had called the killer *Billy, the beheader.*

Inside the court last day of the trial. The judge entered the chamber. "Please be upstanding," said the Clerk and defence barrister turned to the accused.

"I am sorry, I am not hopeful."

The jury came in and sat down. The judge began to speak, the bespectacled man with his white wig, as was the English justice system to proclaim neutrality by the judge and barristers wearing wigs in court. "Have you reached a verdict you are all unanimous on?"

"Yes, we have, your honour," and the Forman passed a note to the judge.

"The jury finds the defendant guilty on all 25 counts of murder. Before I pass the sentence, does the defendant have anything to say?"

The defendant screamed out, "I am innocent. It was Rebecca Stephenson, she set me up."

The French had wanted the accused to also stand trial in France as the DNA proved the Beheader and the Alps slasher were probably the same person. The defence lawyer had explained that the French system is different because the evidence goes to judge, less chance, so better being tried in the United Kingdom, better option with the evidence.

The British government was under pressure to keep the case here and refused the French request for it to go there. Because of the evidence and the unusual, the French government would announce that could state that the Alps' slasher has been punished if they were found guilty in the British court.

The judge spoke from behind his wooden bench. "With the heinous nature of the crimes, I sentence you to 25 life sentences with no possibility of parole. I would like to add, it is the first time in my 10 years as a judge that I wished we still had the death penalty. Take them down."

The courtroom all simultaneously took a deep breath in response to the comments of the learned gentleman. The media went into a frenzy, especially with the judges' comments.

Tabloid Headlines

LIFE TOO GOOD FOR KILLER!

Hang 'em high

INSTAGRAM PAGE 500k Signatures For *DEATH PENALTY* for the Beheader.

The campaign to introduce the death penalty was gaining momentum over this case. Not since Brexit had the public been so divided.

Chapter 75

19 months before French Alps, March 2018

Normally easter is a busy period and this year it was the middle of the range falling beginning of April, easter Sunday, 1 April. But unfortunately, with all the murders, the government had shut the slopes. The staff were heading home, including Rhona. Sharon was very frustrated but hopefully, the background information on Rhona would shed some light.

London, United Kingdom

Harry was sitting behind his desk. His desk was cluttered. He would defend his desk by saying to his juniors, "A cluttered desk was a sign of an organised mind!"

Regular games of squash had kept his stomach down because these days, Harry seemed to be attending functions rather than genuine police work. There was a knock. "Come in."

It was Lilly, one of his favourite officers, thank you. "I have had a strange request for information about your niece. Can you explain what is going on?"

"Well, my profile says it's a man between the ages of 20 to 30, they found semen at the crime scenes and a picture of a man using the stolen bank cards, although this Ms Dubois character has some off the wall idea that it's all misdirection, her theory is that must be a reason that my niece is the only one that has survived an attack, that maybe she has something to do with it, even though I explained she is good at martial arts and quite capable of seeing off an attack and has an horrific scar on her forearm from the attack."

The senior policeman ran his hand through his thinning hair.

"I agree with you, as a policeman for 22 years, it's a bit nuts, so I am not going to cause stress to the family or anyone else by allowing interviews but so we appear to be cooperating, you can get her school reports."

Chapter 76

Rhona was 16 when she created her false persona like it was fated to be. Douglas, the maintenance man from the orphanage, knocked on Janice's office door.

"Yes, come." She stood up from behind the desk.

"There is a girl here. That said, she attended here and wanted to see you!"

"Did she give her name?"

"No!"

"Show her in, anyway."

As the lovely blonde 16-year-old entered the room, Janice spoke, "Hello, Rhona Smith. What do I owe the pleasure?"

Rhona was shocked. How did the woman know her? She left at three. Janice picked up on her unspoken reaction. From her facial expression. Janice pulled a spare seat close to her typical school desk. "Please take a seat, my lovely and let me explain."

From the numerous folders on the shelves, she worked her way until she was happy, she found what she was looking for. She opened the brown A4 folder and amongst the pictures was a picture when she arrived at two and another the day, she left at three. The folder also had information on the trial and about her biological father, who was currently serving life imprisonment for killing Rhona's mum Anna.

Janice opened the draw in her desk and grabbed her black leather personal photo album and placed it on the desk next to the other information. The first few pictures were of her wedding and her husband John, then a little boy and then some more wedding pictures that looking at date she guessed was her son and then the little girl, the picture had the words Rebecca, age 3, written under it in red pen. It could have been Rhona's twin at the same age. The facial similarity was amazing.

"That is my granddaughter at 14," as Janice pointed to another picture. "My son and her, both work and live in Honk Kong now and rarely visit the United Kingdom. They do send me free flights every Christmas for me to visit."

As Janice Stephenson spoke more about her granddaughter, the idea was planted in the 16-year-old's brain. Janice had waited patiently for her to visit and was happy to see her growing up.

As Rhona began to look through her file, she began to cry. "'Ah you OK, dear?"

Janice began hugging the young woman that was the image of her granddaughter. "Why did they not tell me my dad killed my mum?"

Janice open a draw and passed the girl a packet of tissues. "I guess they figured it was quite a destressing thing to know and wanted to protect you from it."

Rhona quickly regained her composure. Clearly, that was the answer to the riddle where the desire that was building in her came from. She had killed a fish and a cat. The cat was the unlucky neighbour's pet that she had persuaded it to come to her with some tinned tuna as the ginger Tom tucked in, she hooked some thread around its neck before hitting it over the head with a stone from the garden. She placed the dead feline in the street, making it look like roadkill.

"I am fine now. It was lovely to see you, Miss."

"Do visit anytime you want," as the grey-haired woman gave Rhona a genuinely loving hug. Rhona left and headed home. She knew her parents were at work and she would wait for them to get home.

Chapter 77

Rhona had gone to Waitrose in Richmond on her way home to pick up a selection of ingredients and a good bottle of French white wine, the expensive Sauvignon Blanc seemed appropriate and some Kingfisher beers as it was curry, she was cooking. Her amazing chicken curry, her signature dish, as voted by her grandparents, aunt and parents.

She got out the wooden chopping board. Methodically, she would get out several small bowls to measure out all her ingredients in preparation. Onions pealed and then cut in half and then chopped down away from her fingers, holding it like a trained chef. She had warmed up the oil in a big green le Creuset pan. The sizzle as the raw onions hit the hot oil. As she mixed in her spices, her thoughts were to the coming conversation. She was trying to think of how she would start.

With onions garlic cooked, she added in the already browned chicken to the pan and finished off chicken and two jars of mango chutney. Just needed to simmer gently in stock for an hour on a low heat. Paul opened his front door; he was greeted by his daughter who said, "I have cooked."

He knew she was cooking because despite the extractor, the glorious smells had made their way to the hall.

"We need to talk!" said Rhona.

Emma was still parking the car. You could see on his face he was not sure if he should be worried.

"Wine, dad?"

"Yes, there is a large bottle of pinot in fridge, not finished. Mum and I will have one, please."

"I did get you guys another bottle." Paul and Emma sat nervously on the stools at the breakfast bar. Rhona was having a *Kingfisher* herself. She poured her parents a wine each.

"OK, I love you guys very much and totally understand why, but I visited Janice Stephenson and understand what happened to my biological parents."

Rhona took a swig of her bottle of beer. You could tell Paul wanted to interrupt Rhona but Emma dug her French tipped fake nails in his forearm, so deep he squealed in pain as she drew blood.

"OK, darling," said Emma. "I am glad you understand why we choose not to tell you."

Everyone was quiet for a few seconds. "Thing is, mum, dad, I do intend to visit him to understand why he did it." Rhona wiped her face with her hand to remove the tears that had surprisingly leaked out. "I am not ready yet but just thought I would share that I know and it's cool you didn't tell me."

Chapter 78

Studying for A-levels Richmond Hill Surrey, July 2017

"Apparently, her room is at the top of the house and faces the river, so that means her view is awesome!" said Rose. They were already halfway up the hill from getting off the bus.

"What's that building there?" asked Rose.

Belinda got out her phone. "It is the Petersham Hotel."

"I bet it's nice to stay there!" said Rose.

They arrived at the imposing town house and Belinda rang the bell. Emma answered, "Hello, girls. Rhona is waiting for you in her room. I will show you."

The girls followed her up the beautifully crafted wooden stair case. Both Rose and Belinda lived in impressive homes too but this was the next league. Rhona stood at the entrance to her room. "I just realised, in the years we have been friends, you have never been in my room."

Belinda spoke, "We have been here for dinner twice and remember, you used to live in Wandsworth, so it was easier to come over to mine in Teddington or Rose's in Thames Ditton."

"OK, girls, anyone want a drink?" asked Emma.

"Diet coke, please, mum."

"Do you have any juice, Mrs Smith?" asked Belinda.

"Paul is obsessed with juice smoothies, so we have orange, apple, pineapple or grapefruit," explained Emma.

"Apple please," said Rose.

"Pineapple please," said Belinda.

"How long are you staying, as I am making scones and can bring some up with tea later?"

"You know Rose is gluten intolerant, mum."

"Yes, I remembered that and I was making a batch for the charity thing I am doing."

Rhona shut the door and the two girls began to take in the eclectic mix of their friend's room.

Chapter 79

Her room was a good size, considering it only had a small dormer window. The view from her desk was she probably had one of the best views in England. "Do you realise, girls, this curve in the Thames is one of the most painted in England!"

Both girls leant over her desk to take the view, being higher up was even more impressive. You could tell it was Rhona's room as OCD affected everything. Her MacBook was measured to sit precisely in the middle of her desk, front and back and side to side. In the draw were spare pens and the metal tape measure.

On one side of her desk was a neat note pad with Mont Blanc pen and two picture frames containing family pictures. On the other side was a lamp and three metal model cars; even the match box cars were highly valuable and boxes they came in Rhona kept in a folder. They represented the three cars she and her father had restored together. Her books were organised alphabetically and by subject, as was her collection of comics. She had a three-quarter bed pressed tight against the left wall.

There were two framed posters and some frames photos posters high enough so the bed could be used as a sofa without touching them. Opposite the bed, on the right, was a wall of shelves. Only the top shelf did not have books but two pieces of *Star Wars* memorabilia. Next to the entrance door was a small wardrobe that had a chest of draws inside with a DVD player on top of the chest, with her table in the middle of the room under the window opposite the door. A two-foot gap remained on each side of the table on the outer wall of the room; tone were Rhona's skis, poles, boots and ski helmet. Belinda, as a fellow skier, loved her equipment.

On the left side was a table with an antique chess table and set. Rose, being a chess player, loved the set. "Where did that set come from?" asked Rose.

"My biological grandfather apparently was a really good player but he died before I was born. But my aunt thought I should have it."

Belinda looked up. "That poster is cool!" she said.

"Yes, it is an original promotional poster for the film *The Empire Strikes Back.*"

Rose stretched up to grab the two items from the top shelf and put the helmet on. "You can get your head in here!" as she flicked on the light on the light sabre.

"Unlike you, Rhona, I am not tall enough to be *Darth Vader*," said Rose. Being petit making her a perfect cox. In the *Star Wars* world Rhona saw herself as a Sith lord or Thanos in Marvel.

"What is the other poster?" said Belinda.

"It's from the 1995 movie version of *Judge Dredd* played by Sylvester Stallone."

Rose picked out one of the three A4 binders, it was the one she had not heard of. The other two had *DC COMICS* and *MARVEL COMICS*. This one had written 2000 AD. As Rose began to look through the binder with the comics in plastic holders. "I have never heard of *2000 AD*." Rose looked at the comic, "Wow, February 1977."

"My dad and grandfather were into them and I continued since. So, Judge Dredd was the most successful character. The concept is clever," Rhona could relate to him. "It's set in the future after a nuclear war and the remaining population live in overcrowded mega cities, so policing is difficult so the judges are judge jury and executioner for all crime. And they drive around on cool flying bikes."

"It sounds great. Do you have the movie?" asked Belinda.

"Of course, I do."

"Can we watch that instead?" asked Rose.

"Maybe next time, let's stick with a marvel movie as planned."

"So, how many comics do you have?" asked Belinda.

"4264!"said Rhona.

"While Rose is coxing and I am at hocky you're out buying comics."

"Yes, something like that, although I sometimes have taekwondo matches."

Rose put the folder back, then notice the bottom shelf was very different: several cook books and three car manuals by Haynes, including a 911 Porsche. Rose looked puzzled. "There are the three cars my dad and I have restored."

"So, are you going to turn up one day in the Porsche?" inquired Rose.

"No, unfortunately, it's worth too much money to drive on the road so will stick with my Kia."

Belinda was looking through another shelf. "So why do you have all these books on philosophy, politics and religion but you're doing science?"

Chapter 80

"Thing is, girls, knowledge is power!"

Belinda and Rose had been in awe of Rhona ever since they met at their school. They had talked for ages and finished their soft drinks. Emma knocked on the door, carefully took the MacBook and put in her draw and positioned the tray with the tea and scones in the exact middle of the desk and double checked with tape measure and then turned and smiled and winked at her daughter.

"Thanks, mum, you're a star."

"There we go, girls." And removed the empty glasses.

"Thanks, Mrs Smith."

As the girls tucked in, Rhona opened her wardrobe and on top of the draws was the DVD player. The girls were confused. "Where is the TV?" said Rose.

"I created this," as she unclicked a catch and the shelves swung open like doors revealing the television. She used Perspex that kept the books in place as the shelves opened, revealing the 32inch TV. "The original room was big enough for me to build a false wall!"

The girls were impressed with her ingenuity. The benefit of having an IQ 195 putting her in the top 5 in the world. The psychologist said it was higher than Einstein or Stephen Hawking. As well as creating a place for the TV, there was also a secret compartment for her special research information.

"OK, girls, so I have all the marvel movies, so let us for fun play a game to see if you can identify the movie from the first line and music." Rhona handed the girls the blind folds.

"If you girls get it right, I have two gifts for my best friends."

Her friends were intrigued by this. This was how Rhona manipulated them, making them thinking they had won something when she was confident they would not get this wrong. As in Harper Lees' *To kill a mockingbird, "Don't ask a question you don't know the answer to."*

Rhona pressed Play.

A famous man once said we create our own demons—music began—*this is a story about a guy in a blue house—all day and all night—I'm blue (da da de.)*

Rhona paused the movie. Both girls shouted out, "*Ironman 3!*"

"Girls, you are proper marvel fans." She gave the girls a hug, she knew they would get it.

"OK, the prize is rent and bills for first year at university. I have spending money for Rose in her gap year but need you to go via Thailand and do me a favour." The girls looked shocked.

"Let me explain," and Rhona took a sip of her tea.

"Last week I had the interview with Rupert Carmichael, the resort manager and he offered me the job as a chef in France. You may remember he was a head boy at our prep school."

"What, the one that was full of himself?" said Belinda.

"Yes, totally."

"But the big news, come on, girls, I need to show you. My parents have bought me a flat in a new development that I move into next week. So shall we watch the movie or do you want to go check out the flat?"

As Rhona took another sip of her drink, "So, as I will be in the Alps for half the year, so figured Belinda can use it and Rose is travelling, then the following year Rose and I will share."

Her friends gave her a big hug. As Rose finished off her scone. "Let's go see the flat!" Belinda nodded with a mouthful of scone.

"Belinda, do you want to come visit at Christmas? I will try to sort something for you."

Rose spoke, "Bet you're going to miss this cool room, though!" Rhona had now persuaded her friends, their next steps.

Belinda and Rose knew she was adopted but when the conversation came up, why all Rhona would say is, "Something happened to my real parents and that's all I want to say!"

After that door had been slammed in their face metaphorically, they never brought the subject up again. She trusted them with her inheritance secret.

Chapter 81

Rhona's knowledge was vast and varied. Shakespeare, Dickens to comics. Rhona had developed a moral code for her victims from her experiences and from literature. Race, sex, colour, religion or sexual preference made no difference to her. She had read most of the religious texts Bible and Quran, studied Buddhism, Hinduism. Rhona's God complex meant she related the most to Fredrick Nietzsche idea of the superman. Or in her case, the superwoman.

1. Make your own values.
2. Accept you may have to hurt people.
3. Understand you are different.

What no one could explain in anything she had read was why she got so much pleasure from killing. Surely, just being a psychopath was not enough to explain it.

One day, she would learn the truth of her ancestry, that would explain her desire to kill.

Chapter 82

Sharon had just finished printing off the emails from Ms Lilly Boswell, when another email popped up in her in box. It was from her boss, its title.

Holiday Request Approved.

Strange she did not put in a request for leave. She ran her fingers through her beautiful hair, it still smelt of strawberries after washing it. She tried not washing it every day as that was not good for the oils in your hair. She had a regular routine Monday, Wednesday and Friday, she did 45 minutes of weights before finishing with a 5-kilometre run on the running machine in the morning at the gym before a nice easy cycle on her way to work. She would put her long dark hair up and not get it wet when showering apart from today.

The crack detective was still trying to figure out the holiday as her calendar showed her the booked days off in her calendar for August when there was a knock on the door.

"Entrez si vous."

The small, attractive Greek Cypriot woman enters the room. "Hi, darling," she said. "Did you get the email?"

"Yes, I should have realised that this was you're doing."

Maria reached over to kiss her lover while placing the two tickets in her hand on the desk. After savouring Maria, she tasted of peppermint as always and always made her tingle from the kiss.

PATHOS, CYPRUS.

"You need a holiday, anyway, boss wants to see you!"

They both left the room together. "Sharon, can I make you a drink I am making the chief a coffee, anyway?"

"Yes, please."

Sharon's office was opposite side to her boss about four offices down. At the far end of the corridor was a small kitchenette for all the staff, with a connecting corridor with offices on both sides. At the opposite end was the stairs, lift and a large briefing room. Maria liked to bake and had brought some cake in and there were some left in the fridge.

"Sorry about the workload, Sharon, but that is the problem with being so good," said chief Louis Bernard.

Where Sharon kept herself in prime shape, the brandy drinking and cigar smoking middle-aged policeman was at the other end of the scale but he was of equal intellect to his young rising star. "I wanted to know if the documents they have sent you through have helped with your theory about the chalet girl?" he paused.

"My equivalent in metropolitan police force, Harry Binder, has been on the phone and they don't buy your theory and won't give permission for you to talk to anyone as they don't think evidence justifies stress on family, effectively wrongly accusing a young girl as they see it."

"OK, read this."

Sharon handed her boss part of Rhona's school report, where part of it she had highlighted in pink. *Although definitely a genius level of intelligence, some of her ideas I find quite disturbing and frightening. Michael Pearson, history tutor.*

Monsieur Bernard took a deep breath. "Over the last few years, I have learnt to trust that your gut feelings are scarily right."

The senior policeman looked at her in face. "Good news Sharon, you have just won the department raffle for two tickets to Phantom of the Opera plus hotel and travel. And while you are in London, happen to run into that teacher."

At that moment, Maria arrived with drinks and cake. "Problem is, boss, we know the school he teaches at but nothing else and it's now the summer holidays, how we going to arrange a meeting without help and the authorities finding out?"

Sharon took a bite out of the cake. "Thing is, Ms Dubois, you do not get to my position without getting some useful friends along the way; I have a friend that works in the French Embassy that is more than just a diplomat if you know what I mean." He winked at Sharon and took a sip of his coffee. "As long as Mr Pearson is not away on holiday, I am confident you and Maria will be seeing Phantom; I will keep you informed."

Sharon shoved the last piece of cake in her mouth and picked up her half-drunk mug of coffee to head back to her office. Everybody in the office was totally comfortable about the two ladies relationship.

Chapter 83

Daniel put the phone down to his old friend. Most of his work was routine diplomat stuff but did enjoy these odd pieces of spy work that came up. Daniel was thinking that Michael working at a school in Surbiton meant he probably lived in one of three possible councils Kingston, where the school was; Richmond or Merton, so would hack the council tax data base or electoral role.

However, Michael had a very active social media presence and one simple message did the trick. The Pearson family had already been away, so he could do a meeting with the French detective in two Sundays time and understood the need for secrecy but not why they wanted a meeting.

Michael got off the phone. "I have had the strangest call from a French Diplomat that wants to meet in secret about something."

Mrs Pearson kissed her husband and spoke softly, "You know, there is only one thing that this can be about."

Michael suddenly went pale. "Oh, the French thing in the Alps!"

Sharon wondered why anyone living in London or Paris ever flew between the two destinations as the Eurostar was so efficient and easy taking you from the centre of one city to the other. Although dinner and Phantom were great, Maria could tell her woman was distracted by the meeting she was to have the next morning.

Chapter 84

It was 10 AM on Sunday and, as instructed, she would come out of the town side of Surbiton station and turn right to the little café where Michael would be waiting for the French detective. It was a lovely sunny morning with a fresh breeze and it looked like from the clouds, rain was on its way as forecasted.

Sharon saw the ginger haired man sat at the back of the café. Daniel had confirmed imagine you're meeting Van Gogh as that was the best description Michael could think about how to recognise him. They shook hands.

"My French is not very good."

They both took their seats in the soft chairs. "It is OK. I speak excellent English, I have been informed."

The history teacher decided to take the lead. "I was intrigued when that man came to see me about arranging a top-secret meeting that no one could know about. I have been thinking about what the French police want to know from a private school teacher in London that is so important. Then it dawned on me, there has been only one student that I have taught that has physically worried me and thought it must be about her!"

Michael began to take out some A4 documents from his brown leather satchel. He was nervous and struggled with the buckles to get the documents out. The satchel had been by his feet. On the blank back of one of the pieces of paper, he began writing the name.

RHONA SMITH

Sharon was enjoying the vegan brownie so much she almost could not squeeze out her first question. "Do you think the young woman is dangerous?"

Before the detective had finished her sentence in her beautiful English with the French accent that the British find so attractive, Michael had flipped over the document he had written on.

The State Manifesto for Murder by Rhona Smith.

The title had two marks, a read circle with a large capital F and then next to it was a circle in blue with capital A, "Start reading and you tell me."

Michael watched the reactions on the French woman's face as she read through the essay, absorbing its contents. After Sharon finished, she put it on the table. "Can I scan this and send it to my boss?"

The red-haired man nodded his approval. Sharon began to carefully scan the documents. "Why the two grades?"

"I went to the principal with my concerns and he just thought it was a brilliant piece of work and that Rhona was jousting with me by making it so dark."

Sharon dabbed the milk froth from her lip. "Well, it's a valid point."

"The thing is, this was only one example. On another occasion, I am sure she followed me home as I walked. I glanced in the car's wing mirrors and I am sure I saw a figure that kept ducking behind cars and trees. When I reached my house, my children ran out to greet me but as I picked up my youngest, I swung her around in my arms and glanced back up the street and there was a figure stood partially behind a tree that I could say 85 per cent it was her," he paused.

"Rhona had this way about her that was quite intimidating, that she commanded the room and could make you do whatever she wanted; I noted she only had two other friends at school, two girls that had also been at the same prep school!"

"Two questions. Did you find anything strange in her friends and can remember their names?" asked the French detective.

"Yes, Belinda Robinson And Rose Coates. They were generally normal but equally academically gifted. I should add, you should also talk to two other teachers that hopefully will talk to you. Her English teacher, Ms Partridge and the careers advisor, Mr Ballentine, David."

Sharon put her debit card on the table. "Can you get us another round of coffees and quickly call my boss?"

Michael watched the French women go outside. "Two more cappuccinos, please."

Finally, someone thought she was not right. The summer sun was bright so was struggling to dial her boss.

"Bonjour." He was clearly not awake yet. In a brief conversation after what she had said, she was given permission to extend their stay and try to connect with the other two witnesses.

Michael was thinking to himself that no TV drama or book had ever written a sophisticated and smart detective as the one he had the fortune to be conversing with as she re-joined him.

"Do you have contact numbers for them?"

"Yes, but let me call them." Michael reached into his pocket and removed his Samsung. "Bella darling, hope not disturbed your Sunday but I am sat a caffe in Surbiton with a French detective that would like to ask you some questions in confidence about you know who, no it will not get back to her. Yes, yes, that would be a lovely idea, also I am giving David a call too. See you in 30 minutes."

Sharon looked intrigued and as she was about to ask a question when Michael made the give me one minute gesture with his hand. Michael put his phone to his ear. "Good morning, David. Hope I am not disturbing. It's Michael. Yes, Pearson, I wonder if you may be free to meet up in the next hour at Ms Partridge's house to discuss the trio?"

"So, you have a chance to talk and meet both the others. Now I can drive us there. I am only parked around the corner."

"That is a bit of luck that they're not on holiday," said the French detective.

"Not really because of two reasons; firstly, the worse kept secret is Mr Ballantine has been dating Ms Partridge since his divorce and the thing about British school system is private school holidays tend to be slightly different to state schools and our school starts its summer holiday one week earlier so it makes sense for us all to go away then."

Ms Partridge's flat had an allocated parking space she did not use, so they could park in; it would be easier if they pick up David from Teddington then head back over Kingston bridge to Bella's upmarket flat that overlooked Kingston bridge.

Chapter 85

The young teacher could not really afford the rent but her parents wanted her to have somewhere nice.

The young teacher opened the door to the lovely open planed living room with its balcony and views. Sharon was interested by the significant age gap between Mr Ballentine and Ms Partridge. On the glass coffee table was a jug of juice and glasses and a selection of pastries. While they were on their way to her apartment, Bella had popped into lift and gone to the Sainsburys local that occupied one commercial unit when the apartments were built.

"Please help yourself," said the teacher.

They all sat down on the two sofas.

"Ms Partridge, my first question I had, I have already answered once I walked in?"

"Really what was that?" Sharon passed Bella a piece of paper.

Rhona is a delight to teach and I am so disappointed she will be picking sciences for her A-levels.

"So as probably only a few years older, Ms Smith being as intimidating as you say, I guess you didn't want her to look your way."

"You're right; I would like to add she is probably the most intelligent individual I have ever met and the books she has read and can quote back to you passages is simply astounding."

Sharon thought she had too many cakes today but one more croissant, as the young woman had gone to the trouble. "Why the comment, the trio?"

She took a bite out of an almond croissant and directed the question at David.

"Well, as a fee-paying school, our academic performance is very important in persuading perspective parents it is worth the cost. So, monitoring our GCSEs and A-level grades and the percentage of students going to a Russell group university or Oxbridge."

Sharon coughed. "Pardon!"

OK, Russell group is the ranking of the top universities and Oxbridge is either Oxford or Cambridge, which is a separate application before main choices. David picked up a pastry.

"We had 8 girls on the Oxbridge program and were confident of getting half of them an offer, then one Monday the trio announced that their first choice was now University College London which is currently ranked fourth so not an issue but it was weird we ended up with the trio getting into the college. We did get one girl to Oxford; out of the eight, another into Imperial college London, St Andrews, Durham, etc. Even got a girl that is currently a lead in the west end, so a high achieving year but it was the way it appears that Rhona wanted the girls to go wherever she goes."

Sharon nodded, she understood. "I am sure you're aware Rhona is in a gap year, as is Rose Coates, although Belinda has already done her first year."

"How do you know this?" asked Sharon.

"Well, I track girls' performance for the next 5 years for our performance statics," said David.

"Do you think any of the girls are dangerous?" asked Sharon. There was a deep intake of breath from all three teachers.

Michael and her fellow teachers nodded.

"Do you think she could kill?"

Bella coughed as she gasped with a mouthful of tea.

"What the Fuck!" said David.

"Look, that is the reason for the secrecy. I am the only one that thinks this and I don't have enough evidence that is why this meeting is just us, please."

You could see the British teachers were blown away by what the French detective had said. "Rhona does not even know that she is a suspect for anything or that I am investigating her, so you can relax."

Chapter 86

Sharon left them with her direct number if anything came to mind and thanked them. Michael dropped her back at Surbiton, as there were roadworks near Kingston station. Sharon was going to walk to Kingston station but it just started to rain.

"You cannot walk in this, you will get soaked. It's no problem for me to drop you back."

Sharon was waiting for her train to Waterloo and, thinking about how productive the interviews had gone, she realised there was something about the station. In a flash *Harry Potter, Half-Blood Prince.*

Yes, google confirmed Surbiton was used for the beginning scene in the movie, more confirmation of her deductive brilliance and how she noticed everything. By the time Sharon emerged from Covent Garden underground station, the rain had blown through and the sun was shining and the love of her life was waiting.

They kissed and started wandering around the shops hand in hand. Tomorrow, she would fully debrief her boss but this afternoon, she and Maria could be romantic in London. Sharon did her best to make the walking through Covent Garden as though she was fully engaged but her head was still preoccupied with the revelations of the morning. It was at the point her phone buzzed and it was a text from Maria. I am at Neals Yards Remedies shop, think I lost you at the last turn. Sharon walked back to See Maria coming out of a shop.

"I brought you something."

"I will try to give you more of my focus in Cyprus, darling."

Chapter 87

Although flat 5 was owned by a company in the Cayman Islands and the electoral role had no occupants, the rent was paid by Simon Brown out of an account he knew nothing about. With the knowledge of personal information, one utility bill and Simon's passport, Rhona had set up a bank account online. Every month, Rhona deposited different amounts of cash into the account, ensuring enough to pay the fictitious rent and real bills. This was a clever missing piece that would seal Simon's fate.

When Paul, Rhona's father, announced he had managed to acquire one of the last Volkswagen beetle of the production line in 2003 from Mexico, he was excited even though the vehicle was worse for wear. The new type beetle was started in 1997 but Paul didn't like it and in fact, product of that one ended 12 years later unlike the previous model with its 65-year history.

It had allowed Rhona to explain she had found a garage to use for storage of the Mercedes and Cortina, to make room for his new project. She explained she had used her Premium Bond money to upfront the rent for a year. Her dad thought it was great and transferred her the money so she could top her premium bonds again and let her move the cars to their new location without knowing where he trusted his high achieving daughter.

Chapter 88

For Rhona, it was time for the next phase until university started in October. Rhona travelled all over London and home counties looking for fly-tipping locations where she could dump the bodies. But she had more preparations to do. The previous summer, she had completed her kill room. Rebecca Stephenson had purchased two warehouses or more accurately lock-up garages, two units next to each other with a drain and water supply meant she could wash things down and be more private.

Rhona had hired a local builder. Dave was the third builder she had interviewed. He fitted her profile because she would need to kill him after he had helped. He was divorced with two grown up kids.

It was August 2017 when Rhona hired Dave, the man from Tottenham, even though he supported Arsenal.

His job was to build a false wall, splitting both garages into 2. Each garage before the work started was two cars wide and 6 deep. After the work with the false wall, it left the front of each big enough room to fit two cars in front of the wall. She would also knock down the dividing wall down so both individual units were connected behind the new fake wall.

Rhona showed him the plan she had mocked up. The title on the paper said The Bat Cave. Dave almost started to laugh. "Can you do this?"

"Yes, can we check out the site first?"

"Let me take you there."

They got into Dave's white transit. The seats were covered in discarded McDonald's wrappers. The writing on the side of the van, **Dave the builder, no job too small.**

"So how many people will you need to achieve my secret bat cave?" She had come up with a ridiculous cover story. "So, I am a chef and import endangered species for people to eat." The cover story explained the reason for the freezers.

"I can do this on my own using a genie lift."

Dave regularly worked out at the gym and was covered in tattoos; he was strong enough to put the steel; being 5 metres, it was not too heavy as the section above it was supporting, was not too big and sliding the steel from the lift to the wall was no heavier than what he could bench press. Dave gave Rhona a list of materials to order.

The local *Travis Perkins* got her the pallet of bricks and ordered the brick slips. Brick slips are just partial bricks that can be stuck on to look like solid bricks. She hired 5 Acro props, these a tubular steel supports that are adjustable to height that is needed and 5 wall props, they look like big shelf supports. Multiple bags of sand and cement and the steel from local steel merchant. The mixer Dave already had and the special door mechanism she was able to order from the website he had told her about.

"I am fascinated by how you do the wall thing. Can I watch?"

"Yes, you're paying."

Also, the 45-year-old from Tottenham thought if a bunch of weirdos want to eat tigers, etc., who gives a fuck, plus this young woman was nice eye candy and she was keeping him topped up with tea and biscuits. Dave carefully chiselled out 5 holes at 1 metre intervals, then removed the brick in each of that location so it was big enough to fit the wall prop. Once all 5 Acro props and wall props were holding the wall up, he removed a bigger hole and placed the premade concrete padstone, a large concrete block at each end. This is what the steel would sit on.

From the other side, the genie lift, which is like a portable manual forklift in a U-shape with forks sticking out and vertical arms that raise another set of forks vertically with a counterweight, Dave raised the steel up as he cranked the steel up it made a clicking sound as the steel rose and was level with the padstones. He was beginning to sweat through his t-shirt and it was the first time Rhona had noticed how incredibly muscular this middle-aged builder was. For an older man, she could understand why he said he did OK with the ladies.

Chapter 89

As Rhona watched Dave, she said, "Do you fancy a tea break?"

They sat on two plastic chairs in the summer sun. Dave reading the *Sun newspaper* as Rhona was looking through Royston's suit case as some of his clothes she had kept as part of the story he had run off but also as memento.

"Do you want something to eat as I am off to place a bet, anyway?" said Dave.

Rhona thought about Subway but there was no way he would get the complicated way she liked her sub. "Yes, please, quarter pounder meal with strawberry milkshake medium. Thanks."

Rhona handed him a twenty-pound note. After lunch, it was time to put steel in the gap.

He slid the steel over and then moved the lift away. There was a small gap between the top of the steel and the props supporting the wall above. He then began to take handfuls of dry sand cement mixture and jam them into the gap. "Why do you not use wet?"

"Because it can shrink once that is set. We can take the props away and knock the remaining wall away."

So Rhona now had a 5-metre-wide opening between the two garages. Dave Roberts also installed a hoist and made some bespoke shelves with his table saw. This table would also be the instrument of Dave Robert's demise. The table saw is a sturdy metal framed about 650mm by 450mm with a circular blade that cuts from below whatever is guided over it.

In the left-hand unit, a metal door was disguised with brick slips. These are the fake front of bricks that are stuck on to look like whole bricks, the secret door would slide behind the wall at a press of a button that was also hidden. In front of the door were two classic cars. A red Mercedes 380 SL, exactly like the one the character Bobby Ewing drove in the popular 70s series *Dallas*. The other one was a 60s white Cortina Mark One, Lotus edition, with the distinctive green stripe. Ford had teamed up with the Lotus to race.

The love of classic cars was something that she had acquired by helping her father Paul with his passion and both her and her father could strip and rebuild engines. In the other unit were spare parts and tyres and wheels in front of the false wall. The garages had a large metal bath with chipped enamel with hoist above it and 6 industrial size white freezers. Below the hoist, in the corner, she hung plastic sheeting from the ceiling to reduce blood splatter to just that part of the room.

Also, she had adapted a table with strong eyelets to attach handcuffs to hands and feet. She had also stuck sound insulation panels all over the walls and installed a secret camera outside that detected movement within five metres of the front of her warehouses and sent the information to her phone. Rhona had picked Dave Roberts because he had no close family because of divorce and no one to miss him.

"You have done a good job. Let me offer you a beer."

Rhona decided Dave was not a risk for now so with only Royston missing, she just let Dave go and paid him a bunch of cash and said, "I have your number; I may have something for you next year."

Dave was a cockney that went to Southend for his holidays and never wanted to go away on holiday abroad as he disliked any foreigners, so he had no passport but did have a driving licence.

Chapter 90

Rhona had been back from France only a week and was feeling restless then she membered and looked through the contacts on her phone, Dave the builder. "Hi Dave, do you remember me you did my garage?"

"Oh yes, the crazy chef Rebecca," responded the Tottenham based builder.

"Can you meet me at the garage, I want to talk about another job?"

When Dave arrived at the garage, Rhona was waiting with a beer for him.

"I can only have one as I am driving!"

Dave was not so high and mighty to not on occasion to drink and drive but he couldn't do his job if he lost his licence, it was the same reason he was never to be seen driving badly or speeding despite the reputation of White Van Man. Rhona knew she had put enough sedative in the beer.

Dave woke, his hands were tied with handcuffs and he was on the table.

"What the fuck!"

He did meet her moral code as a victim, being a bigot and racist. The assassin pressed the button and the blade started to spin with its forty teeth with lethal cutting power. Deadly like the great white shark with all its teeth. She pulled down the goggles and pushed him across the table as the blade cut into his neck, blood from the carotid squirted Rhona in the face, all over her goggles; she wiped her goggles so she could see.

She heard the crunch as the blade hit the spinal vertebrae. Dave's head was hanging loose over before the last cut from the spinning wheel. Dave's head was the honour of being head number one on the shelf in the freezer, she attached a tag with his details through his right ear.

After she had wiped the van down, Dave the builder's white van, was found abandoned in Asda. She had parked it up at 3 AM then ran the 5 km to her car, just a nice 26 minutes in the night air. It would be impossible to sleep with the mix of hormones in her blood. She organised her momentos to look at the missing pieces in her collections over her table, like a stamp collector, before going to a fair planning possible purchase.

Chapter 91

She took cash and driving licence out of his wallet and entered the date and his information in her pink diary.

She also kept information electronically on a memory stick, each victim had their photo on there. She had several books that stamp collectors use. The first few pages had the 15 passports in it organised by nationality. Thirteen English organised by birth town and a German and an Australian. Driving licences would be her mementos if passports were not available. She wanted sets of five or ten, so four more Germans; she had four from Manchester so one more or six from Manchester to complete the set.

Her god complex was ridiculous, she considered herself a savant of killing. She needed another doctor. She placed Dave's body in the metal bath, then put on her plastic gloves and poured the deadly liquid over the body. She wanted to destroy Dave's body because as a chance to experiment with how effective acid was at disposing of bodies.

It was amazing how quickly the sulphuric acid melted the flesh and the calcium in bone and enamel in teeth took longer, leaving a red soup. This she transferred to the bucket and poured down the drain at the back of the building. Society becoming so promiscuous was making things easier for Rhona. Rhona had to consider the size of her victim so she could carry the bodies, even allowing for bloodletting.

She changed her car for something bigger, she just explained to her parents that the dealer was offering a great deal and she wanted to go electric with her new black Kia Niro, now blend in with the new uber drivers that were getting these. Although she just needed a bigger car. The first thing Rhona did was strip out the GPS from the vehicle, as she did not need anyone to be able to track her movements.

Chapter 92

Belinda Robinson was born at Kingston hospital in the maternity ward exactly four weeks after Rhona Smith on the 26 September, unlike Rose Coates having entered the world straight in water, being born in a water bath in her future home the following April.

All three girls were best friends at Twickenham prep school in Hampton Middlesex. And had all gone to Surbiton together with full academic scholarships, much to their parents' relief, although both Belinda's parents and Paul and Emma gave the fee money, they saved to charity, including money for more computers for the school. All three were such geeks they were pretty much just them.

Rose and Rhona had deferred their university place but Belinda was going now to do Psychology and Rose, Mathematics. With 9 A-stars and one A between them, Rose studied double maths, so four A-levels. Academically smart bunch of girls.

Chapter 93

Where many people struggled with some of Rhona's obsessive and compulsive behaviour, Paul and Emma had adapted to it. They felt so much love for her, it almost hurt. Belinda and Rose could relate to it. They also had similar control issues, although not as severe as their friend. They would debrief at school about home problems.

An example of this was, she remembered at 14, Rhona spoke, "I lost it last night that fucking philopena cleaner moved my laptop."

Rose spoke, "Do not, people that is just who we are, we need our things the way we do?"

Paul and Emma took Rhona to see the psychologist again. "We are concerned about the obsessive-compulsive disorder."

"Well, it may be just because she sees the world differently. I would say she is on the spectrum."

The lady gave her loads of test the last maths one Paul was blown away written on a piece of paper was a sequence of numbers.

"16 06 68 88 _ 98. Can you tell me the missing number?"

Within ten seconds, Rhona said 87.

Paul took a deep breath, he was flabbergasted then Rhona took the paper and turned it upside down then it became clear 16 became 91, 06 became 90, 68 89, 88 stayed as 88, then the missing number 87, before finishing with 86.

"Your daughter may have some socialising issues but she is clearly from IQ point of view in the genius category."

The previous night Rhona had got back home after school chess club; only Rose could beat her in the team, which did vex Rhona a bit about her friend. She opened the door to her room. She knew things were wrong, she took out her tape measure from the draw, her laptop was one cm off, being in centre on her wooden antique desk.

Dinner time was often a ritual; Emma had a book with the way her daughter liked her food. Examples of her behaviour were evident in her food; Sunday roasts, Rhona needed her meat in the middle of the plate but gravy had to be on the plate, first each side of the meat had to be an equal number of Yorkshire puddings and potatoes. Carrots in one, Yorkshire and pees in the other. If there was more than one green like Brussels, then the pees and Brussels mixed up and still be in the Yorkshire.

Chapter 94

Paul and Emma had moved to Richmond so it was easy for school runs as Twickenham Prep in Hampton is a 5-minute drive from there and equally quick to lady Eleanor hills private school that her mum was an ex-student of and hoped her daughter would end up at the same place.

However, Rhona had chosen Surbiton with her friends, instead of her mum's old school. Her mum had questioned her choice but Rhona wanted her and Rose and Belinda to be together and knew with Belinda's mum being involved with Surbiton School, there was no way she was not going to go there.

Chapter 95

During their A-levels, Rhona had worked on her friends subconsciously to influence their decisions, for Belinda and Rose, to drop their application to Oxbridge; she wanted them at University College London with her. She was confident if both girls applied, they would get an offer and although UCL is one of the top universities, she was sure their parents would put pressure on them to take the more famous institutions if they got an Oxbridge offer.

Rhona's plans were London, she was not confident of achieving her plans if based in a rural setting. London was easier to disappear, plus getting bodies to storage. Both Belinda and Rose had a big part to play, even if they were not aware.

The only disadvantage of London was all the cameras but with help from her aunt, under the guise of a school project, she had managed to get some essential information. It was the opportunity to meet Harry.

"Sir, this is my lovely niece. She is doing a school project about the police, sir!"

The senior police officer put out his hand as the savvy killer noticed something useful.

"Nice to meet you and thanks for allowing this. It's been amazing!" as she shook the senior policeman's hand.

Rhona had a map showing all the cameras tracking roads, so she could avoid them when required.

Chapter 96

Rhona never had any intention of going to catering college, it was so her parents would not object to the gap year and part of her cover. Being a graduate of University College, London, was going to be part of her serial killer bio. That she would realise to the world, hopefully from the sanctuary of her Thailand home.

She had looked at the most famous alumni from that distinguished educational establishment and Rhona Smith was going to top the list of famous alumni. She read it, this is what she envisaged the list would like, in terms of famous, as she wrote it on an a4 piece of paper and folded it and put in her diary. She had amended it as she thought it would read.

1. RHONA SMITH: Most Prolific Serial Killer with 500 confirmed kills.
2. Mahatma Gandhi: Successfully lead India to independence from the British Empire.
3. Chris Nolan: British film Director of my favourite movies' *Batman Trilogy, Inception, Interstellar*.
4. Chris Martin: Vocalist and co-founder of Coldplay.
5. Sir David Attenborough: BBC journalist.
6. Alexander graham Bell: Inventor of the telephone and founder of A T and T.
7. Robert Browning: Playwright.
8. Ricky Gervais: Controversial British comedian.
9. Francis Crick: Discovered DNA.
10. John Stuart Mill: Philosopher and member of parliament.
    The list of famous people went on but for the purpose of her diary, that was her list.

The irony of The greatest person associated with peace would be replaced as the most famous associated with evil doings as far as society would understand.

It made her smile.

Chapter 97

On one occasion, Rhona claimed to be looking for a room. The three students that shared a house had advertised that they had a spare room. The three were staying in London for the summer, as they had paid rent for the year, anyway. The couple needed the library with their research requirements. She had called them from the advert on the social media. Introducing herself as Belinda using her friends' details but with a different photo.

Rhona was now staying with brunette hair like her friend Belinda but she also wore glasses with no prescription in them. "Why do you have a spare room?" asked Rhona.

"Toby graduated and got a job with the BBC in Manchester," answered Oliver. Oliver was a single guy and had become best friends with the other couple.

It was a Saturday night during the summer. The three-bedroom house had been turned into four by using the extra reception as another bedroom and the smaller third bedroom was now a joint study for them to use. Rose was due back from her travels in August and move into Rhona's just before the start of term in October. She had been there just a week when she suggested played the Never Ever game.

"What is that?" asked Oliver, the shy boy from Taunton.

Elizabeth and Martin were masters' students. Elizabeth Explained, "Someone asks questions and we must answer honestly. If you have not done the activity, the questions asked, then you take a drink but if the three of us have done it, then Belinda takes a drink."

Her real motivation was in establishing poor morality for her code Rhona's last question caused them to all look down. "Have you ever cheated on someone you have been seeing?"

It was a question that none of them would have answered honestly sober but alcohol has a way of loosening tongues. During the last round of the night, Rhona managed to drop something in the shots. Once the sedatives kicked in, Rhona transported them to the garages. They all woke in her dark garages. The last man, Martin, physically defecated himself as she pushed the blade into his chest. Each one was lifted to the bench to have their heads removed.

During the summer, Rhona had joined several social media groups for new students to meet up with different people and figure out future targets. Her friend Belinda as was providing her with social introductions as role as second-year student, exactly as she hoped.

Chapter 98

Rhona was absorbing the atmosphere of the popular LGBT bar in Soho, London. The dance music was loud, it was a remix of one of years and years songs playing in the background, so Rhona would have to focus to hear conversations. She found herself naturally wanting to dance to music but had to focus; she was supposed to be upset. Rhona had been to this bar in her blonde days with Angela.

"Can I buy you a drink? I am Lawson." The tall man stretched out his hand.

"Marcus and gin and tonic, please!" As the barman handed Marcus his drink, Rhona was watching from about a metre away and was able to tune into the conversation even though the background music was loud. "Thanks for the drink."

Marcus went to kiss Lawson. Lawson stopped him with his hand pushed into his chest. "Steady on, mate. Can we get to know each other first?"

"Don't worry yourself, you're probably a cock tease."

Marcus turned and pushed through dancers to head to a different part of the bar, taking his drink with him. While Lawson was still in shock at the incident, she decided to strike.

"I am so sorry," and started to cry. "My girlfriend has just broken up with me and gone off and told me to sleep somewhere else tonight but I cannot really afford that."

Rhona's performance was so good that the kind man felt compelled to speak. "I have a spare room if you want to do that."

Lawson Could not understand why he had just offered a stranger somewhere to stay, it was his good heart.

"Really, you sure? I am Veronica." She sniffled and wiped her fake practiced tear with the napkin from the bar that had been under the gin of tonic of Marcus.

"Yes!" He took a deep breath and "I have had a horrible night so want to leave now."

For the Veronica persona, Rhona just used an oyster card to travel and cash.

"No worries," said Rhona. "I live in Finchley but I am leaving now."

Rhona was trying to work out if she had picked a good target as she walked with Lawson to Tottenham court road station. On the busy Friday night, the 30 minutes on the northern line, you could see that he was wondering what he had done.

She knew she should reassure the man and reached across. "It was really kind," and spoke in her well-educated voice of her Veronica persona, "I am not a psycho or serial killer or anything!" as she looked up at the tube map. She thought when most people make that joke, of course, it's a true statement. His flat was only 5 minutes' walk from Finchley central.

She stayed with him for five nights and established he had led a morally good life but after ten years of marriage, needed to be honest about being physically attracted to men. He explained he wanted to meet someone the old fashion way, not by using a dating site. Rhona suggested that come out to people that he did hobbies with, like fellow members of the squash and golf club and before too long someone would approach him.

Rhona gave him her fake email for Veronica Stone and she was keen to know how he got on. A month later, he was dating a guy that he had played squash with for 5 years and never knew. Lawson was a criminal barrister; you never know he may be useful in the future. She gave him her email, Veronica.Fictus@gmail.com.

Lawson, being classically educated, picked up on the reference. "You know Fictus is Latin for fake?"

Rhona spoke, "I just thought in a world of fake news. I wondered how many people would pick up on that."

"You sure you are going to be OK back at your parents?"

Rhona gave Lawson a hug. "Yes. Take care!" She had proved to herself she could resist killing if someone did not fit her code. She added the kind man to the front of the diary.

Another night she tried something similar but asked someone on the tube, having followed them from the bar. They had offered a sofa bed in the house they shared with three people; to thank them, she offered to cook a meal. A week later, they were wrapped in plastic in her freezer. Even people with low morality could still be kind and generous, much to their downfall. She had 24 headless bodies ready, a random mixture plus several students. No real pattern exists in the group from age, sex, colour, religion or sexual preference.

Chapter 99

Rhona had considered escorts/prostitutes as victims as they fitted her code but they were too easily be linked in the first few phases. Same with dating sites, it was easier; she thought for those victims-to-be, to try to trace back to her via computer or phone. There had been too many serial killers over the years that had already done that and after her achievement, she did not want linking with their efforts. One of the most famous was Peter Sutcliffe.

Her next set of victims would be different. All employees from London embassies. They would still have their heads when discovered but have a hand's missing. The first thing the police would find would be a bag of hands. She would put in a note with the bag of hands. "Hands around the world," that made her laugh.

Then it was time to switch to her embassy killer profile. She was targeting French, Italian, Canadian and American embassy staff. Then probably Spanish. Rhona spoke fluent French but her Italian and Spanish were also excellent. She was learning Russian, German and Thai, all at the same time. Learning at the same time made things easier, so she had a picture of a visual, say cat and the three words in each language would come to mind, Kot, Katze and Kat.

Rhona's research found out that the American embassy staff went out at Battersea, now that the embassy was based at nine elms from 2018, moving from its historical location in Grosvenor square. The purpose-built building with better security was a modern-day castle with a moat around it and gardens, so vehicle access to the building was via an underpass.

Having secured four of his colleagues, Chester was the next obvious target. The striking physical specimen had played college football as a Tight End before his shoulder dislocation, which ruled out any professional career as his shoulder could pop out painfully at the slightest impact. This Physical impairment was going to save his life and jeopardise Rhona's. He was sat upright on a cold concrete floor, the room was in was poorly lit. As he began to wake up, he realised his hands were in handcuffs behind, his hands hooked over some sort of hook; all he could see was a light like the ones dentists use and that girl's voice.

"What is going on?" he asked.

"Time to die," as she lunged for him, he swerved and unhooked the cuffs and saw the keys on the table; in the motion, he had partially knocked Rhona out.

Now, he had ascendancy but it was dark. Where was his jacket and phone? He felt along the wall, still woozy, as Rhona was still on the floor recovering from Chester's blow. He found the switch and 6 fluorescent lights flickered on and he could see the door. He unlocked the cuffs, dropping them on the floor. He passed the cars, which he did not notice as they were under the tarpaulin.

Stumbling out of the area of garages onto the side road and felt his wrists where the cuffs had been and they ached, it was his dislocated shoulder that was bad, he was sweating. He bashed it against the lamppost and click, it was back in. Painful but the adrenaline was managing it, sweating profusely in the cold night air as he stumbled onto a bigger road.

The side street was badly lit and it was quiet, only a few cars were zooming past on the main road that ran past the industrial area but with no houses anywhere to be seen or get help. He figured he needed to get out, he could not see the person he had hit.

What time was it, he thought. It was difficult to focus. He was foggy and could not see properly, his tag watch, maybe 11 PM. No wallet, fuck, there was a bus stop but no money, his wallet was in his jacket. Patting his jeans, he found his gold American Express card, it had been the last card he had used to buy drinks and had forgotten to put it back in his wallet.

On this chilly summer night, it would prove to be his escape as he got on the bus, tapped his card. An out of breath Rhona was just turning the corner and saw him getting on the red escape vehicle.

"Fuck!" She had messed up again. She had not made the wall hook to allow for someone that must have somehow got his shoulders over his head. A bit like getting out of a straitjacket.

She remembered if you could dislocate your shoulder. That must have been what he did. Yes, point 57 in her book; Harry Houdini, the most famous escapologist of all time, could dislocate both shoulders. She had missed that. She would change the restraint system. Fuck. small thing get you caught. She howled to the night like a wolf. Hopefully, the drugs she had given him would significantly impair his memory.

179

Rhona knew she had been too over confident. Her arrogance could now lead to her downfall. Did she run, she had enough money. No, she would sit tight for now. That had been her third date with Chester, so she had already stolen his passport and copied his keys but now had nobody. But when everyone was looking for the beheader, Chester would disappear.

Chapter 100

Chester was still feeling rough and groggy when he woke the next morning but would make his way down to his local police station, which living near Clapham junction, it was Lavender Hill. *Google* said 10 minutes to walk to the location.

Chester was a mess, his head was pounding, he could not remember much; he knew they had drunk and he vaguely remembered running away from being handcuffed and his shoulder was sore. He needed a coffee. Where was his wallet and he could not find his jacket this morning, so had put on his Stanford university hoddie.

The degree in politics and European affairs had made him perfect for working in the American embassy. Would they believe me when I cannot remember myself but four of his colleagues and friends were missing and he and three others had been interviewed in connection with the missing colleagues, so hopefully they would believe him.

The black coffee with two sweeteners was hitting the spot. The morning sun, it was lovely on his face but he needed his sunglasses because of his headache. He was going to double up on medication, taking both paracetamol and ibuprofen.

The large female black officer at the reception desk asked him what he wanted and looked the big American up and down as she sucked through her teeth. He gave a quick explanation and was asked, though she looked at him again. Weird *white American boy,* she thought.

Dawson was the police constable on duty, so he took the statement; he knew this was under the authority of Paula Patel. "You have three things, partial name and her description and approx. time of abduction and possible bus; so, leave it with us, Mr Peterson."

It was Sunday, so he knew just to send an email to Paula and cc his boss. After 45 minutes, Chester thanked god, the headache clearing. And then remembered a detail as he was leaving the station.

"Someone will call you," said Dawson as the American made his way home, feeling better that the medicine was kicking in.

He said, "I do not know if I imagined but could have sworn, I saw a nurse uniform and red wig/hair."

The police man both believed him and felt they were happy he had given them useful information. Dawson shook the American's hand. "Take care."

Chapter 101

Paula tried not to work on Sundays but she was just looking at her week ahead as she sat at her kitchen table. As they were having a late breakfast of bacon and eggs, her husband was rustling up. She was working out what night they needed Parvati, her mother-in-law, to baby-sit for date night when the email arrived; the title read, **American diplomat claims to escape kidnapping.**

Paula immediately grabbed her phone that was charging and stood up and paced around the kitchen as she began to dial the number at the bottom of the email and put the phone to her ear. "Police constable Dawson, I will cover it with your boss at Lavender Hill but can you come to my office first thing tomorrow?"

Dawson had never been involved in anything so dramatic, just luck that he had swapped shifts for a friend that played football and they were doing well and their semi-final was Sunday morning in some amateur league thing.

Paula had an unprecedented number of missing persons. In 18 months in London, they had 70 plus. What was strange was how many were adults; they had ten that were studying at University College London and 25 from embassies in London, that was weird.

Paula said, "What does he remember?"

Dawson looked at his notes. "He thinks he was drugged and says it was a woman. He had three dates, Becky something and his passport is missing and something about the nurse uniform and red wig."

He turned over his page. "All he remembers is he woke up in a warehouse or garage and found his way to main road, got on a bus to Cricklewood bus station and got a cab from there last night. But that is all he remembers. He doesn't remember the number of bus."

Paula was thinking that was a lot of videos to check when Dawson continued, "I took the initiative to check, mam; there are 13 buses that go to that garage."

"Oh shit," said Paula, "but only 3 that includes the number 3, which he did think maybe in the number, which helps us narrow down the search."

"OK, I want to go to the garage and check the video on all buses with number three with a two-hour window of 10 PM to 12," ordered Paula.

Chapter 102

Dawson headed down to the garage and he spoke to Neal, the manager of the facility. The manager gave him a tour of the facilities, he then explained, "We have the footage on these discs from the routes and date you are interested in. The toilets are there, you can watch the DVD in here and in here is a small canteen."

The manager went across to the window and pointed. "Food wise is a Lidle supermarket opposite or turn left out of the garage and you will find a subway about a ten-minute walk!"

The bus drivers were all perplexed to see a policeman turn up every day to the garage. Neal tried to reassure everyone from the mechanics and drivers it was nothing to worry about.

They had shown the picture of Chester to all the drivers working that night but none could confirm that they recalled seeing him getting on the bus, unfortunately.

After a week going through each disc, he was just drinking his tea and as he was rescuing the chocolate biscuit that had fallen into his cup as he had over dunked. The process of rescuing the biscuit meant he almost missed the footage. He rewound and there he was. He finally saw him, he had found the footage. "Boss, I have it!"

It showed Chester getting on the bus at 11.05 PM and getting off 65 minutes later.

"Neal, I have him getting on this bus and off at the garage."

The manager Neal showed him a route map based on that. It narrowed it down to three possible stops. "I would guess these three stops are where he may have got on."

He would relay this back to Paula. "We have narrowed it down to three possible stops!"

On the table in the conference room, Dawson marked the stops on the large map that was on the desk, so these and these are warehouses and that is nine warehouse areas it was most likely to be.

"Some are just old garage lockups. But probably not the garages, as Mr Summers described a large room, wider than these garages."

Chapter 103

With so many cases this year, the doctor from last year had become a cold case. But this information, his description, something triggered in her. She looked through her journal from before, red head, prescription pads missing, attractive blond, hiding her face from CCTV, a nurse tunic to go use the prescription pads and wig to hide being a blonde. Something to think about.

When Rhona got home after Chester had escaped, she couldn't believe she had made the mistake. She iced the bruise on her face. After hot and cold treatment, within the week, it was pretty much invisible; any trace of the contusion and certainly was undetectable with foundation make-up. She would have to learn from this mistake and hope it was not going to result in her downfall, like so many she had read about.

Chapter 104

Paula Jones now Patel, having taken her husband's name, was from Portsmouth and had been raised with her older brother for the most part by a single parent as her father was in the Royal Navy as a skilled engineer and away for most of her childhood.

She only had three memories of him as a child. The first two were happy with family holidays, taking the ferry across to the Isle of Wight where they always stayed at Park dean Caravan Park at Nodes Point located near the little village of St Helens. The biggest asset of the location was a stunning view across the bay. They would always need a three-bedroom static caravan because she and her brother shared but they were only young and a room for granny. She still remembered the tacky children's entertainment and the two songs they would dance to. *Big fish little fish cardboard box* and *the cha cha, slide to the left, slide to the right song.*

Being young children, she had not picked up on the strain her dad being away so much was having on her parent's marriage, if anything, her child's interpretation was looking after her Alzheimer's suffering grandparent, which was causing the biggest stress to her mum. Paula had noticed her father kept a daily journal and had a picture of the three of them. The picture was a lovely one with Susan, her mother and Peter, her brother on Sandown pier in his journal.

Her dad bought her first journal and he had sent her one for her birthday every year from 6 onwards. The covers had got less girly as she got older. Her first diary was baby blue with a pink unicorn on the cover. It was a stormy Wednesday she remembered that changed the course of her life. The sad memories like yesterday, plus since her father had given her a journal every year, she was 14, as she never missed a day to scribe her daily activities and thoughts.

There was a knock at the door, her father was apparently off the coast of New Zealand at the time because the Destroyer he served on had suffered a serious engine malfunction and were stuck in Auckland, waiting for parts to fix the engines. Her mum answered and the two police officers came in and as Paula came down from her room to get another cup of tea.

She had been studying for her GCSEs. She immediately noticed her mum was sobbing and was being comforted by a female officer. The young police officer had to deliver the news, her brother had been killed in a car accident. It was where she understood the importance of family liaison and the supportive role of the police to destressed families. She also learnt the valuable lesson, sometimes things happen outside your control. Apparently, it was no one's fault; both drivers had been killed when the other driver's car brakes had failed when he was trying to avoid a flooded part of the road.

Paula helped her mum with the difficulties by looking after her gran and her father being away gave her empathy towards other families with difficult circumstances. The funeral was the last time in the next few years Paula would see her dad as he moved to New Zealand as he had met someone while the Destroyer had to stay longer when the repairs were done. To help her mum, Paula chose to do her degree in social studies at Portsmouth University, staying local.

After Graduating, she got a job locally with Social Services but she was frustrated with budget cuts that made her job harder. Three years later, her mum remarried and her gran was now in a home. She had no need to stay locally when a job opportunity came up. She seized the opportunity and applied.

Paula was not confident she would get it, but did think she had done an excellent interview. She was astounded when she opened the letter with the metropolitan police logo on the back of the envelope. It confirming she had the job. Her mum and step-dad were looking at her. "Well, tell us?"

Her mum squealed, "Yes, Yes Yes." And jumped into the air with the letter in her hand.

Family liaison/missing person's role within the metropolitan police. They were excited and she had to indicate when she could start and was a set of instructions but that was it, she was off to London with the blessing of her mum. And her successful step-dad gave her some money for rent to help with the deposit.

Gerry was a genuinely nice man and had taken to his step-daughter as he had always wanted a girl as well as the two sons from his previous marriage. He had lost his wife to cancer and he and Paula's mum, Janice, had met at group grief counselling.

Chapter 105

Paula was out on a date with her boyfriend Daksh, he owned a successful independent pharmacy. It was love after their second date at the movies with him, they were seeing *Guardians of the Galaxy Vol 2* when she started crying. The song was playing Brandy (*you're a fine-looking girl*) was playing and the scene was Kurt Russell explaining the song is like him, a sailor that loves the sea too much to stay with the girl.

Paula regained her composure. "I will explain when the movie is finished."

She explained about her own father. She explained the movie made her think about her father that had moved on to a new family abandoning them and losing her brother, so the emotional similarities to the film.

She felt her experience meant she could read people emotionally and the untimely death of her sibling. They dated for three years before they had got married and not long after that Paula had fallen pregnant. Daksh's mother looked after their little boy, as were both at work.

She had been back to the Isle of Wight once but stayed in a lovely hotel interestingly close to the old holiday park as a kid, her fiancé at the time could afford it to see the famous music festival.

Chapter 106

The police had checked out 6 locations, it was Paula and Dawson with Chester. "OK, I know we said garages will not be big enough; let's go there, anyway, as we have been unsuccessful so far," said Paula.

Rhona's phone pinged as the app on her phone was picking up movement outside her bat cave. The secretly hidden camera showed a suited woman, Chester and a policeman in uniform. All checking out the 8 garage doors. Her camera could see a wide area with its fisheye lens. The camera lens was cleverly hidden. Chester spoke, "It is those blue doors I am sure."

Rhona decided she needed to act and nip this in the bud. Rhona slipped on her mechanic's overalls and jumped in her car and parked around the corner, then arrived. The night Chester had escaped, Rhona had bleached her hair and was now a stunning blonde again.

"Can I help?"

"We need to see the garage. Is this yours, yes?"

"What the fuck is that shit doing here?" said an apparently angry Rhona with her cockney accent as opposed to the eloquent, privately educated girl.

"Excuse me!" said Paula.

"That man attacked me." And pointed at Chester, that looked shocked and was totally dumbstruck. The only time he had ever shown aggression in his life had been as a Tight End for Texas state university before his shoulder problems.

"Can you open please?"

"Yes, no problems," as Rhona took out a set of keys from her pocket that had a batman logo key ring. She uncovered the items, removing the green tarpaulin. She removed it to expose the two vintage cars. Paula could see confusion on Chester's face that he had no recollection.

"Wow," said Dawson, the uniformed officer. "A Mark One, Cortina." He was something of an enthusiast. The distinctive white car with the green stripe, the car a collaboration of Ford and Lotus for racing in the 1960s.

"OK, clearly nothing here. Do mind coming and giving a statement?" inquired Paula.

"No problem but happy to not make an official complaint, do not need the stress."

Her statemen read, "Chester told me he was interested in seeing the cars but I explained it was probably too dark but it was just a way to get me somewhere dark when he tried to get me to do stuff, so I suggested it would be better in the back and as he got out of the car to get in the back, I drove off and left the dirty drug taking bastard!"

The statement was a powerful accusation by Rhona. It proved effective.

It was his word against hers and clearly the units were not like he described. No real evidence and the garages were not big enough. They did not match his description of his recollections of the room he claimed to be held in. Paula was still sure this woman was someone to watch. But could not explain why. Rhona could see on Paula's face she was still suspicious. Rhona may have to accelerate things.

Chapter 107

Paula Patel had an eventful day with the statement from Ms Stephenson. She did not like the idea that, according to her information, it was Chester that was the predator but maybe he had taken drugs and was not remembering clearly. Although it was over a week ago, so could not prove it now. It could be he was angry at being rejected and nothing more than that.

Paula knew from colleagues false accusations were all too common about lots of things, making their job harder. Something did not feel right but she was too busy to dwell on this dead end; she entered it in her police records but also made a note in her personal journal. Paula had too much on her plate than potentially a minor incident. With no evidence of wrongdoing apart from contradictory statements.

One of her benefits of her journals is she could often find information, especially if she knew roughly the date, rather than database search or going through lots of filling cabinets. Also, some information never made into files if rules as too vague or irrelevant. Although she loved family liaison part of her job, her boss so the potential in her as a detective and was encouraging her to look that way as well in her exams as possible career progression. Harry Binder was good at spotting talent in his staff and nurturing it.

Chapter 108

Chester liked hot chocolate to help him sleep, as he suffered from insomnia for a long time. Rhona would exploit that. The key, that she had made a copy of, fitted in the apartment lock; she entered when he was at work and then added 5 drops of the liquid in the bottle of semi-skimmed milk, should be enough.

It was one in the morning when she crept back into his apartment. She used her torch, so no one could see lights turned on in his apartment that late. The drunk hot chocolate mug was by his bedside, empty on the table; his book had fallen on the floor and the lamp was still on, the medicine had literally knocked him out. She tried to shake him, he was out cold for another 6 hours. She worked quickly, binding him in gaffer tape.

The way that Rhona wrapped her victim's bodies is so tightly it was like the *Alien* movies before the creatures jump out of the eggs on their faces to implant their off spring. Police would like to re-interview Chester. She thoroughly washed out the mug. Picked up a suitcase and threw in a selection of his clothes to demonstrate he had left. The contents of his suitcase ended up in a charity clothes recycling unit. Shame for some of the nice clothes to go to waste.

Chapter 109

Autumn Before Going to the French Alps to Work, September 2017

With Royston safely on the ground and Angela and Simon still believed they were in a relationship with Rebecca Stephenson. Rhona understood the intellectual hypocrisy of killing for low morals when she was dating multiple people but hers was a higher calling, justifying the actions.

Rhona had arranged to meet Rose in Phuket during the autumn before she went to work in the Alps and Rose was to continue onto Australia in her gap year. Simon and Angela were not happy about why their girlfriend was having a holiday in Thailand with Rose on her own.

"Thing is, darling, originally we were both travelling together but then I got the job in the Alps, so I agreed I would just meet her for a week before she goes onto Australia. Just two girlies, a third wheel would make her uncomfortable."

This sentence, along with a nice cooked dinner and a massage, had satisfied both her lovers to accept it.

Rose was excited about the flight; the longest flight she had been on was to Tenerife with her parents, only that was only 4 ½ hours, whereas this was 11 ½ to Bangkok was something to look forward too. She was staying overnight and getting another quick morning flight on to Phuket. Both hotels were slightly better than backpackers would normally choose but that was part of the deal.

Rhona had found three things online but wanted Rose to check them out in person and then organise appointments locally before Rhona would fly out to join her and they would do some tourist things together before Rose continued to Australia. Rhona had an appointment at ten.

"Hi, I'm here to see Tony Jones."

The Australian realtor was shocked when the beautiful young woman came in. Even in flat deck shoes, she was at least 3 inches taller. "My friend Rose has said you have three possible purchases that would suit my requirements."

They got into his airconditioned BMW. "I thought we would see the two beach ones first."

As they drove, she looked through her phone at her notes. "I hope you do not mind but how has an Antipodean ended up being an estate agent in Thailand?"

The burly man spoke, "I left Sydney and travelled around all of Asia, Malaysia and fell in love with the place."

Rhona nodded because she equally loved the place, especially the food. "I was only 60, 40 that you were Australian, not New Zealander because your accent has softened," said Rhona.

"Strictly speaking, I am a New Zealander, as was born and lived in wellington until I was 8, then we moved to Sydney, so my accent is a mix!" The burly man rubbed his chin. "I assume you know this island was devastated in the tsunami in 2004. So, many of the hotels have been repaired or redeveloped but there are two sites that are still available with beach front locations."

Rhona nodded that she knew about the devastation. There were beautiful views next to the beach amongst the rubble and damaged palms when the powerful waves struck. One of the things she did not like was both locations had big hotels close by. Tony was trying to impart knowledge but not come across as a mansplaining.

"The third location was situated on a hill above Phuket town, it was a rundown colonial house from the days when explosion of tin mining industry had been what had caused this part of the world to thrive." Rhona nodded, she already knew this but let the man have his moment.

"Tin is still being excavated but tourism is the largest part of the Thai economy." The house, or what was left of it, had stunning views of the Phuket town below and the sea.

"What about the monkeys?" asked Rhona.

"The hilltop was popular with tourists because of the views and monkeys. However, the rundown building was just back in the trees. They tend to go where the food is and with an appropriate fence. Probably will not have a problem," said the Australian/New Zealander.

Rhona had sketches of what she thought she wanted to create but the hilltop house had given her food for thought. "Can you drop me off at the architects on Thalang Road? I will need some time to decide."

In the car, she drew out some ideas for the hilltop location and ripped the piece of paper out of her book. "I will be in Thailand for another 7 days and hope I have a decision for you then."

The main architect's English was not good enough, so his secretary translated. Rhona had only just started to learn the language. As well as developing the possible beach locations, she wanted a basic idea for the hilltop location.

"OK, these were some initial ideas I had," plus she handed him the new scribbles she had just done. She gave a fist full of Bhatt as a deposit and her drawings. She hoped her Thai would be good enough during whatever development she decided on she could converse with the architect without a translator in the future.

Chapter 110

Rose had spent the day at the beach while Rhona was busy. That night, they went to a night market and tucked into street food. "One green curry and one red curry please," said Rhona in slightly broken Thai.

Although not great, the waiter understood that the woman had tried and it was close enough. "So, was it a successful day?" asked Rose as Rhona tucked into her green curry.

Rhona put her finger up to indicate she would finish her mouthful before answering. "Totally and at the end of the week, hope I can show you, also thinking we go and get taxi to the temples and the big Buddha."

Rhona was inspired by the Buddha's massive structure that was sat on Nakkerd hill, the imposing 145 metre concrete structure that dominates the area. Walking around it made her believe she had a higher purpose in choosing her victims based on poor morals. They then had then a day of sunbathing.

"I booked us an island, hopping trip to see the limestone caves and **James Bond Island** and the floating town with its 100 per cent Muslim population in the largely Buddhist country," said Rhona.

Rose was excited about another day of sightseeing with her bestie. This part of the world had inspired Rhona since she was 13, when she had visited with her parents. They wandered around old Phuket town.

"Do you know why the buildings are brightly coloured and look Mediterranean?"

Rose looked at her blank face at the question. "Particularly Portuguese. It is because the European trade in tin and drugs back to Europe."

Rose and Rhona got on the boat with the other tourists. She was looking forward to doing this tourist thing but was thinking how many of these people she could kill given a chance. In this location, vulnerable tourists that could easily disappear, especially backpackers.

It had been a month since the doctor's demise but she needed to wait until France. Thailand was her escape plan and you do not shit on your own doorstep or cliches like that. The limestone caves were impressive, the way the sea had carved into the structures and with rain water seeping from above through the rock, leaving stalagmites and ice cream looking structure in the tight narrow cave.

The tourist guide on the boat explained why the island was called James Bond Island as he was making everybody laugh as he had picked an English tourist out and his wife and was calling him Mr bond and Miss Money Penny. He explains why that tall island is called James Bond Island. And its Thai name means nail because of its shape.

"Well, it forms the evil lair of the baddie in the James Bond film, *Man with a Golden Gun* out the top of that solar panel, coming out deflecting sun like a laser," in his thick Thai accent.

"Which *James Bond* was it?" asked Rose. "Wasn't it Sean Connery back in the old days," she continued.

"No, it was Roger Moor," said Rhona.

Rose's movies were Harry Potter and Marvel and romantic comedies.

The initial drawings were perfect. What they had come up with, for the hilltop location, was inspirational. She arranged another transfer from the Caymans and walked around the sweaty streets to the estate agents.

"OK, Tony, I will go with that one." She tapped on her phone and money was transferred. Tony sorted out the legal stuff and Rhona Smith now owned a property in Thailand.

"OK, Rose, let me show you."

The taxi took them to the top of the hill, they walked over to the rundown building on the hillside. "So, I own this site and going to have something new built here."

"Wow, the view from here is unbelievable."

"This is our secret."

Rose hugged her friend. "Of course."

The girls separated at the airport, Rhona home to England and Rose onto Sydney for her trip around Australia and now New Zealand, as she would not need to get a job to cover her costs, thanks to her friend's financial contribution.

Chapter 111

After getting back from working in France, she needed to get the numbers up as quickly as she could. She disposed of quite a few more in the next few months and it was so much easier than she realised her charm and looks were such an aphrodisiac for people. It made her realise why it was probably difficult for good-looking celebrities not to cheat, as they must get hit on all the time. She was beginning to think she was too hard on people in her judgements but so be it, that was the code she had and not changing it now.

"Stay focused, Rhona," she constantly said to herself on her nights out on the hunt.

France had been very productive for a shortened season. In future seasons, she could sit in her apartment block and using the garage that came with the apartments. She could work her way through guests without anyone knowing. Rhona picked up her pen and wrote in her diary.

As far as I know, I have made only two mistakes. I messed up Chester and Kylie. Kylie, I have covered and equally Chester had led them to her garages but that Patel lady did not look too keen to believe in anything he was saying. I have now taken care of him.

Diary Entry, April 2018

She would be heading back to Thailand to check on the progress of the construction of the project before starting her first term at university. She had one more group, possibly two, in her sights for this year.

The Coach and Horses was quite a popular location with the Italian embassy and the Canadian high commission. For the Canadians, she was using her new Deborah persona. With green contacts and glasses with brunette hair again and her accomplished accent. The Mayfair based establishment with its black-and-white mock Tudor facade did special deals for embassy staff on food.

Sam had come onto her straight away, he was bewitched by her. The young Canadian was dooming his self and fellow staff he lived with. The night they met, he was out with Richard and Richard's girlfriend, Susan. Samuel introduced his friends. "Hi guys, this lovely lady is Deborah."

Sam's friends were off to the cinema. "What you seeing?" asked Rhona.

"The film with Emily Blunt, *A Quiet place* and it has got the guy from the American office, her real-life husband, John Krasinski."

"Oh yes, it's supposed to be a good post-apocalyptic sci-fi monster thing," said Rhona. They stayed for some more drinks. "Nice to meet you, enjoy and let us know if it's worth seeing?" said Rhona.

"Where do you live, by the way?" asked Sam.

"Wandsworth!" was Rhona's answer.

"I am in Putney. Fancy getting some food with me in Putney and then it's only a short cab drive from there for you to get home?"

So again, she had made someone chat her up and invite her back Like Dracula must be invited into your house in the legend.

"Yes, that sounds like a plan."

Within the house in Putney lived Samuel, Richard, David, April and Britney and they all worked in the high commission of Canada in various roles. Sam was the only single person. Richard was seeing an accountant originally from Manchester. David dating a girl from south London, Niomi that was quite religious, as was he. April's boyfriend was coming over from Canada soon to visit so it would all be about timing if she was going to maximise numbers. Britney was seeing a guy that worked in the city. Lawrence was a particular knob, to the extent that Rhona was looking forward to his disposal.

Chapter 112

After a few weeks of dating Sam and in timing with April's boyfriend visit, Rhona had agreed she was cooking for everyone. Niomi was vegetarian so tofu curry for her and chicken curry for everyone else. Niomi did not really believe in sex before marriage but had eventually given in after 6 months that she had fallen in love. She had prayed for forgiveness for having sex outside of wedlock. Rhona had decided to spare Naomi because she felt she was fundamentally a morally good person, even if Niomi herself did not believe it herself.

"Thanks for cooking. Can we all say grace, please?" Niomi gave a little pray and everyone began to eat. "That was Delicious," as the black girl looked at Rhona.

"Thank you," the Croydon girl said. She paused and looked at her. "I was trying to work out your accent. Is it Birmingham?"

"Just outside the place called Walsall."

"Oh, thanks again. Is it Deborah or Debbie?"

"Either is fine!" said Rhona.

Rhona had practised over 15 British accents and facts on figures on the locations so even a local would not detect she was not a native from whatever location she claimed to have originated from. The benefits of superior intellect. Her ability with languages is she could have a long run as the embassy killer. The different looks she could create made her think of the children's guessing game **Guess Who?**

It was her hair she had to think about with constant changes, *very Madonna* like. She had everything she needed; a fortune, an incredible intellect and an un wavering focus and desire. She had read that although Napoleon and Hitler were at the higher IQ ranges; it was their charismatic nature that allowed them to manipulate others for their own personal goals.

For example, when Hitler became chancellor, he refused to take a salary although made it compulsory for people to own a copy of his book. Again, master manipulator. Rhona thought Hitler was evil with no redeeming features, somehow her calling was different. Having approximately in 500 million pounds in a Cayman account helped, although it was restricted to access 50 million until she was older, but it was more than enough for her plans.

Chapter 113

It was a great Saturday night, everyone was sitting around the table, just finishing the food, the chicken and mango and tofu and mango curries had been a big success; only Rhona's plate had some left, she moved her plate over to Samuel. "You can finish mine."

"Are you OK?"

"Yes, had a bit of a bug but did not want to spoil the evening. I need to be excused."

Rhona went upstairs and shoved her fingers down her throat, it did not work. Unfortunately, her skill as a lover meant she had no gag reflex; she was prepared as she drank some liquid out of a bottle and heaved her meal into the bowl. As the poisoned dinner hit the white porcelain of the toilet. To be sure Rhona did not want to take a risk with a dose, so she had the vegetarian curry. The previous week, they had played the Never Ever game and she had established they all fitted her code but one.

But this week, the Jenga set was out. She came back down and the residents had cleared the table and were now in the lounge part of the room. Only Niomi had appeared to had not done anything, her only vices were she drank wine, had a tattoo of Jesus on her shoulder. She did attend church every Sunday, so always set her alarm so she could get to church early to meet her mum even if she had stayed at David's.

One by one, they declared they were feeling tired and the poor performance at *Jenga* was a clue that the additional ingredient was having an effect.

"We are going to bed."

Each couple disappeared. With Niomi being the only vegetarian, she only had a mild sedative which Rhona ate. It was easy to add a strong sedative to the chicken curry. Rhona waited after she had sex with Samuel for him to fall asleep. It took her two hours in her car to transport all the sleeping guests to the bat cave and in a few hours, they would wake chained to the wall with amended security connections after the error with Chester.

She injected one by one with adrenalin to wake them up and explained their low moral standing and each one was stabbed through the heart and then each body was moved to saw table and had hands removed. In one freezer, she added them to the bag of hands and the other were hands with tags and later she would melt down the remaining body parts in the metal bath.

She calculated she did not have enough space to store all her bodies. Lawrence awoke as Britney, his girlfriend, was being killed. He screamed and defecated himself. Rhona could smell it. Maybe have to rethink the waking up bit but loved the fear in their eyes. Niomi had totally slept through her alarm, it was 11 AM, not 7 AM and where were David and everyone. She was quickly in panic and dialled 999. The police swiftly arrived, although it seemed ages.

A lady in a black suit said, "I am Paula Patel. Can you come back with me to the station, I need a statement?"

Back at the station, the young black girl Niomi explained the names of all the people; it was only Sam's girlfriend, she only knew her as Debbie or Deborah something. Rhona was confident that sparing Niomi was the correct thing to do, she did not fit the code and she only knew her as Deborah, a brunette, she had worn contact lenses as well and it had come up in a conversation about it being unusual having green eyes.

Rhona's natural colour eyes were blue. She had lenses in dark brown, a light brown and green. Plus, several sets of glasses and the opportunity to dye her hair as required.

"What I know is she has green eyes but needs glasses, brown hair, tall, from Walsall and a job in advertising sales in the west end."

"That's been incredibly useful," said Paula.

She could see the girl was in shock and a councillor would meet her to help her get over the shock and not to worry about what had happened to them. The foreign office had been asked by the police to explain the missing people from embassies but to date it was only English-speaking countries. Rhona would raise the stakes with the Italians, Spanish and her Russian was getting good.

Russian opened many of the old eastern European countries like Ukraine. She spoke French. It was German she also needed because she reckon that gave her another 11 countries where it was a dominant language. In Rhona's different personas, she could not change her height but could wear supper flat shoes and stoop to make herself to appear shorter. Sparing Niomi was just like her ATM stunt in the Alps, with a totally incorrect description of the embassy killer.

Chapter 114

Charles de Gaulle Airport, Paris, August 2018

Maria and Sharon were sitting in the boarding area waiting to be called when Sharon's phone rang. "Hello Michael, how are you?"

Maria was pulling on her arm. "We are being called. Tell him we will call him back!"

"I will have to call you back. I am about to board a plane." She put her phone into airplane mode.

"No worries, I am free all day," and the phone went dead. The two ladies picked up their hand luggage. Sharon was putting their bags above in the overhead storage.

"Do you need anything out of your bag?" Maria asked.

"No, darling, but I wonder what he wanted."

"I know it is all you can think of now," said Maria and kissed Sharon on the cheek. The case was at a standstill without access to her parents, who surely knew their daughter best and her aunt was out of bounds, as that would get straight back to her boss.

Maria slept most of the flight but Sharon was reading Professor Thalia Galanis' book as they would be having dinner with her in a few days. While her partner slept, she noticed her shiver, seeing her goose pimpled arms from the cool airplane air so covered her with a blanket. Sharon hated the smell of planes, the recycled air.

The cabin crew were asking passengers to prepare for landing. Sharon woke up Maria. "Darling, I know you are desperate to call that man back but can you help me with our bags first?" said Maria.

As they watched the luggage machine go around, it was not going to be difficult to spot their silver samsonite cases because Maria had personalised them. They had luggage straps as Maria had said cases break and get lost so straps and tags. They certainly stood out with the distinctive rainbow LGBTQ colours and matching tags. The women were proud of what they were. The noisy conveyor belt rumbled around with the strain with all the luggage from the full flight.

The strong detective reached in and grabbed effortlessly the 20 kg bag and swung it onto the trolly. Maria was watching bags emerge from the rubber straps that stopped you from seeing behind the curtain as if bag handling was the *Wizard of Oz* and to see the magic of individuals hauling bags onto a conveyor was a dark mystery only for the privileged few.

"I see the other one," said Maria.

Sharon had worked out it was 25 seconds for the bag to reach her. The loud conveyor dominated the noise of the room. In her head, she counted down. 5, 4, 3, 2, 1 bag. Both bags on trolly and through passport control.

They left the airport, the temperature difference was lovely. Paris had been 17 centigrade, dark rainy morning and here it was sunny blue skies, 31 centigrade that was striking from emerging from the airconditioned airport in early August on the beautiful Mediterranean island.

"I will make the call from the taxicab." Sharon removed a layer and tied her lightweight jacket around her waist.

"Hi Michael, I am free to speak."

Michael cleared his throat. "When we met, I forgot that I had met Rhona's parents a few times. They are totally cool individuals; they are very successful and when Rhona was given an academic scholarship, they donated equivalent fees to the school; they also told me they knew Rhona had some unusual traits and had her visit a psychologist because she is adopted but everyone they saw said having OCD is part of being so smart." There was a pause. "I hope that helps," said the teacher.

"Thank you, that does help." With Sharon in the back of the taxi making her call, Maria was sat in the front with the driver jabbering away in Greek.

Sharon needed to call her boss with the latest information. "Hi, I know I am on holiday but just received some information. Apparently, Rhona was adopted and her parents have taken her to see psychologists. Thought if we can find out what orphanage and then might understand the circumstances of her adoption."

Sharon heard her boss cough.

"It would be good to understand why Lilly Boswell did not mention her niece was adopted or the circumstances around that."

"OK, leave it with me. Enjoy your holiday!" said her boss.

Chapter 115

Pathos, Cyprus

Sharon and Maria were enjoying the mid-morning sun at their hotel. Maria had positioned their sun loungers for maximum sun worship, with a small table next to them and a parasol for shade later. Their sun beds were so close Maria could let her arm drop and she would be touching her lover. She preferred the big head phones that cover your ears but for sun bathing purposes, she had the pod type in as she listened to a mixture of *David Guetta* and *Calvin Harris*.

Maria sat up and turned off her kindle, she was at the end of a chapter of the romance novel she was reading called *The Wedding Date* by Jasmine Guillory. She switched between music and reading all morning. Her partner was so different, Sharon's massive brain struggled to turn off. They were supposed to be relaxing but Sharon had already worked her way through several sudoku puzzles and cryptic crosswords both in French and English.

The detective was so focused on the intellectual challenges and the interview information that she had not noticed a large English boy had been deliberately splashing them by jumping into the pool. Maria took her headphones buds out of her ears and started to swear at the boy before a fat burnt woman came over and grabbed the boy by his arm.

"That is naughty, Nigel," she said in English! She pulled him away and turned to face them, she spoke, "Sorry, ladies."

The boy huffed and turned to his mum. "They are Lezzos, mum; they were kissing."

It was clear the mum was lecturing the boy but they could not make out the conversation as they walked away, out of earshot.

"That was rude," said Maria.

"Did you notice how burnt they both were? God has a way of punishing people in ways that are not always obvious." Sharon laughed and gave her lover a hug.

Sharon thought back to the day she got the tattoo. "Let us go for lunch," said Sharon.

Chapter 116

Maria was a secretary in the department when she was picking up the gay vibe from Sharon. After 6 months of being together, Sharon turned up at Maria's flat with a small, wrapped present. She handed her the gift. "Happy anniversary."

The DVD was *West Side Story.* "I do not understand, I have heard of it but never seen it, so do not know what it is about."

Sharon kissed her lover. "Let me explain. It is a musical version of *Romeo and Juliet* that came out in 1961 based on the Broadway musical. Tony is Romeo and Maria is Juliet. Its two rival gangs instead of Montague and Capulets in Verona, Italy, it is the Sharks and Jets set in New York city."

Maria grabbed Sharon by the shoulders and pulled her face towards her and said, "So, are you my Tony?"

"Owe," winced Sharon and pulled away from the embrace.

"What's the problem?" Sharon carefully removed her top and on her shoulder was a new tattoo, it was a large red heart with black letters that read **MARIA**.

Both women began to cry. They kissed and Maria was careful with her hands.

Chapter 117

"OK, then, let's go for early lunch, darling," said Maria.

Their hotel was only a 5-minute stroll to the main Pathos harbour that was covered with small gift shops and lots of different restaurants.

"We have not eaten here yet." It was a cute little Italian restaurant which had about 15 tables, each with four metal chairs and white and red stripped table cloths. It was hot, even with the sea breeze, so they took a seat under the canopied part; although being early, still there were only two other occupied tables with hungover tourists, clearly having late breakfast. As well as Italian pizzas and pastas, they also did all day breakfasts to keep the English tourists happy.

Sharon's detective skills were not really being put to the test, sun burnt English man tucking into his plate of fried food, with one reading the English paper *The Sun,* some headline to do with the bank of England and Theresa May. Sharon was thinking how illogical the British had been to leave the EU. But as she watched the two overweight men tuck into the plate of processed food, understanding the direct correlation between health and food did not take a detective of her skills.

Sharon was not a French food snob, certainly saw the appeal of the three main famous English traditional dishes of fish and chips, sausage and mash and Sunday roast beef. Two years ago, she had been to a crime seminar in Cambridge and got to try punting and a ploughman's lunch at a pub in Cambridge.

Sharon understood research gave a detective an edge; for example, she had found out that the origins of fish and chips were from a Portuguese immigrant to London in the 15th century. Sharon was still convinced the first three victims were misdirection to give police a fake description. In many ways, her theory about the English girl was out there but the teacher's information, both from her visit to London and what he had said yesterday, just made sure she was right. She needed to put all the pieces of the puzzle together.

The waiter guided the ladies over to a table. Maria could tell Sharon was lost in deep thought. Maria browsed the menu and ordered in Greek for them.

"Mushroom and ham pizza and Greek salad and two diet cokes, please," said Maria.

The wind was blowing the salty sea smell into the café; when their food arrived, it made Maria reminisce about her childhood in Cyprus. Maria's family was originally from Pathos. As well as sun relaxing and meeting her aunt, there were several interesting archaeological sites to visit. Pathos had been improved as it had been a European city of culture the year before.

Chapter 118

The holiday had several things on the agenda; they were visiting some of her relatives, particularly her Aunt Thalia. She was a renowned professor at Athens University and Sharon was keen to meet her.

Maria and Sharon's relationship was largely physical, both shared a spiritual connection. Sharon thought María was the most attractive women ever and being with Maria was one of the few things that could get her to relax. "Maria, do you think the ranking police officer would cover for a serial killer if they were related?"

Maria looked out to the fishing boat that was coming back into the harbour. "Yes, I love you and I would do anything to protect you. Also, how many cases in the past were protected by relatives or partners?"

"Let us pay and go back to the hotel, I want to get through another chapter or two this afternoon before we meet your aunt for dinner."

Sharon had read the first three chapters of Professor Thalia Galanis' book **Political Systems, Genes upbringing and society understanding the nature of the human condition?**

Maria allowed Sharon two more chapters before she had something else in mind for afternoon relaxation. After some fun on the bed, Maria suggested second in the shower. It was the application of after the sun that led to thirds. Having fully recovered from activities to each other, showing their genuine love. Maria was on the floor.

"Why are you on the floor?"

Maria looked up at Sharon. "Will you marry me?"

Sharon kissed her woman. "Of course."

They kissed again and Maria went outside to call her parents to tell them the news. Sharon, however, was now desperate to read the next chapter of the professor's book before dinner. **What makes killers?**

Chapter 119

The professor had arrived that afternoon from Athens. She had been offered jobs at numerous universities around the world but liked to be close to the home she knew and especially as it was easy to pop to the villa that she inherited from her parents just outside Pathos.

The flight was quick and cheap from the Greek capital to Pathos, only 109 miles across the sea but sometimes, she would get the much longer ferry and read through the journey *The Slow Boat to China,* as she described it.

It was on one of those journeys watching the sea and feeling the breeze on her face, the idea of the last book struck her. This time she was excited to meet up with her niece and her partner, the French detective whom she had read about. She had not seen her niece for six years. Thinking back to that day caused tears to roll down her cheeks. The professor decided to cook some traditional Greek food tonight for her two guests.

Maria spoke in Greek, asking the taxi driver to pick them back at 11.30 PM. The villa had high walled grounds and the stone had been rendered with a metal fence gate and TV intercom on the white-washed wall. The height of the walls obscured the ground floor of the building and the lovely gardens and pool.

Maria pressed the button and the face of a forty something women appeared on the screen. "Yasso," said the woman.

There was a buzz and the gate unlocked. The stone path lead through lovely gardens past a swimming pool that was lit up and the sound of trickling water as the pool recycled and cleaned itself. As they passed the pool, Sharon was thinking she would like a midnight dip. They reached the house where a woman came out wearing a cook's apron.

Before Sharon could assimilate her surrounds the woman had hugged and kissed her. So, this woman was not only at the cutting edge of genealogy and psychology but also a great cook and likeable person. Thalia was pouring the three of them a glass of red wine when Sharon touched the professor on the arm and spoke, "Sorry, it's been a tough year."

The professor finished the bottle into her glass and slumped back down onto the soft cushioned chair and took a large mouthful of the red alcohol. "I am flabbergasted," as the woman sat down.

"How do you know that?"

Sharon pointed to darker marks on the walls. "The paint on the walls have faded due to sunlight but not where there have been pictures, the other pictures are of family, so it is fair to assume the ones that are missing were of you and your husband," she paused. She let the other two women take in her deductive skills. "Because you are missing you wedding ring and you still have the white mark, so sun has not had a chance to colour it in, it's therefore recent. I assume divorce or separation, because if death, you would still be glad to have the pictures on your wall and Maria would have been invited to a funeral."

The professor clapped, "Yes, cheating shit but fuck him."

The alarm went off on her phone. "I need to take the vegan moussaka out of oven and its grilled halloumi for starter."

"Sounds amazing," said Sharon enthusiastically.

They began eating. "I even know the young girl he was shagging because my loyal gardener Nicholas told me he had seen them kissing in the pool, but enough of that nasty business," she sighed.

"I bought a copy of your book with me. Would you sign it and I have my notepad, I am working a case and I think your theories may help."

The Greek professor nodded, "Of course!" and disappeared into the kitchen.

Maria had never seen her lover at work. "My god, that was amazing. How you did that?" Sharon smiled and kissed her lover with tongues. "Please stop, otherwise I will not make it through dinner," and they both laughed.

Chapter 120

Over dinner, Sharon was desperate to grill the professor more about her theories.

The professor began to explain more about her ideas. "I do not believe. It is a coincidence the way our western democracies are split into three parts." She finished the last piece of food on her plate. "The executive that makes the laws, the legislature that votes on those and makes sure they are OK and the judiciary that enforces them." She paused for her guests to take that information on board. "So, if we compare that to humans, the executive is our genes, the way we are parented is the legislative, the society we live in is the judiciary."

You could see on the faces of the two guests they were intrigued by Greek women's proposition. "So, how does that link to us being human?" questioned Sharon.

The professor took a sip of her wine. "I assume you understand Darwinism and the survivor of the fittest. We have evolved to survive and part of that survival is to kill."

Her guests nodded, they understood. "It is why most of us can serve as soldiers and kill as part of that duty." Sharon and Maria both indicated their understanding again as they took mouthfuls of the excellent moussaka. "To sum up, I believe we are genetically programmed to kill but most are taught that killing is wrong and some that killing is always wrong, hence pacifists and society tell us when it is OK to kill like war. Or countries that have capital punishment."

"Why do we get murders?"

"Two possibilities, they are not brought up to follow the rules or something additionally that strengthens that ability at a genetic level. Many of the scientists are still not decided as to which is more important, **Nature or Nurture,** just to add to the confusion. I believe we are killers but brought up hopefully that apart from special circumstances we should not, which is why killers can come from any background but the worse are often where this predisposition is reenforced."

Rhona was brought up 1500 miles away and had not read the Greek woman's book but had the same belief.

Chapter 121

Rhona was trying to decide if it was time to give the police something and if she did, whom would she contact. A quick phone call and lunch was set up. Rhona was meeting her aunt. It was a pizza express.

"How are things going? Have you got over the attack now?"

"Yes, studying has helped."

She had contacted several people on her class list and three of them were now in her freeze. Just as the pizzas were arriving at the table, Rhona began to speak, "I was wondering why you were in the Alps for the things that happened and wondering how it all worked?"

Lilly cleared her throat and took a sip of her sparkling water. "Can we start first, I am starving?"

They both had a slice of pizza and Lilly started, "Charles Robert is the head of police for the area and they do not normally have such serious cases, so called in their star Sharon Dubois, who is like their star detective for France and I was called in for two reasons," said Lilly.

"So, like a Miss Marple," said Rhona.

"Yes, so firstly because I am a profiler and that 80 per cent of tourists in the area are British, so she wanted a British connection."

Rhona nodded as she munched through another slice of the Hawaiian pizza. "Why that American chap?"

Lilly put her finger in the air to indicate wait as she finished her mouthful. "Well, the killer has been using icicles as a weapon and he has had experience with that in America."

"So, if a similar thing happened here in London, who would be in charge?"

"Well, that would be my boss, chief inspector Harry Binder. I need to get back quickly. Can I drop you off?"

"No aunty, the tube is just there." She put her hand up and the black cab pulled over.

"Where to lady?" The cabbie looked closely in his mirror and then turned to look at her. "Wow, are you?"

"No, I am not but I know I look like her."

"I have had lots of famous people in this cab. I had Tom Cruise in here once, he is short, whereas how tall are you?"

"5 feet ten. Scotland yard, please!"

"So, you a copper."

"Yes, murder profiler."

The cabbie finally shuts up with his cockney banter and Lilly could think. She loved Rhona and knew she had made the right decision. Paul and Emma had raised a confident, smart, together young woman and Lilly was sure that would not have been the case if it had had just been her.

Chapter 122

Back to Thailand Before University, September 2018

That was the plan. "Going on holiday with this guy been seeing but not serious."

"Do not waste all your allowance on holidays," said her father.

She had managed most of her travelling without her parent's knowledge but the Thailand trip would clash with Emma's brother's wedding. Simon was not aware that Rebecca entered the country as Rhona Smith. It was a shame she could not get his expert opinion on her project, as she could not have him knowing about her connection with her escape plan.

The first couple days were typical, good food, sun and sex and alcohol, but she was desperate to check out the development, so Rhona added some extra medicine into his beer. The next morning, he had the hangover to end all hangovers. "Why don't you take it easy in the room until it lifts and will pop into town as it's a market day?"

"I do not remember drinking that much."

"Maybe it's the sun, look at your shoulders."

They did look burnt. She had switched the bottles so when he thought she was putting a high factor cream, it was a low one, so completed the illusion.

While Simon was resting in their room, the Thai architect was pointing out the development. They stood at the top of the hill, looking down. In Thai she spoke, "That's the lining for the infinity pool."

The small Thai man said, "Yes, it will stick out and appear to be floating out of the hillside, as water splashing over will run back on its self underneath. Those columns, over there, form the underground car park."

Rhona was impressed with how efficient the local builders were with the development. Her money was being well spent and understanding Thai helped, as the architect explained to the foreman how important this build was. She rode back in the architect's car, thanked him before getting a few things from the market before getting the taxi back to the hotel.

Simon loved the holiday as they went their separate ways at Heathrow, he turned to her. "When am I going to meet your parents?"

Rhona gave him a kiss. "Soon, I promise!" Knowing she was lying.

Chapter 123

The advertisements in the UK press read:

French Govt Garrantee Safty For Skiing 50% Off The Price

French government will subsidise all winter holidays for the season plus military presence to guarantee 100 per cent safety. Despite these headline and ridiculously cheap holidays, bookings were still down 50 per cent. Rupert was relieved that bookings were down because he was so short staffed because of all the resignations, lots of half empty chalets, it just about worked.

"Rhona darling, need your advice; my mum and dad don't want me to go back and work this winter, even though there is going to be French army all over the place," said Sophie.

"Well, my parents are worried, so we are off to Canada but honestly darling, you have nothing to worry about," said Rhona in a soft reassuring tone.

"Talking to you has reassured me, thanks, honey," said Sophie. "Also, sorry we couldn't get to come over to see you in Ibiza this summer but promise, get something in the diary for next summer."

Rhona had been too busy racking up her numbers, maintaining the hormonal fix. The Humberside girl, like Rose and Belinda, was under the spell of the charismatic killer.

Rhona had wondered how long people would debate why if she achieved her goal and what the focus of the Netflix documentary would focus on. Even Rhona did not know the full story to why yet herself. She was trying to ponder what actress could play in a film. She knew from how they made *Lord of the Rings* with the hobbits, she did not necessarily be small.

I think, I would like the girl from the hunger games, maybe she was too old now. Jennifer Lawrence. Only an inch shorter, so I guess it depends how long I take, she thought.

Chapter 124

Whistler Canada, Christmas 2018 Holiday

The seven of them were waiting in the lounge. The Boeing 787 was now in position and the jet bridge was connected to the plane. Rhona watched through the window as luggage was being put into the hold and the lift, installing the food for the long flight to Vancouver.

"It's exciting," said a voice over her shoulder.

"Yes, totally," said Rhona as she looked at the teenager in the face. She was totally aware the 15-year-old pubescent boy had a massive crush on her.

"Please don't hassle her, Myles," said Belinda. They had organised the seats with Paul and Emma in two on left, with Paul getting closer to the isle, so Emma could watch take off from the window, then Rhona, Belinda, Myles and Maddie in the middle three and then Susan and Michael.

Susan knew her 15-year-old had a crush on Rhona. The window seat next to Susan was a native of Vancouver who had been on a visit to London but was returning for Christmas.

It was about 30 minutes into the flight and Rhona had been looking through an Air Canada tourist magazine with the big red maple leaf logo, giving details about their fleet and great places to visit in Canada.

"I cannot believe we have not done this before, considering how much both our families love skiing." Michael preferred snowboarding and did both to a high standard.

Because of its costs, skiing is largely a sport for the affluent professional classes. Whereas most people can book a cheap flight and lay on a beach. Skiing required lessons initially, the hire of equipment and passes for access to the lift system. This holiday for both families was into the multiple thousands. Skiing was certainly an indicator of your economic class.

Chapter 125

Rhona was looking forward to Canada for several reasons. Her family and she had only skied outside France twice. The trip to Austria was good, the resort was like something out a chocolate box tin with the design of the ski lodges but all three of them did not like the runs as much and they did not speak German at the time.

They had also done a trip to Italy, so Rhona could show off her Italian. Paul had refused to go to Switzerland, as he felt it was overpriced, even though they could afford it. They had also not done North America, either USA or Canada, because of journey time but they did not trust what the French government were saying about the security and they had been invited to join Belinda and their family to whistler for Christmas and New Year for a ten-day trip.

Rhona thought it gave her the chance to collect the 4 missing Canadians she needed for her set.

It was funny how things were often connected, her activities in the Alps were now leading to this opportunity in the continent of North America. Rhona reached across the aisle and grabbed Belinda on the knee. "It should be fun."

Myles was engaged in some movie as was his sister Maddie, she was only 12 but was already a great skier. Maddie and Myles were watching the screen, watching some popular movie.

Rhona was thinking about connections again. Her love of books she had read *The Hobbit* before Sir Arthur Conan Doyle as the creator of the world's most famous detective *Sherlock Holmes* but reading this, led her to reading another piece of work by him, *The Lost World,* a story about a professor Challenger discovering a lost world in the Amazon jungle with prehistoric creatures. It was made into a poor movie even for B movie standards in the 1960s.

After reading this and finding out about being adopted, Rhona came up with a story that her biological parents had been explorers and were still alive, lost in the Amazon jungle. This essay had won her a junior writing competition. She had since then read Michael Crichton's book *Jurassic Park* and watched the

Spielberg movies based on his books. Yet again, how things are linked. It was why she believed there must be a reason for her dark calling just needed to know where to start. One day, she would be given a book to answer these questions.

Chapter 126

The nine and half hour flight had given her time to think about how she was going to do this as it was a new, not pre-planned deviation to her original ideas in her diary.

The girls agreed to share a room to save money. Rhona was confident in ten days she could achieve her objective. The third day there and Rhona spotted a celebrity. "Look Belinda, two ahead of us," said Rhona.

Belinda responded, "What the fuck!"

The Hollywood couple were trying not to attract too much attention on this holiday, as they were both set to start filming after the holiday.

"It's *Mila Kunis* and *Ashton Kutcher* queuing in front of us for the lift," Belinda whispered with her hand cupped to avoid her voice being overheard, even though they were several metres away.

"Let us cut them up on the slope." She was confident, she could out ski the Hollywood couple. They were in the chair. Belinda turned to her friend and said, "Let's see if we can get a selfie instead."

Rhona looked at her. "Think I may have a secret weapon to get them to agree."

As the girls got off the lift, Hollywood stars were just about to go down the run but several other people had spotted them. Rhona then shouted something out, it was loud and lots of people turned towards her, including the Hollywood actress. Belinda thought it was something out of *Star Trek*.

"Was that Klingon?"

"No, it's Russian. I asked if she would do a selfie."

As the girls slid towards the actors, Ashton was asking what the girl had said. They were within two metres when Rhona spoke again, "Thank you, you are making these two British girl's holidays."

Mila spoke, "Your Russian is good."

"Just decided wanted to learn. Guess it was fate."

The girls knelt in front as Ashton took Belinda's phone and took the perfect selfie. "Thank you very much, that was very kind," said Rhona.

Rhona was a ruthless killer but it was her capability to be so charming that was so disarming.

Chapter 127

The weather was perfect, as was the skiing. After several nights out with Belinda, Rhona had decided Buffalo Bills Bar was the best option. With another few nights having hung around until closing at 2 PM, she had got to know the staff and the owner that was attracted to her. His flirting was significant. The four staff would allow her to achieve her goal in one hit and hopefully, if she timed it right, hide it so she and her family would be gone before anything was discovered.

The two guys were chatting with her, drinking beer at a table as the two girls finished up loading the dishwasher. Although she could not confirm the girls fitted her code, they certainly flirted and kissed different men on different nights, so appeared to be morally compromised. She would make an exception that she did not know for sure to get the four she needed. Her code was just a rough guide as *Captain Barbossa* explains to *Elizabeth Swann* In *Pirates of Caribbean Curse of the Black Pearl* movie that the right to "parley, it's just guidelines, not strict rules".

As the Wednesday night ended, "OK, I am done. I need my bed," said Belinda.

"Can I walk you then, darling, as part of our Canadian hospitality?"

"Thank you, Lucas. That is incredibly sweet but I am 60 seconds away."

Belinda gave him a kiss but it has been a lovely evening and Belinda left the bar and walked into the cold night; she looked up at the stary night, she knew Lucas fancied her but she was not as keen and they were going home in a few days. Logan locked the door behind her. Rhona watched as Logan slumped onto the table, knocking his bottle onto the floor.

Lucas looked shocked but as he got up to check on his boss, he found his legs went weak and fell onto the floor. Both girls came running, though Mary Jane and Charlotte were looking confused but alert, even if tired from a long shift. They had not drunk anything from their beers, they had been too busy. In one swift move, Rhona had managed to slit both girls' throats; they both held their necks trying to stop the blood.

With all four young Canadians dead, she adjusted the meat in the freezer and stuffed their bodies into it. Two nights before, as part of chatting her up, Logan had shown her everything and Rhona had hidden an icicle in the freezer. Rhona had pretended to go to the toilet to retrieve the weapon from the freezer as they were closing the door behind Belinda, leaving.

It took her 30 minutes to mop the floor so anyone looking in through the window, the next day, they would not see anything strange. Thursday, the bar was closed anyway and Rhona's party of seven was leaving early on Friday morning. Rhona had been able to use the hotel that had an office facility to print something off.

Chapter 128

Due To Unforseen Circumstances The Bar Is Shut For Rest Of The Season.

Rhona stuck this on the inside of the door, locked up before dropping keys in a nearby bin. Through several conversations, she knew about where they lived and after she had killed them, she took their keys and one by one got her souvenirs. Lizzy had a passport but Mary Jane only had a driving licence. Both the boys had passports. The keys she dumped in the trash. The four items for her collection were in her secret compartment in her case.

It had been a great holiday on all fronts. She was looking forward to giving the British police their next headache.

Chapter 129

As the 787 was gaining speed for take-off and Rhona was unwrapping a sweet for ear balancing purposes. She was sucking on the sweet caramel boiled confectionary as the four bodies in the freezer were being discovered in the cold food storage appliance. As the plane lifted off, Rhona was thinking of the physics of flight.

"So, Myles, you're smart. How does flight work?" she paused. "If you know the answer, I will give you this 100 Canadian dollar note I have left for you to change up."

"It is to do with the shape of the wing; as the plane speeds up, the air moves faster over the top of the wing in relation to the underside so that means the pressure is higher below the wing then above causing in lift," said the boy, smiling confidentially.

"Wow, impressive. Oh, you cheat." She grabbed his phone; he had not put it on airplane mode and was still getting internet from Vancouver airport. The alarm was raised by two extra staff that Rhona was not aware of that worked during the day for deliveries and when the food delivery driver could not get hold of anyone, both he and the two staff were concerned. The police broke the door down and within an hour, they had found the bodies stuffed behind the steaks.

The winter vacation location had increased its police force over the years, as the popularity had grown to more than just a ski location. With the increasing number of celebrity homes, they had also decided to be more vigilant.

To that aim, James Campbell had gone to see the main guy at Beverly Hills police station for advice about the police issues related with high concentration of celebrity residents. The chief of the Royal Canadian mountain police generally did not have such serious crime, he had delt with a killing when a man had pulled a gun at a robbery and unfortunately, the arresting officer had to shot the man but apart from that, it was drunken brawls or minor domestics.

This was a horrific multiple murder. As chief James Campbell looked at the wounds, he remembered. "Fuck, the Alps' slasher is in town."

He rang his superior in Vancouver and it trigged a double response, an extra 50 men were coming and an expert from the United States.

Chapter 130

The extra Mounties arrived. Professor Rothstein was looking closely at the pictures. "This is not the slasher, it is a copycat."

James Campbell looked at the expert. "How do you know this from these pictures of the victims?"

Samuel scratched his head.

"You see, the entry wound, it's by a left-handed person, not right-handed like the Alps killer."

James was impressed that he could tell that. "The Alps killer left semen behind on his victims and these had no such left behind product, this piece of information was never released about the crime scenes, which again makes me think we have a copycat."

The Celebrity Ski Resort Of Whistler Has Copy Cat Killer

Rhona had been home in England about four days when the story broke about a copycat killer in Canada.

She smiled at them, thinking it was a copycat, as she wrote in her diary the new development with her left hand before switching back to her right. She had been confident they would call on Rothstein to check on her work. Rhona was naturally right-handed but through training even her piano and guitar playing found it easy to swap hands.

Chapter 131

Since her holiday in Cyprus, Sharon was still desperate to continue with the Alps investigation despite other work load. Her boss had some news about the adoption thing.

Sharon had no time, as her holiday had been cut short by an emergency call from her boss.

"I have this case that is far more important and the media do not know and only the people on the boat and about three others know what I am going to tell you but you're to head straight back to the Mediterranean; there has been a murder on the president's boat."

The initial incident looked like some failed attempt by a disgruntled terrorist group but Sharon had worked it out, it was a domestic killing of a husband getting rid of his cheating spouse and trying to make it look like something else. So not politically motivated.

Sharon went into see her boss immediately after returning from the boat and being thanked for clearing up the mess without anyone, including the media, finding out.

Sharon enters the office. The French police chief pointed to the chair for her to sit down.

"I Spoke to my counterpart. Ms Boswell was embarrassed and did not want to be judged by you as a woman."

Before her boss could finish, Sharon jumped in, "In what way?"

The French police officer would have scolded any other officer for interrupting him but he had a soft spot for his talented detective.

"Rhona's father is in prison for killing her mum and as her only living relative, Lilly Boswell became her guardian but decided her career was more important and subsequently, put up her niece up for adoption but I understand, does still play an active role as her aunt to the girl."

Rhona's father being a killer just made more sense to her when the news broke about the copycat. Sharon was keen to know more.

Her work load was still massive and the season in the Alps had been incident free but the French authorities had wondered if it was because of their military presence.

What Sharon was able to do was have a video call with Samuel Rothstein. He explained she should get James Campbell's permission before he could give her anything other than the headlines and not discuss his conclusions. James had heard of the famous French detective. He was happy to discuss the case.

Sharon wondered if Ms Smith was in the Vancouver area at the time.

Chapter 132

Rhona decided the next order was Italians, Spanish, then Russians. It was the middle of February and into her second term of her first year but it was time to move things along to the next part of her strategy.

The Chester fiasco time for some changes but also accelerate the stakes and her king's gambit play. Rhona had used her "nowhere to go" strategy on Luca and his fiancée. Rhona had watched them several times in the bar and listened to their conversations, she understood as her Italian was excellent. It was the fifth night she had been on their sofa bed when she got them chatting about previous relationships. Their answers were perfect for her code.

Rhona turned up the music in the lounge as she could hear them having sex as the small one-bedroom flat was all one level. It was the garden flat of a big Victorian house that the developer had been able to convert into four rentable flats. Luca shouted from the bedroom he said, "You need to turn that down, the music, otherwise the neighbours will complain."

Rhona shouted back, "but I can hear Sofia ride you like a cowboy."

Luca started to laugh and it caused him to slip out. "Concentrate, darling," said Sofia and reached down and put him back in.

The two Italians were of slight build. She could hear them having sex and Sofia was on top. Rhona stabbed her in the back, missing her spine and penetrating her organ of life. She squealed out in agony. In a split second, as his girlfriend was squirting blood all over him, she took the second knife and slashed Luca's throat; she carefully removed her overalls and placed them in her bag. She then cut off a hand of each of them and picked up their passports from out of the draw.

She left the blood and two hands for the police to find. The hand thing significance would only become apparent later to the police. After two hours, she had both bodies perfectly wrapped in plastic and transported back to the lair, leaving the bedroom and lounge floors covered in blood. She wanted the police to know foul play for embassy staff but then they would get the other victims. It would create even more confusion, stretching their resources to the maximum. She knew from conversations with her aunt how thinly stretched the resources of the police were and she would add to it.

Chapter 133

The commissioner of the embassy had called the police. It was Monday morning, two of his staff had not arrived for work or answering their phones, so he was concerned as they had not followed the sick protocol. He was transferred to Paula Patel. "How can I help?" she asked.

The commissioner explained in his perfect English with a beautiful Italian accent. Almost Shakespearean as being from Verona. They quickly spoke and she got the address details of the two Italians, Luca Conti and Sofia Moretti, lived in Ealing. Two cars arrived, a police car and an unmarked vehicle in the quiet road. They parked just down from the address. The dark-haired lady in her blue suit knocked firmly on the wooden door twice but no answer.

The young police offer emerged from the garden. "Cannot see anything from the garden, mam."

Just as Paula was thinking what to do and typing on her phone, a red Ford Focus pulled up, a bearded man got out with slick hair. "Are you Frazer?" she inquired.

"Yes," said the letting agent and produced a set of keys with key ring number 5 for Hook Avenue, it is a ground-floor flat. The uniformed officer took the keys, opened the door with another officer to check if it was safe.

Paula was just about to enter when she heard the young police constable shout out, "Oh my god!"

When Paula entered the room. "OK, let us all get out of here."

Even though the curtains were closed and the room was dark and without the ceiling light on, it was still possible to see the room's horrific scene. There was a shaft of light from the crack in the curtains that was reflecting on the red, gooey floor.

"Thanks, Frazer," as the three police officers left the building.

"We will need these keys for a few hours and I need you not to tell anyone anything."

Paula made a quick call to the forensic team and the murder squad; the street was a hive of activity, with numerous police vehicles and the area near the house and people out walking their dog to walk on the other side, two young officers were given the job of directing residents. Signs had been placed closing off the road. The first bit of evidence was that embassy staff were not just missing but the victims of foul play.

After that Harry insisted, he wanted Raymond and Paula to coordinate because they had a killer and were concerned. They were about to get a bad surprise with all these missing embassy people and now two dead bodies that could indicate more to follow.

Chapter 134

Harry was looking stressed behind his desk when two officers entered his office.

"OK, Paula and Raymond, with the discovery of two members of the Italian embassy found murdered, it's clear to me we may have a connection with all the missing members of embassies and these two homicides, so I would like both of your departments to work together."

He stood up, using both hands leant on his desk. "OK, crack on. Let's see what we can find, dismissed."

The two officers scurried out of the office.

Well, the first thing we have are two survivors, I will get them in again for interview. Niomi was available the next day and unfortunately could not add anything to her statement. After numerous voice messages to Chester's voice mail, Raymond said he would go and check out his flat.

Having forced the lock, Raymond and a police constable were looking around the home. The police constable shouted from the kitchen. Washed mug on drainer and fridge were empty. The police constable joined Raymond, he was just going through the wardrobe. The draws appeared to be half empty and the bed was neatly made. Police constable looked at the senior detective.

"Looks like he left, sir."

Chapter 135

Paula in her smart suit may look the same as her murder squad colleague but by contrast, Raymond Forrester was brought up in a large middle-class family with two older sisters from Ilford, Essex. He had attended Ilford Grammar School and gone on to study forensic science at London Metropolitan University with its world class labs in this field of study.

Using modern technology was making it easier to prove suspects were guilty. One of Raymond's first jobs was using modern techniques on cold cases and with changes in the double jeopardy law in 2003 that now allowed someone to be retried for the same murder if new significant evidence was available with the improved forensics.

Raymond had been brought up with holidays to the Caribbean and the Far East and even Hawaii, very different to a caravan park of Paula's childhood. Their intellect and work ethic meant they got on well. They both loved 80s music and their careers and family, *level 42* and *Jimmy Sommerville* was played in the car when the two police officers travelling together.

Chapter 136

Over two years, she killed eighty-one people in London, taking her tally to 99 with the Alps and Canada. Each London kill was allocated a tag either through the ear of a head or wrapped around a finger; if she had destroyed the body, the heads or hands placed on the freezer shelf. The bodies wrapped in plastic and placed in another freezer.

If she used Simon's pickup, she could get rid of the 24 beheaded bodies in one trip in one night. She would dump the 24 bodies with no heads as they were all in her freezer with labels in their ears. All the bodies were from her random pickups or students associated with University College London, her embassy ones were for the future; all the embassy staff kills had heads still attached but no hands.

However, she was systematically melting down their bodies for space in the freezer as her last batch of kills would be different again and those bodies would be found again with a different calling card.

Chapter 137

It was two days in June and Simon was feeling a bit under the weather, so Rhona said, "Why don't you come round and let me look after you?"

Yet again, Rhona drugged him while she borrowed his pickup truck. She had dropped twenty-four bodies off at the site that had just recently installed a closed-circuit television camera. Yet again, in her disguise. She returned the pickup to the car park and fell asleep next to Simon after she had washed off all the make-up.

The back road, behind the abandoned building sites, was for ever been fly-tipped, the site was to be a new massive housing village development but delays due to infrastructure problems meant the road had become popular with fly-tippers as little traffic used the road. The only traffic was dog walkers, who used it as a quick way to get to the park. Several dog walkers, including Mr Davidson, had forced the council to have CCTV cameras installed.

It was a Sunday morning that badger, his black Labrador, with its white chest ran ahead and found the black bag. She began ripping into it as the contents of the bag were revealed. Mr Davidson knew instinctively to stop Badger from what she was doing. She had eaten two fingers off one hand before he had her back on the lead and stopped her. Badger barked as that was nice tasting meat.

He tied her to a lamppost as he made the call on the warm morning. The retired accountant got out his phone, which he hated. Both his wife and children had insisted he should have a way of communicating, in case he got into trouble on a walk. They called him a troglodyte because he hated technology. He was moaning about all the TV channels with sky Netflix and Amazon until his wife kept finding him shows he loved via one of those services.

This Sunday morning was up there with one of the strangest things in his 80 years. He got his phone out of his pocket, his daughter had loaded his phone with his favourite classical and opera music. He had been listening to *Katheryn Jenkins*, the blonde mezzo-soprano from neath south Wales singing *Hymn to the Fallen* when Badger was barking and pulling the contents out of the bag. The other things were in the warm sun, the frozen bodies were defrosting and beginning to ooze. The pungent smell of death hit him in the face, up his nostrils, causing the retired accountant to gag. He dialled 999 and was asked what service.

"Police, I have found a load of dead bodies," he said in a shaking voice.

The call handler immediately asked her supervisor to continue the call. She took over while her colleague called the police with the address. "Please stay calm and please wait for the police, someone will be with you in ten minutes, sir."

When the first police car arrived, an ambulance arrived behind them. Mr Davidson was sat on the dirty road cuddling his dog. In the slight breeze, he had positioned himself up in the wind. The two officers that were first on the scene were equally affected and one threw up the contents of his lunch. His colleague was not too sympathetic. "So, did you not enjoy that big mac then?" and chuckled at his junior's misfortune.

They walked over to Mr Davidson as the sick officer had a drink of water to wash away the bile taste from his mouth.

The police had managed to keep the find a secret for a month with the cooperation of Mr Dawson because all they could gather from the video capture was a hooded figure and black pickup truck.

Now, they had received another clue, they felt they could release the information to the news. The news channels were abuzz with the news that 24 headless corpses had been found in London. Billy, the beheader, by the tabloids was what was buzzing over the internet. 19 men and 5 women. All the victims appeared to have been sexually assaulted with semen in either vagina or anus. Rhona had used a sex toy on the bodies post mortem and syringed a correct amount of fluid to give the DNA match.

Chapter 138

Harry was in the conference room waiting for the senior and junior staff for the emergency meeting. All twenty-five staff sat waiting, the senior officer entered and walked past his officers to the front to address them. He looked stern faced. "This morning we finally had to release to the media the discovery of the bodies we made last month," he paused. "With the disappearance of two members from the Italian embassy, you are away, the teams from homicide and missing persons have been working together but after an extensive analysis of the news is interesting if not disturbing," Harry paused and asked Lilly to take over.

"Having checked with fingerprints and DNA we have and no embassy staff amongst victims, I am not surprised because at the crime scene in Italians, we found two hands that matched the blood of the victims. It's likely the killer for the beheaded victims is different because different killers traditionally collect different trophies."

Harry took over and pointed for his colleague to sit again. "We have a capture showing a hooded figure dropping the bag out of a black pickup and we are trying to establish the make and model but unfortunately, that and the number plate are not visible. Unfortunately, the company that recently installed the camera to stop fly-tippers has done a poor job and they will be getting a reprimand for their contract."

Chapter 139

"We have one new lead. This DVD was sent to me anonymously."

The big screen turned on as the officer pointed the remote control at it and pressed play. It was very dark but the scene showed a black pickup truck arrive at the front wooden gates of a building site. The number plate was not quite clear. A hooded figured got out of the truck and opened the gate and entered the site where there was footage from the other camera as they were motioned sensitive. Something that was about the size of a body was dropped into the trench. The electronic disc caught the hooded figure going to the site hut before the footage ended.

The lettering on the wooden gates said **Oakhill Developments Hampstead.** Raymond stood up. "How did we get this, sir?"

"An anonymous envelope. It was addressed to me by the metropolitan police with urgent in blue ink," said the burly police chief.

"Isn't that a bit strange?" asked Raymond.

Harry pointed to Ms Boswell again. "Not necessarily. Often serial killers switch between not wanting to be caught and wanting the notoriety of their achievements. It is part of their narcistic character."

We believe the pickup truck is the same one used in both pieces of footage.

"I think I can say the item being dropped into the trench was a body, so I believe we have two good lines of inquiry," he paused. "I want someone to go see Oakhill Developments and another to talk to experts on vehicles, see if we can narrow down the model of pickup, as I suspect there are a lot of black pickups in London."

The police did not release the information about the DVD or the camera capture footage, they just put it down to amazing police work, which made Rhona laugh when she saw Harry give an interview from the Hampstead site. This victim was related to the others and the next of kin had identified the body.

Chapter 140

July 2019

Rhona was watching the press conference on her phone as the girls were waiting to board their plane to Ibiza.

She had booked the apartment for the holiday two months before. "Hi darling, I have booked an apartment for Belinda, Rose and I; so, coming to San Antonio for a week as we planned and have some sand, sea, sun and sex."

Sophie began to laugh.

"Belinda, Rose and I are all single," Rhona wrote in her diary, even serial killers need holidays.

Rhona had made an Ibiza playlist and was absorbed in the music when Rose grabbed her arm to ask her a question. "Do you like this fragrance?"

Rhona leant in and smelt her neck. "Yes, that's lovely."

Her friends' approval was enough for her to buy the bottle of Dior. She turned the music back on perfect *Venga Boys*. *Whoa, we're going to Ibiza, woah back to the island.*

Rose was paying for her perfume and Belinda looked at her dancing friend. Rhona noticed her friend's confusion, so placed an ear pod in her ear and both girls smiled. "That's a perfect choice," said Belinda.

The girls had several drunken nights out partying in San Antonia when it dawned on Rhona how easy this would be to have a kill location. She would check out online the cost to buy something here. She often showed off her Spanish by ordering drinks.

It was the fifth night that the girls were being invited for dinner at Sophie's. "I would like you girls to come for dinner, Glen is cooking and I have stuff to tell you," said Sophie.

"OK, I am intrigued." Rhona spent all day sunbathing by their apartment pool, trying to think about what her northern friend was going to say and keep abreast on the news.

That was it. The police announced they had made an arrest of 34-year-old man in connection with their inquiries and could confirm the body that they dug up is related to the headless ones they had found.

Rhona grabbed the room key. Rose was asleep in the shade, her fair skin struggled.

"You OK, babe?" said Belinda, whose Italian heritage meant her skin copped with the sun and after a few days was like some sun kissed goddess as the incredible fit hockey player wore the skimpiest bikini.

Rhona gave her the thumbs up sign. "One minute, just need to check something."

Rhona entered the apartment and locked the door behind her. She opened her suitcase and revealed the hidden compartment and took out her diary and scribbled the events news. She returned the diary and returned to the pool. Belinda spoke, "You, OK?"

"Yes, just needed the loo," she lied. And applied some sun screen, things going to plan.

Chapter 141

Ricky Jones, chief executive of Oakhill Developments, was sat in the office. His PA entered. "There is a policeman here to see you, sir," said the small dark-haired woman.

"OK, show him in."

The detective thrust out his hand in front of him. "I am detective Raymond Forrester and I need to ask some questions about your development in Hampstead, also what vehicle do you drive?"

"I have a silver c-class that is parked outside but we have several small company logo signed vans that are used by staff to get materials," said the executive.

The detective wrote in his little black notebook. He looked back up towards Mr jones. "OK, so during the build, who had keys to the site?"

"That's easy, my permanent operations manager Bill Giddings that overseas all our projects and self-employed site managers for the day to day. I can give you Bill's number, he can tell you who we used for that project, but being such a high-profile one, it was either Johnny Philips or Simon brown. Or I can call him for you. And confirm."

"Hi Bill. Can you confirm who was the manager on the Hampstead job? Yes, great, thanks, talk later." Ricky hung up and scrolled through his phone. "Yes, it was Simon and this is his number," and handed the phone over and the detective scribbled the number into his notebook.

The detective arranged to meet him at the nearly finished apartment block. The block was in three phases, the third phase was where Rhona had dumped the body of Royston. When Simon Brown turned up in his black pickup, Raymond smiled; that was a load of work saved in trying to get an expert to analyse the DVD for the model, although it would be needed for trial.

As Simon got out of his vehicle, Raymond had already sent the picture to his colleague in the office that was going through the footage with an expert to work out the model.

Raymond immediately arrested Simon on the spot, much to his shock and read his rights. Simon kept repeating as the uniformed colleague put on handcuffs. "Murder. Murder. What the fuck!"

Raymond knew a quick DNA test would be enough to get the ball rolling.

Chapter 142

The next day, the police had quarantined the front garden area of the block of flats, an archaeologist was called in and using a Ground Penetrating Radar machine, they could see the skeleton in the concrete and a yellow JCB, the process like underpinning.

Before long, quite a few people were watching what was going on. The body was preserved by the plastic and they quickly identified it as the missing doctor. Inside, wrapped in plastic, was his phone and, although out of charge, was undamaged. All the major TV networks had cameras at the scene as the JCB began to dig.

"It has been confirmed," said the attractive reporter, "that a body of a male has been found."

Within the next 12 hours, the police were able to confirm that the new body was connected to the other victims and the next of kin had been informed as to the victim.

Chapter 143

Rhona had calculated the truck and phone was enough to arrest and probably charge and once they investigated, they would find all the other incriminating evidence. She stopped thinking about it, the three girls had arrived at Sophie's place. Glen answered the door for the ladies.

The girls were all dressed in t-shirts and shorts; it was quite a sultry evening in July, temperatures on the island rarely drop below 21. Tonight, there was a breeze making things more comfortable. Sophie's apartment was close to the sea and although it did not have sea views, you could hear the water and smell the salty air.

After they had finished the delicious risotto and the second bottle of wine, Sophie got up. "OK ladies," she held out her hand to reveal the lovely diamond ring.

"AHHHH," from the girls.

"What the fuck! You're only 24." Rose and Belinda were thinking she was up the duff.

"I am not pregnant, by the way."

Glen stood up. "We got engaged in secret last year because we know we love each other and never want anyone else and like to start a family young, which we know is a bit old-fashioned." He kissed Sophie. "So, we would both like all three of you to come. If you do not have a plus one, I have a few of my single rugby buddies coming," he said.

Sophie took over, "I have my sister, Daniella and two friends from school but if you are up for it, Rhona darling, I would like you to be my maid of honour for the hen and wedding." She continued, "Hen is in September in Leeds and wedding in October at Rise hall in Yorkshire."

Belinda said, "Oh cool, that was that TV series. How can you afford that?"

Sophie made the pray sign. "Thankfully, Glen's dad is helping my dad."

"Is that the one that they made the TV show of with *Sarah Beeny*?" asked Rose.

"Yes, totally," said Belinda.

"We are totally lucky that both our dads are putting the money up," said Sophie as the Humberside girl beamed.

Rhona was not sure about being a bridesmaid and wedding but a new experience and maybe new opportunities. "I am totally touched. You want me for this honour," said Rhona.

The girls all squealed and jumped around as Glen looked a bit embarrassed. Then opened another bottle of fizz. In the middle of this, Rhona's phone pinged to tell about some vital news she was tracking.

"Just need to check something."

She went onto the balcony that looked at the back of the apartment block to the pool area. The pool provided light in the otherwise dark back area of the apartment block. She grabbed her pods from her pocket and put them in her ears.

Chapter 144

It was the BBC and a press conference, yet again by the MP for Epping. The strong man had succumbed to emotions as his eyes looked red and cheeks were flushed.

"I have the sad news to inform you that the body that was recovered was that of my son and with the news, his death is related to the other bodies found. I have been to see the prime minister and she assured me extra funds will be released so this killer can be found and brought to justice as fast as possible."

There was a lot of mumbling from the audience. "David Jones, Daily Mail. What can you tell us about the arrest?"

"OK, the man we have arrested is helping us with inquires and we will keep you informed if he will be charged."

The footage finished, Rhona took out her EarPods and re-joined the celebrations; things were coming together.

Rose passed her a glass. "Cheers, everyone," as she smiled at her brilliance.

The rest of the holiday, the girls discussed the nitty-gritty of the hen night and the wedding.

The hen was going to be in Leeds. It was another possible kill location. Rhona did a good Yorkshire accent and in her research for one of personas, she was from Roundhay in Leeds's suburbs.

Sophie explained the hen would be the three of them here, her sister and two school friends, plus another girl that was working with her in Ibiza and her mum Elizabeth, Rosie Glens mum and her French friend could not make it but Renee was coming to the wedding. Her work colleague Coleen had gone home to have an operation. But will be at hen and wedding.

Belinda spoke, "Your mum!"

Glen answered, "That's to keep you girls out of trouble."

Everyone started to laugh. "Cheers again," said Rose.

That night, Rhona added Glen's name to the safe list in her diary.

Chapter 145

The junior officer had now powered up the phone they had found with the dead doctor.

The text messages were transcribed into documents.

The last message on the doctor's phone had been sent from 0899765589. The number was traced to Simon Brown. He was charged later that day. The Crime Prosecution service was happy; they had enough now, it was just about building more for the case. They were happy there was enough to charge.

Harry informed his counterpart in Paris that looks like they have caught the killer and DNA matches the semen they had found on the victims in the Alps, even if the kill method was different. Where The French chief called Sharon into his office.

"Take a seat. So, just got off the phone with Harry in London. He is emailing some files but looks like the person they have charged for the serial killings in London is a DNA match for the Alps slasher." He let his detective take that in. "Anyway, he is 34, called Simon Brown."

"No, but that can't be right. It must be Rhona. I am sure."

Chapter 146

The Saturday night Rhona had made her first kill. She had taken the doctor's keys and phone, prepared the doctor's flat, it was stripped of any evidence of a girlfriend. She had the doctor's phone; on the Sunday Rhona was staying over at Simon's, he had been to the gym. While he was in the shower, she sent the following text.

"Stay away from her or you may not see another day."

After sending the message, it pinged the doctor's phone before she then deleted it from Simon's sent box and his deleted messages. She placed the phone back on the table as he came out of the shower.

"What you doing with my phone?" he said with his towel wrapped around him.

"Just checking you are not cheating on me."

He laughed. "Are you joking? You are the most amazing thing to happen to me in my life."

"But you did sleep with me on the first date, so worried you're too easy and if I get a job abroad, then will you stay faithful?"

She began kissing him, so he would quickly forget the conversation. Sex is a great way to change the subject.

Chapter 147

Rhona was not sure about when the start of the case would be but guessed Simon would talk about the flat. At portcullis house, he had been at many times. Rhona knew a tall girl that looked like Rebecca Stephenson; even with glasses, different colour eyes and hair was asking for trouble, so it made sense to avoid the apartment block until it was done.

In the bottom draw of one of the chests was a black hoddie with Royston's blood placed there along with Simon's DNA after it had been on a boil washed.

She was right, the flat was investigated as his statement mentioned it was the location of the real killer. They quickly found the hoddie.

The young officer shouted out with his gloves, "Sir, think I have the hoddie," as he carefully handed the black garment to put in the plastic bag Raymond was holding.

"Good work. Let us keep looking."

Chapter 148

Emma was sat at a big glass table in their Kings Road offices with Swatches of material and wood samples, plus several drawings trying to work out the pitch for the client for the scheme for their new extension when her phone vibrated and *September, the earth wind and fire* song played as the dedicated phone ring for her daughter as it was the month she was born.

"Hi, darling. What do I owe the pleasure?"

"For my summer break, I *know* only live 5 minutes away but wondered if I could stay with you guys for summer in my old room, do walks in Richmond park and have a movie fest play chess, etc.?"

"That sounds great but you must have some degree work to do."

"A little bit but good to have some time off, going to see my friend from working in the Alps. You know, the northern girl I told you about, Sophie and Rose and Belinda are coming with me to see her in Ibiza in July but thought nice to be there for August and September. Maybe see if dad is ever going to get that Volkswagen finished."

There was a pause. "We would love that, darling," said Emma.

She had been shopping on the King's Road when she called. In their shop, she entered.

"Oh, darling, that was a surprise," said Emma. Paul came and gave his daughter a hug. It had been just over 5 years since Rhona had found out about her father.

"OK, mum and dad, I love you both very much but I am old enough now to meet my real father. I have lots of questions, particularly about my mum and why."

Emma took Rhona's hand and kissed her on the cheek. "Darling, we totally understand that this day would come but we warn you, it may be quiet upsetting," said the only mum Rhona had known.

Paul stood in the background and wiped a tear from his eye. He knew this was a significant day as it was the day Rhona looked beyond them as her family.

"One question, you have waited this long. Why now?" asked Paul?

"I now feel mature enough to come to terms with meeting him. It is a bit like the scheme they run of victims meeting the perpetrators, it is called restorative justice. I think I will maybe visit in the next 6 months, need to get myself psyched for it," said Rhona.

Chapter 149

She was enjoying her time with her parents and even managed a couple of random pickups and the letter arrived she was expecting.

Rhona opened the white envelope and read the contents.

You are cordially invited to the wedding of Sophie Rawlinson and Glen Cooper at 3 PM 7th October 2019, the Venue Rise Hall Manor house, grade 2 listed building in Beverley East riding, Yorkshire.

The Monday was the compromise to get to the venue. There are rooms available to guests on a first-come-first-serve, so the sooner you reply the better room you can get. All 31 rooms have been taken for the event. For those guests who do not know the area, this building was restored in the TV series *Beeny's Restoration Nightmare*. Rhona Smith plus one. Please RSVP as soon as possible to establish catering numbers.

Please ring the hotel directly or email below for reservation of your room.

077890-547-4567 or email risehall@weddingroom.com.

Rhona turned the lid on the bottle of whisky and poured out the contents onto the two ice cubes, causing the distinctive clink sound where the force of the falling liquid moves the ice against the cut glass. The last two years had been full for Rhona and a wedding maybe a pleasant distraction or even an opportunity.

The Hen the month before should be fun, plus she had exchanged details with two men that were in their last few weeks, even if not aware. Although she had only met him once, it was clear Sophie was totally in love with the young man she had dated since she was at school.

The personal trainer she had given ski lessons to, along with Sophie, was very attractive and charming and could see the appeal. If she was going to use the wedding as an opportunity, then she would need to scope out the venue beforehand but how? Then it dawned on her, she would go to Hull and see her friend and they could look at the venue together, interested in her plans as well as chief bridesmaid. It was part of her job to get rooms ready.

Chapter 150

Rhona agreed to be in Hull for a few days to see the venue and meet with her best friends.

Rhona would sleep on the sofa in the loft conversion that was a hobby room most of the time.

"We are meeting Chloe at my favourite breakfast café called Nibble, where her other friend Amy works."

They arrive at the coffee shop. The red-haired waitress came out, "Do you have a table?"

"Yes, number 55," the wooden spoon had written on it.

A blonde girl followed out. "Lorna, you have met my best friend Sophie before."

"I did not recognise you, sorry."

"This is my friend, Rhona. That is because I am lucky enough to work abroad."

The red-haired waitress looked at the girl. "Wow, a celebrity!" said the woman in her strong Hull accent.

"I will take my break now," said Amy to Lorna. "I guess you're Rhona," said Amy, having not heard the introductions before.

Sophie's phone pinged, Chloe was parking up and the message told her what she wanted.

The curly-haired girl approached the table without anyone noticing and then Sophie squealed when she spotted her friend.

After the introductions, Rhona spoke as a specialist at accents, "I thought you went to school with Amy and Sophie but you do not have a Hull accent."

The food arrived and Chloe began to explain, "I went to Leeds university for psychology and then got a job for a charity in the city." As they tucked into the food, Chloe spoke, "Got everything organised, girls, for our party night, even got a good deal on the rooms in *Premia Inn!*"

Chapter 151

The Hen Party, Leeds, Early September

The night out in Leeds had been a big success; the girls had all had a good time and Rhona managed to look like she had a full vodka and tonic in her hand when, in fact, it was just tonic with a slice of lime.

As she had hoped, three different men had hit on her and they all had her green cased phone number. Future victims, although they did not know it. The group was booked into several rooms in the Premier Inn in Leeds. Because it was Rhona's birthday, the night had been a double celebration.

Rhona's aunt arranged to meet her again, not just for her birthday gift. Rhona had got back from Leeds on the train to kings cross, missing the *Harry Potter* announcement that they do on 1 September. Although she had not read the books, she had seen the movies as she wanted what the fuss was about. Similarly, she was strangely attracted to the twilight saga.

Chapter 152

1 day after Rhona's 21st birthday, she wanted to meet her niece on her own.

"I guess you are spending some of your inheritance but it is meant to be for your future, not just holidays."

The 50 million pounds was more than enough for her plans but this was a fraction of what was in trust. She took a package out of her bag. "Here, my gorgeous girl."

It was a small box that had been skilfully wrapped as Rhona carefully opened it to be respectful of the careful nature of the wrapping and she might keep the paper to reuse. The purple lined jewellery gift box contained a beautiful white gold necklace chain with the word Rhona.

"Oh my god!" and grabbed her aunt to give her a big hug and kiss.

"Also, I have this." Lilly began to cry as she handed it to her.

The envelope was in her hand and scrutinised the strange seal. Lilly watched closely for Rhona's reactions as she read the letter. The handmade cream coloured envelope from Indian cotton. It was sealed with a red wax seal as used in historical times. It was a strange black creature symbol, almost like a dragon with a cross.

She cracked open the envelope and there was a small piece of folded paper with the same symbol in the corner embossed into the paper. The letter had a smell; Rhona took a deep breath through her nostrils. She was trying to place it. Her aunt picked up on Rhona smelling the fragrance. "It's Jo Malone, your mother's favourite perfume."

Rhona read aloud. "If you're reading this letter, then it is because something has happened and I cannot be with you but know this: I love you with all my heart and watching over you from where ever I am. I love you, my royal princess, Rhona."

"What does mum mean?" asked a confused-looking Rhona.

Her aunt answered, "Well, officially the Romanian royal family ended in 1946 but well, we descend from a different branch."

"Really, that is cool, is that how we ended up with the right to dig for oil."

"Yes, exactly!"

Rhona was feeling emotionally overwhelmed, so changed the subject as she tried to stop tears from coming.

"I have been meaning to ask you aunty many times what made you join the police, especially as you graduated with a first-class honours degree in psychology and could probably do anything?"

"Well, while I was studying, one student was murdered and three other students went missing and were never found again. I was interviewed as I knew two of them." She continued, "One was a girl that was in the same hall and the other was a boy that was supposed to meet me but never turned up. I became interested in the process of investigation."

"OK, I must tell you, I have a meeting with my father in prison in the next 6 months."

"Oh, OK darling, he is a sad, bitter man. Let me warn you," said Lilly.

Rhona looked across at her aunt, who was halfway through her cake. "You must have known I would want more answers."

It was strange, Rhona thought that her aunt was so put out, but maybe it was a twin thing. Rhona had finished her coffee and biscuit.

Her niece waved and gave her aunt a kiss on the cheek and left. Lily called over the waiter, "Can I have another coffee and the bill, please?"

The conversation made the 42 year blonde think about 22 years ago.

Chapter 153

Lilly loved her degree and enjoyed Loughborough, although she was not naturally the most outgoing person. Even members of the rugby team found her quiet but she was such an amazing player and physical specimen.

Andy worked in the student union bar. She remembered she had found him very attractive and he was equally tall, if a bit too skinny for her developed frame. He loved her for being so tall. It was probably the fifth time he had noticed her and the first time he had been fortunate to serve her and hand her the cold pint of larger.

He plucked up the courage to ask her out. They had walked in the woods on that third date and for what reason she could not explain she had throttled the life out of him while he was still post coital. She could still recall the beautiful sunny warm day, the light filtered by the canopy of the trees above as they walked deep into the woods to find a quiet spot to have sex. They were not doggers and did not want to be seen.

Even now, Lilly could not explain why, as Andy was thinking about what to do with the condom. She decided to take off her belt just as he was tying up the latex protective equipment and put it in his backpack, so when they came across a bin as dog walkers do with poo bags. He reached down and felt that Lilly's brown leather belt was around his neck and she was pulling from behind with all her strength.

He was desperately clawing at his neck but the skinny man was no match for the powerful rugby player. After she was sure he was dead, she carried him to a nearby river and dropped him in to wash away any DNA. The other three girls she just did not like and it was surprising how easy it was to get rid of their bodies. Those were the only people she had killed.

She read there was medication that they used in the criminally insane and she began taking the medication for bipolar disorder that also helps with psychotic tendencies; the medication took away the desire and she felt lucky she had been instinctively clever and ended up being a cold case.

Lilly felt her killing was like being an alcoholic, she had loved it and if one more, she would have been hooked again, but thank god the drugs she took killed her desires for that. To quote alcoholics, anonymous, she was 22 years clean.

Chapter 154
Wedding

Rise Hall

The wedding suite was full of excited women.

Sophie and her mum, Elizabeth; Rosie, her sister Dianella, Renee from France, Chloe and Amy, her friends from school; her colleague she worked with in Ibiza, Coleen. Amy was trying to attach one suspender to her left white stocking while Chloe was doing the other. The Basque was doing its job of maximising Sophie's figure, pushing up her small bosoms, they looked twice the size. The Northern Irish girl spoke, "Jesus' girl, when he gets you on his own later, it would not surprise me if you conceive tonight. You look fucking unbelieve."

Sophie blushed. "Stop it, Coleen."

All the other girls were nodding and Rhona, having dabbled both ways, was also thinking the same but she was playing being a girly girl. Belinda and Rose were waiting downstairs, there was already far too many women in the room as it was.

The white dress was stunning. Her mum helped her get into it as she raised up her hands. A blue garter and sparkly white shoes, almost Cinderella like, completed the look.

The girls took several pictures and the photographer Maggie had captured a lot, plus some video of her getting ready.

Chapter 155
Prosecution Begins

The Prosecutor was confident he was a master of his craft; he was tall and his clear diction allowed his voice to resonate through the magnificent room that smelt of history. Or whatever they used to clean the floor. As far as he was concerned, this was the best case he had been given in years. The high-profile nature of the case would not do the writing of his future memoirs any harm either.

Julian knew his colleague, Sarah, very well. They were in the same chambers and now found themselves on opposite sides. What had surprised him was that she had not been able to convince her defendant to take a plea of insanity, it was the only option, he thought, but they were now starting and he stood up to make his opening statement. Even with jury selection, he managed to bump the two he wanted off.

"As I stand here!" Julian slowly made his way towards the jury box of the twelve individuals that would decide Simon Brown's fate. "What I imagine goes through your mind is, surely you must be crazy to kill 25 people and butcher by beheading 24 of them, exhibits prosecution 1a and 1b, your honour."

The judge spoke, "The folders you have contain photos and details of all the exhibits for your consideration. For both the prosecution and defence."

It was not a question but at least five members of the jury found them self-nodding acknowledgment unconsciously. "Well, your job is being made easier despite what your instincts are telling you."

Julian was skilful at speaking and calculating how much time to leave before he continued like a royal Shakespearean actor, "The defendant had the right to plead innocent by way of insanity but has not chosen to do that, so it is not your job to decide if the defendant is crazy."

He knew he needed to pause again and looked down at his expensive black patent shoes. He had different shoes depending on the case, just one of Julian

Masters's idiosyncrasies. He wanted that part to sink in as he rubbed his chin and walked towards the defendant.

"Very simply from the evidence, the prosecution will present, we believe that you will have no doubt that this man." You could see Simon was getting angry and Sarah was having to ask the bailiff to restrain her client in the dock. Julian waited for Simon to regain his composure. "Like I was saying, no doubt that a reasonable person would agree, the facts prove his guilt; that is our case."

Again, the skilful barrister paused. "You will be shown several pieces of evidence and expert testimony to back this up."

He took his glass of water and again strode across the floor. "I urge you to listen carefully, as some of the evidence is complicated."

Julian always knew stating this was always risky because it could come across as arrogant but he knew the defence, they were mounting and his expert colleague had a couple of points that might just work. As the case was stating, a beautiful young woman was starting the happiest day of her life. Having got dressed just as Julian had finished his opening statement 221 miles south.

Chapter 156

The dress was perfect as Sophie, looking like a princess, appeared to float down stairs holding the arm of her father for support. Her bridesmaids, including Rhona, guiding the magnificent train behind her. The colour theme was purple, so the wedding room was covered with sashes and balloons of purple and ivory and matched perfectly the dresses of the girls. The smell of vanilla and roses filled the wedding room as the guests waited in the room and turned their heads as the music started and they saw the amazing looking bride float down to join them.

Glen stood nervously with his best man. The school friends had played rugby together at school and now, for an amateur club. Glen had been a personal trainer but had been promoted to manager of the successful gym, in part to his charismatic style with members. His best friend was a chef in a local restaurant. Although they both supported Hull city football, it was their choice of rugby league was their only difference of opinion.

Glen, a lifelong Hull Kingston Rovers' fan, whereas Glen's best man, Rob, was Hull. It was like the rivalry between Everton and Liverpool in the Mersey city or United and City in Manchester. In Hull, you were one or the other. Glen was tying his lace that he had noticed had come undone. He looked up and checked Rob had the rings, he didn't want *four weddings and a funeral* moment where the best man had forgotten the rings.

His best man gave him the thumbs up and opened his hand, revealing the two platinum bands. Glen began to smile as the music playing the unmistakable voice of Adel.

There's a fire starting in my heart, reaching a fever pitch, it bringing me out of the dark; finally, I can see you crystal clear go ahead and sell me out and I'll lay our ship bare, see how I'll leave with every piece of you.

As the romantic music played, it occurred to Rhona this was highly unlikely something she would ever experience but she would be immortal as the legend of Rhona Smith, so probably worth it.

Don't underestimate the things I do. There's a fire starting in my heart, reaching a fever pitch, bringing me out of the dark.

Rhona was impressed she was not a romantic person, but rolling in the deep was just the perfect song to walk down the aisle The lyrics were having the desired effect on the congregation.

After the vows and the book was signed, everybody headed outside in the early October that was still pleasantly warm.

The confetti was being thrown and Sophie turned around to throw the bouquet over her head. Rhona knew that being the tallest she had the best chance but a wife and kids was not her destiny, so she pushed behind in front of her, "Agh, what" as Belinda stumbled forward in her heels on the grass and caught the bouquet.

Rhona smile at her friend. "Maybe you meet someone today. Looks like a few good-looking men today." Rhona was thinking maybe she could add a few more names, as she had two follow-ups from the night out in Leeds already.

The reception was like Leeds, with Rhona pretending to drink and another name, surprisingly it was Coleen, no wonder she loved the underwear of Sophie but was yet to come out about she was not a gold star lesbian as she had been with two guys and technically had not been with a woman yet.

Chapter 157

"You will hear from several witnesses and I believe you will have no doubt as to the guilt of the defendant." Julian cleared his throat.

"I call Peter Davidson." The young bearded man looked 18, he was 29. "Can you explain to jury your role?"

The young man looked over to the jury. "I analyse video captured footage to double check that it's genuine and not been tampered with."

Julian put his hand up. "Great, we have two pieces of footage. Can you explain them to the jury?"

"Yes!" as he spoke, the footage was being played on the screen in the court. The footage showed the bodies being dumped at the fly-tipping site. "We are 99 per cent confident that this is genuine as this was taken directly from the security contractor's mainframe." Julian used his trick of turning to the jury and smiling. "We were also able to enhance the feed and get more information about the truck."

"Objection, your honour. Mr Davidson was not being asked about that."

Julian jumped in, "Just trying to save time, your honour."

"I will allow," said the judge.

Sarah was trying to not allow any sign of disappointment. "On the side, there is some damage," said Peter.

Julian pressed the play button again. "OK, Mr Davidson, this was the DVD we received anonymously from the site. How confident do you think this is?"

Peter again looked at the jury. "Not to confuse but you can do some technical computer work on video using algorithms that tests for inconsistency that often the human eye can't detect but the software, so we are 95per cent sure its genuine."

Julian decided to grandstand, " So 99 and 95 per cent that these are genuine."

"What we got from the video, we see a black truck with the same damage and the same hooded figure, use keys to open the gate before the second motion activated camera picks up on something being dropped in the trench. Lastly, the hooded person climbed down the trench, we believe to make sure whatever was in the trench is not found, the person heads to the hut," and 2 minutes later, the feed ended when the DVD was removed from the recorder.

"For the record, we submit these as prosecution 2a and 2b, your honour."

The judge looked across at the jury. "The DVDs will be available to watch in the room when you make your deliberations."

Again, many jury members nodded they understood.

"Thank you. That's all I need from this witness."

Judge asked, "Would you like to cross Ms Shearsmith?"

She looked at her notes. "Yes, your honour. How many black pickups are there in London?"

The young man looked up to think. "Over 500!"

Sarah was pleased with herself. "And it's not possible to tell what model!"

The young man stood his ground, "but the damage."

"Surely you agree working pickups often get damaged and could be many with the same damage. Thank you, Mr Davidson," as the female barrister sat down.

"Mr Davidson, it's fair to say we can all agree you have skilfully shown the court that someone drove the truck that was the same truck. But we cannot say who."

"Again, the witness was making a point. But has defendants' truck and site keys." Julian had watched the battle of words enfold and was confident the prosecution had won that point.

"I call my second witness, chief inspector Raymond Forrester."

The policeman being a good Christian man, swore on the bible to tell the truth. "Can you explain to the sequence of events that led you to the defendant?"

The policeman took a black book out of his suit jacket. "Well, as you saw in the video, the development site by Oakland developments, so I conducted an interview." As he spoke, the inspector referred to his notebook. "I met with Ricky Jones, the owner, who confirmed two people had keys for the site, Bill Giddings and the project manager."

"OK detective, in the exhibits prosecution 3 in folder are three pictures next to each other, the still from the video of the hooded figure, a picture of the defendant. And Bill Giddings."

Unfortunately, a jury member began to laugh and was incredibly embarrassed. It was clear the 25 stone bill Giddings could not have been the hooded figure.

"So having established the defendant was a possible, we arranged to meet at the sight and when the defendant turned up in a black pickup, we decided to arrest him and found his DNA was 99 per cent match, we then dug up and recovered another body that was dropped into the trench." Also, without a question, the detective continued.

"The death of that victim was different he was murdered by a knife wound to the chest."

Julian put his hand up. "One second detective, the wound to the victim is prosecution exhibit 4. We did not find the murder weapon but pathology establish it was a right-handed person."

Then Julian turned to look at the jury as he asked the perfect question, "What hand does the defendant use?"

"He is right-handed."

Julian went back to his desk. "Detective, so apart from the victim having been murdered by a right-handed man, what else is linked to the victim?"

"We found traces of the defendant's DNA on that body to what was discovered on that body."

"We submit the DNA analysis as exhibit 5, your honour. You also discovered a phone with the exhibit p 6 and transcript of last message received on it."

The detective nodded. "Can you please say yes or no for the benefit of the stenographer!" said the judge.

Again, before the barrister asked the question, the keen detective was in full flow.

"The threat linked back to the phone register by the defendant."

You could see on the jury's faces that Simon was done. "We then retained Mr brown in custody as we waited for forensics and search his flat. We did not find anything at the defendant's home but he claimed he had been set up by his girlfriend. We decided to give the defendant the benefit of doubt and to be the professional police force we are," as he beamed with pride, "we went immediately to apartment 5 Portcullis House."

Sarah knew what was coming but, "Before we go any further, I suggest we break for lunch," said the judge.

Chapter 158

The bailiff brought the various choices of lunch requests for the jurors. As they were being distributed, the ex-military man had asked everyone just to call him Stephens. "I think it would be good to take an early roll call."

Not surprised, the majority were already thinking guilty; it was 8 guilty, the other four still not convinced.

Stephens looked at a woman, she was not convinced yet. "I need to know why and what the defence has to say."

"How about you, as for some reason, Stephens thought, everyone should already be convinced?"

"I want to hear about this girlfriend first."

There was some mutters amongst themselves as they could not access their mobiles so had nothing to do. Although then a set of celebrity photographs were brought in the room to correctly identify. The members had worked individually, as instructed, on each set of photographs.

Chapter 159

"Can you explain what you found there at apartment 5 Portcullis House?"

"Bank statements that appear to show Mr brown had another account with numerous cash payments going into account and payments for bills for a utility in the defendant's name for the apartment. The electoral role showed no occupants, however, as if was trying to keep the apartment a secret."

The detective continued, "We were able to establish it was payments for rent owned by an offshore property company."

Julian now asked a question that he knew his colleague would object to. "Is it usual in your experience for builders to have so much cash?"

Sarah stood up from her table. "Objection. I believe the murder detective is not an expert on tax and fraud."

"Sustained," said the judge.

"Sorry, your honour, what else was found at the defendant's apartment?"

"The black hoddie we see in the video with the defendant's DNA and traces of who believe was the first victim the body from the trench."

"What do you think was the purpose of this other property?"

"Objection, pure speculation."

"Sustained."

"Could it be reasonable to assume this property was a kill room?" The policeman nodded.

Sarah shouted, "Your honour."

"Mr Masters, I had already ruled on this point; any more of your renowned antics and I will put you in contempt."

Julian covered his mouth so no one could see his smile.

"What about this girlfriend?"

"The defendant said her name was Rebecca Stephenson but the only one we could find was 6 years older living in the far east."

"I understand you have a video of her FaceTime interview," said Julian.

The video was played by the court.

Can I ask you, Ms Stephenson, have you ever met this man? The video showed the detective had emailed her the picture.

I have the email now; no, definitely not.

When was the last time you were in the UK, Ms Stephenson?

Not for five years.

Would you be able to prove that?

Yes, but I would need permission. Hopefully, with the contents of all the meetings I have attended, the minutes contain the attendees of those meetings.

Thank you, Ms Stephenson.

Two of the not guilty jurors were beginning to sway.

"So, exhibit p 7, the video we have seen and P8 shows the prove that the woman could not have been in UK."

The video was turned off. "What did the defendant say when you showed him a picture of the Honk Kong-based lady?"

The detective looked up towards the defendant "He said it was definitely her."

"What do you think happened?" asked the barrister.

"We interviewed some witnesses that confirmed that a lady fitting her description had visited the site a few times, so we worked on the theory that one of the victims was a missing person with my colleague Paula Patel. I am convinced we had identified her," she paused.

"Her name was Charlotte Rayburn and exhibit was a picture of the girl," who did look like Rhona and Rebecca Stephenson. "Exhibit p9 for prosecution." It was a bit of luck in Rhona finding her. "We think when the defendant found Ms Stephenson's social media account, he decided that was the missing girl he could use as his alibi, not knowing the lady was Hong Kong-based."

"For the doppelgänger debate, we set the jury a test and they do not know the result, it is to prove how easy it is for us to miss-identify people; as exhibit for the jury, we gave the jury a test and they don't realise the results of it yet."

The stenographer was working hard to keep up with this bit. "The jury were given a set of different celebrities where some sets had the correct names under them, others did not."

Julian approached the detective, then turned to the jury. "How good, detective, in your experience, do you think they did?"

"Well, as they are famous celebrities, I would expect a better performance than random stranger identification; hopefully, 40 per cent correct."

Julian looked at the jury. "Would it surprise you only 15 per cent correct."

The jury looked disappointed. "It's fine I did this test with my well-educated chambers colleagues and they only got 5 per cent, so shows how hard it is."

The jury began to smile again. But Sarah knew Julian had weaved his magic on the case.

Chapter 160

Exhibit 10 celebrity photos and jury results.

The group was as follows. Some of the pictures have the correct names under and some we have switched the names around.

Jessica Chastain and Dallas Bryce Howard, picture 1

Mila Kunis and Sarah Hyland, picture 2

Amy Adams and Isla Fisher, picture 3

Margot Robbie and Samarra Weaving, picture 4

Natalie Portman and Kera Nightly, picture 5

Katy perry, Zoe Deschanel and Emily Blunt, picture 6

The last picture has Emily Blunt with blonde hair against Sarah Paulson, picture 7

The jury were confused at the point Julian Masters was trying to do but Sarah knew it was to undermine some of the testimony of her witnesses to come.

"OK detective, thank you very much."

"Do you want to cross?"

"No, your honour."

"My last witness is Doctor Mary Argyle, an expert psychopathic behaviour at Broadmoor."

"Doctor, you had a chance to spend time with the patient and the jury may struggle with how, apparently, a person can suddenly become a killer."

"You have heard of the term natural born killers and there has been lots of writing on the subject that by our nature, we are all killers, which is why we can become soldiers but our upbringing and society teaches restraint, but sometime it takes some event to cause what we call a psychotic break."

The barrister nodded and looked at the jury. "We think he killed the man he saw as his rival, then in the same rage killed his girlfriend and that released the beast."

"What about the DVD thing?"

"It's not unusual for killers to switch between wanting to being captured and admitting to their crimes to then denying them."

"Do you want to cross?" asked the judge.

"Yes please. Although you're an expert because of psychopaths' nature, you cannot be 100 per cent sure either way, isn't that right, doctor?"

"That is true."

Finally, a point of victory for Sarah.

"That concludes the case for the prosecution." And Julian Masters closed his folder and winked at his colleague. He went over to her. "Nice last point."

Judge said, "We will end the day and the defence will commence tomorrow."

Chapter 161

For days, she had tried to explain the evidence was overwhelming; they had failed to find this woman, the one they had interviewed did fit the description but had established not left Hong Kong in 5 years.

"Your best chance is to plead not guilty by way of insanity and hope that at some point, the real killer is found."

Sarah was sitting across from her client; she doubted his chances, she knew her colleagues' tactics and had seen his psychiatric report, but she knew she had four-character witnesses could raise enough doubt. Simon Brown was adamant about his plea. Even her own psychiatrist said he showed no characteristics of a multiple killer but that was what made study serial killers so fascinating.

"Put me on the stand so I can tell the jury about lending her my truck and clearly on both occasions, she used it to do what she did," said Simon.

"Problem is, Mr Brown, its considered the worst thing you can do. It will allow my colleague to cross-examine you and with his skills, he will make you admit to doing it without realising it."

Chapter 162

The experienced defence barrister stood up, she was not confident. It was not the first time she had been to this famous court. Her colleague was formidable but he had everything, she had one weapon only and it was weak, he had destroyed her witnesses before she even had a chance.

Sarah Shearsmith stood up and looked at the jury. "Our defence is straightforward, my client did not do it, he was framed. As the police officer in charge stated, they had no clue as to the killer of the 25 headless bodies until the disc they received in the post showed a body; the proposition is that maybe my client felt guilty. Or more likely that a third party sent the disc, the unknown person we saw on the DVD, hiding their identity with the hoodie.

"My client's DNA was not on file so only after he was tested did they have a match. I will show with my witnesses there is enough reasonable doubt that my client cannot be proved guilty."

Even as Sarah was saying it, she was not convinced but was showing her best poker face to the jury.

Chapter 163

"I call my first witness, Mr Ricky Jones." He took the oath. "Mr Jones, can you explain to the jury who you are and your relationship?"

He looked directly at the barrister finding her attractive. "I own and managing director of Oakland developments, that is a luxury home contractor." He took a minute. "Simon brown is one of my most successful project managers and a good friend that I have known for several years."

"Can I ask how much money he earns?"

"Around 80k a year as a self-employed contractor."

"Defence exhibit one showing his earning; Mr Jones, it's been suggested that Simon maybe engaged in cash work elsewhere."

"Well, it's true, several builders do this but I think Simon has too much money, plus with weekly meeting with Bill Giddings and monthly updates with me, he would not have time."

"One last question: did you ever meet this girlfriend?"

"No, but he told me he was in love and was thinking of proposing."

Sarah knew she had not wanted that because she knew her colleague would twist it.

"Thank you. I am finished."

"Cross, Mr Masters?"

"Yes please, your honour. So, Mr Jones, you cannot say 100 per cent that the defendant had no way of fitting in side work."

"No, I can't."

"You mentioned the defendant said he was in love if ever there was a reason to kill it was a rival, yes. I guess."

"Your honour."

The judge spoke, "Members of the jury, you're to disregard the last statement."

She then called the carpenter and the bricklayer but all she could do was to use them for character witness because the idea of their being another lookalike made it look even more like a conspiracy theory.

She decided her psychiatric witness would only provide a chance for her opponent to cross, so hoped she had created enough doubt.

Chapter 164

"You have a simple choice, substantial weight of evidence or some complex conspiracy theory that is as farfetched as not landing on the moon. This is an example of Ockham's razor. For those that are not familiar with the term, it means when you face two opposing ideas, it's often the case that the simplest explanation is the right one."

Sarah would try to sum up and give her client a chance.

"We know from witnesses that the defendant was a good man and couldn't be sure that it was not someone that had borrowed Simon's truck. We know from the amount he earned, he had too much money to worry about cash work for this flat and no significant cash comes out of his bank accounts. He would have been busy meetings with his colleagues.

"Witnesses confirmed he adored his girlfriend;.the prosecution psychologist could not say 100 per cent that he was a killer. I think I have established enough doubt."

As Sarah has finished her summation, she couldn't look at the jury; she had done her best but even she thought he was guilty.

The judge did his best to give an impartial direction to the jury. "I must urge you to evaluate the case based on the evidence you have heard, not personal preconceptions."

The jury only took 30 minutes to deliver the crushing verdict for Simon Brown.

Chapter 165

November 2019

Rose would share her flat as a fellow first-year student. Belinda was happy, she had saved money that first year and had made friends from the first year to now houseshare with.

The student had chatted the girl up at the fresher's stall. As a second year now, she agreed to help at the stall with anyone that was interested in university radio. Rhona had a Sunday University Radio show where she interviewed key members of the university, from heads of departments in the various faculties to key students like the captain of the girls' hockey and football team. The show was a desert island disc type format; the guests would give her a choice of music to play and discuss favourite books and movies and for students, their career goals they had.

Her next victim, he was back at her flat; the boy from Manchester thought he was going to get laid by Belinda, something he had drunk too much. She bit his lip, ouch. "Why did you do that?" he questioned.

"Because it confuses your brain," said Belinda, except unfortunately for him, it was not the blue eyes of Belinda but the successful serial killer eyes of Rhona.

"I feel cold and wet." He shivered. She got out from under the sheet and they were both covered in blood. Rhona got up and was dripping from her legs and torso and the small razor-sharp blade was in her hand.

"Sorry, Mark, I am Rhona and you're dead."

She was going to use false names beyond Rebecca, as that name had done its job. She had sliced his femoral.

Still, no one was aware of this other flat, so she could still bring people here like she did with Royston. Now the case was done and Simon had taken the fall and was starting his sentence she could use this flat again.

She did not feel too upset for the Simon Brown; in about six or seven years, he would have a hell of a story that he would tell she had even given it a title.

I Dated a serial killer but survived!

Chapter 166

Her parents were back in the Alps and rebooked the last chalet. Skiing with their daughter was the best.

She took a day out for her parents, she faked injury the day before saying her knee was sore to visit her apartments. The last job of Francois Matter before he left for Australia was to find a replacement to manage the apartments for her. After several failed interviews, the answer was obvious: Juliet Blanc, that rented the space for her café restaurant, would do it in exchange for rent. It was the perfect solution for someone that would do a job but too busy to take an over curious interest.

With the problem of the previous season and Rhona going to whistler, this was the first chance Rebecca Stephenson would meet her manager. Rhona was going to try to fit in a visit to Sophie, although Sophie had just handed her notice that this was her last season as Coleen was correct, they were not sure if it was officially a record but they had sex so much they both had to stop with soreness.

Rhona arrived at the bottom of the run, her friend was sat at the café with a bottle of oringina for her friend. "How was the honeymoon? Already suspecting?" as she looked at her chest. "You do not have to answer you're pregnant!"

Sophie jumped into the air and squealed, "Yes!"

Rhona gave her friend a big hug and hoped to come up north later in to see her and Glen. She had some following up to do.

Chapter 167

It was February 2020, a new term at university. Time to push on with embassy kills. The skiing was good with her parents, plus she had used the garage in the apartments to hide two bodies.

The Spanish staff were outside the Indian restaurant, Kutir. The two young Spanish diplomatic staff assistants were talking in Spanish, moaning about their boss. From their accent, Rhona guessed them from the Catalonia Region. Rhona appeared to casually walk by; even though they had been so passionately involved in their conversation, they had not noticed she had been stood there all the time.

"If you hate it so much, why do not you quit?" She turned away as if the comment was not from her. The two Spaniards looked gob smacked.

"We cannot just work here now, the whole Brexit thing and we love being in London."

Rhona, being so much bigger, pulled the two of them together and put her arms around them in a three-way hug. They were desperate plus there was no reason to suspect this woman was not genuine. They got into the back of her car. She spoke as they headed to her spare flat, that was now available.

As they chatted in Spanish in the back of her car, she explained, "I have an importing business across Europe and I have a vacancy for Spanish speakers. That's why, I was there as someone told me that restaurant is popular with staff."

Both passengers spoke, "Si," it made sense.

They let her make them a coffee as she explained they could share the spare bed or use the sofa. Of course, they woke in the dark on a concrete floor like many before. The coffee time had given her a chance to talk to them about their personal life; Carlos was a player thinking his accent gave him an edge over British girls and the only way to describe Anna was a slut.

Chapter 168

The package arrive addressed to high commissioner of Spain. The stout man carefully opened the box as he sat behind his large oak desk in the grand room that was his office. His secretary was just about to ask him a question when she noticed her boss had gone pale. He then appeared not to be able to breath and collapsed to his side off his chair onto the floor. His secretary had not even seen the box on his desk, she had been too engrossed in work and now was concerned; her boss was having a heart attack.

She dialled the emergency services, who were there very quickly. The first paramedic was happy he was OK but told Isabella they would take him to be checked out. As he was talking, the other paramedic opened the box.

"Fuck me. Frank, look at this."

He looked like he was going to chuck up. "Jesus Christ," shouted frank as he took his mobile to ring the police number.

It was less than an hour since Raymond had got there to take the box away. The embassy located in the heart of Belgravia, what he did not expect was to find the two recently severed hands in Ziplock bags. It was a left and a right hand but DNA quickly revealed the hands were from different people and it did not take much detective reasoning from the new joint team that this was the hands of the two members of the Spanish diplomatic core.

Chapter 169

Harry was beside himself, he called a private meeting. In the room was Harry's secretary, Linda, taking notes, Paula Patel, Raymond Forrester and Lilly Boswell and Raymond Forrester.

"OK, this doesn't leave this room. We just put one serial killer away in October now looks like we have another," sighed the stressed-out senior police officer. Harry pointed to Lilly. "So, we have officially had another serial killer, we had two hands from Italian diplomats, again left and right, one from a woman and the same again. These are likely to be trophies."

Lilly looked at her notes. "We can assume any embassy staff could be at risk."

Harry took a deep breath. "I have already spoken to the home secretary and the foreign secretary this morning and they are informing all foreign embassies to tell their staff to be extra vigilant." Harry coughed. "Also, we have been given extra funds, so no limit on overtime or taking staff from other departments or even other forces."

"Wow!" Paula exclaimed, "that's unprecedented, surely."

"Yes, spoke to my grandfather and my father and neither recall having a crisis that gave such power, forces have coordinated before in manhunts but not like this." Harry took a slurp of his tea. "It's 10 AM now; by 4 PM, I would like a briefing as to a joint strategy plan you guys have come back with."

Harry was looking at his computer at holidays, he fancied Tuscany. The stress he and his wife would need to get away. The three officers burst through the door. Harry checked his phone and shut down the lid of his computer. "only 2:30. Have you got a strategy already?"

"No sir," responded Raymond, the other two officers could not maintain eye contact with Harry; they knew this was going to be a strange conversation.

Raymond cleared his throat as he leant across the desk towards his boss. "We have had a development; we followed a proper chain of custody on the box, recovered only myself and Rosy and David from forensics have had contact with the box. So, the box was totally clean apart from three samples."

"Sir, can I recommend you sit, sir?"

He did as he was told. "I guess you found the ambassadors and the paramedic's DNA and hopefully the perpetrator?"

Like a chorus, all three offices spoke, "We hope not, sir. The other DNA was yours!"

You could hear a pin drop as the information hit home.

"Harry was angry. For fuck's sake, we have someone that must have access to the department, I want you to get internal affairs involved."

Chapter 170

It was time, thought Rhona, to visiting her father.

Rhona was shown into the room, there were several tables with other prisoners sat at meeting their families. Rhona saw the man at the far table; she knew instinctively that it was her father, Gregor.

"How are you doing?" The middle-aged man burst into tears, she reached across the table and hugged her biological father. Rhona wanted to know everything about her father. She wanted to know how he had met her mother and why he had killed her. She had so many questions but she would visit him numerous times and understand if he was, were her killing was grounded in.

All his letters had been returned by Paul and Emma, saying not yet ready on them.

The uniformed guard stood nearby to the grey-haired man and was watching the crying man. "Hello dad. How you doing?"

The question was a so matter of fact it threw him off his response. "What are your adopted parents like and how is that bitch aunty of yours?"

"Lilly is lovely but if you are going to be abusive, then I am leaving now," and Rhona stood up so aggressively the plastic chair pushed back under the table and whacked Gregor on the knees with force.

"Owe, sorry, please do not go." He started to cry again and reached out with his hand.

Rhona took it. "OK, dad; let's ask each other one question, each taking it in turns, OK?"

Gregor took a sip of water out of the plastic cup. "OK, what are Paul and Emma like?"

"They are amazing, they have a successful house renovating business, so that has allowed them to spoil me and I have been lucky enough to have been privately educating and am now studying at one of the best universities in the world."

"OK, wow, that is a lot."

"Now my time, how did you and mum meet?"

"Well, I had just emigrated from Romania and my father was a chef, so we established a restaurant in Clapham on the strip that is called the pavement." Gregor rubbed his stubbly face with his left hand. "It overlooks the common and was very popular." He took another sip of water. "I began to have a bigger role as my father was getting sick."

"Is that my grandfather that loved chess?"

"Oh yes, my dad and I loved chess. He died of lung cancer at 52, unfortunately his love of cigars, with the stress of it, my mum was never the same and she did last to see you born, but not long after that, she had a heart attack."

He looked Rhona into her reddening eyes. "Do you remember her? You were only 14 months when she died. Having got over my father and mum was struggling, I was waitering when this stunning tall blond walked in and I told Anthony I would personally take her order."

Gregor was getting enthusiastic recalling this information. "I rushed out from behind the counter like a crazy man, wiping my hands on my apron and showed her to a table; thunderbolt, for me, love at first sight."

Gregor began to cry. Rhona reached over and began to hug her father. "I can still remember the day, it was raining and she ducked into the café to wait out of the rain. I handed the beautiful woman a menu. Can I get you a drink while you decide or just a drink?"

"I was going to just have a drink but the eggs benedict sat on soda bread has caught my attention," she said.

I then boasted to her. "By the way, the soda bread is homemade." I brought over her diet coke I decided to talk to her. "I have not seen you in my café before."

"No, I am waiting for my sister Lilly. We are meeting an estate agent to pick up keys on a flat we are renting in Grafton square, we are just moving into the area."

"OK, sorry," said the uniformed guard, "time's up."

"OK, same time next week and I will bring a chess set, will ask if we can have a double session."

The tall, black, slim guard unlocked the door turned. "Stay sitting, Gregor. I don't want trouble today."

At the same time, they were leaving the room, two visitors were being shown into the room to where two other prisoners had been sat at their tables.

Chapter 171

"Can I see the warden, please?"

Rhona was shown into the office. A small wiry bespectacled man was sitting behind his desk on his computer, looking stressed. He sat up. "What can I help you with, young lady?" feeling frustrated, he had enough on his plate.

"My name is Rhona Smith and I wondered if we could allow me to have longer sessions and a private room with my dad as I have not seen him for 20 years."

"Which prisoner is your father?" asked the warden.

"Gregor Niculescu," said the young woman.

You could see the cogs wearing in his head as it came to him. "Rhona, yes, he killed your mother. I am so sorry."

He explained it was against policy. "Do you have any problems I can help with as I am very smart?"

The warden looked perplexed at what the young woman was saying. Rhona leant across his desk with a stern faced. "If I can solve your problem, I get the extra time and a private room."

"What tells you I have problems?"

"I can see it on your face, the way you were looking at your computer as I walked in. Look, Mr Hayes, you have nothing to lose!"

"Well, I am looking at these accounts and need to find a way to save 5 per cent from the budget!"

"OK, give me ten minutes."

"Wow," Mr Hayes was impressed. "So just be changing the shift pattern you have reduced it. I would have never have worked that out," said the grateful warden.

"You could also try shopping around on food sources rather than excepting the current supplier deal, may find another 5 per cent there."

"OK, Ms Smith, deal is a deal; next weekend is double time. And a private room."

"Thing is, Mr Hays, I want to understand why he killed my mother and will only get that by getting to know him first."

Chapter 172

She was going to bring him a special cake laced with an undetectable poison that would induce a heart attack.

Rhona passed through security. "What is in the plastic container?"

"It's just a cake for my dad."

"Can I try some?" asked the guard.

"No, sorry." The Ikea box with its deadly package.

"It's great to see you again," as he kissed his daughter on the cheek.

"Tell me what you studying at university and what are your hobbies?"

"I am doing pharmacology because fascinated by drugs and medicines." Rhona looked away from him as she was lying. "My hobbies are skiing, chess," as she pulled out Gregor's father's chess set. "I bake with mum." And placed the Ikea container on the table. "And rebuild cars with dad, we have done three."

"Wow, that is a lot."

"Well, I have a ridiculously high IQ, so I need to do lots. I also collect comics," and wanted to say the next thing but stopped herself and bit her lip so hard she drew blood.

"Your mum was super intelligent also." Gregor had picked up on it. "You were going to say something?"

"No!" but looked to the ground and thought, yes, I kill people.

"Can you play and tell me more about the romance with my mum?"

"I loved your mum and I didn't kill her." Gregor began to cry.

"Guard, I need the toilet quickly, please." Rhona went to the toilet. She didn't know what to think about what her father had just said. She returned and knocked on the private room. The guard opened the door. Rhona looked across the room with horror.

"NO," she shouted as Gregor brought the cake to his mouth both the guard and her father looked perplexed, she was at the table in a blink of an eye. "Your nut allergy." Rhona removed the cake from his hand, "Did you have any?"

"No, that was my first piece. But I don't have an allergy."

"Sorry was thinking it's my adopted dad that does. Guard, can you get me some water?"

When the guard left the room. "OK, dad I was angry but I believe you now that you did not kill my mum. I am studying pharmacology degree and what I put in your cake would have caused a heart attack and be untraceable."

"Fucking hell, Rhona."

"Sorry, dad."

"I will try but it has been a while since I have played."

"It was a coincidence that your mum and I both originated from a small place in Romania called Bran near Brasov." Gregor looked away from his daughter and began to sob.

"I have a confession to make, I cheated on your mother with the nanny; it only happened once, it was a stupid drunken one-night thing. I am not making excuses but I do not think I deserve this as punishment."

Rhona thought for a moment, it was more than enough to end up on her table but this was her father so exceptions were made. "I was convinced she did not know. I told Lilly and she promised she would keep it a secret as Anne's heart would be broken as she loved me so much, anyway six months later Anne has disappeared and I am being arrested and they found me guilty for her murder."

"You need to know I am innocent. I loved your mum. I did not kill her. They never found her body. She was depressed and I think her sister helped her disappear as punishment."

"That sounds farfetched, dad."

He reached over and took his daughter's hand as he started to cry.

She believed him and felt it was now her task to use her phenomenal intelligence to work out how to get him out of prison to put her killings on hold while she worked out how to do this.

Rhona was still processing the incredible revelations. What happened to her mum if she was the killer, why not kill him if she was angry at cheating? Maybe she loved him too much to kill him and setting him up was the best thing to do but then she had to stay in hiding. Maybe she is secretly watching me, hence the letter.

Chapter 173

Having visited her father, she needed answers and hopefully her aunt could give her some. Lilly answered her phone. "What can I do for my Favourite Niece?"

"I am your only niece, silly," Rhona coughed. "I need to see you. It's not right I think my dad is innocent. You need to help me!" and Rhona began to cry.

"Look Rooney, I don't know what he has been saying but he is a liar and cheat!" said the policewoman.

The word cheat hit Rhona like a bullet. It was like pieces of a puzzle had fallen into place. "Can you meet me at **The Little Mediterranean Cafe** on the common tomorrow I want to know what you know about my mum's disappearance?"

Lilly took a big deep breath as she processed the information and what her niece thought she knew. "10.30 for brunch, I have got to go now, sorry work."

Lilly double checked, her phone was off, then sat at her desk with the piles of work; there was no connection with the latest victims, apart for they all worked in embassies and now four hands left as trophies. Embassy staff had kept going missing. She could not think about work what was she going to do. She picked up her phone and left a message. "Anna, my love, it's time!"

Rhona had asked her aunt to meet at this location as it was where her parents had met and wondered if he had told her the whole story, she was on her second cappuccino when the waiter finally asked her, "You look familiar. Do I know you?"

Rhona looked the man straight in the face. "Maybe I believe you know my aunt and used to know my mum and dad but I was only 2." Sipping her coffee, she continued, " I believe the last time you saw me, 19 years ago."

The waiter manager joined the dots. "Rhona Nicolaescu.!"

"Yes, although it's Smith, as I was adopted. Pleased to meet." Rhona stood up from her table to shake the middle-aged man's hand.

"So pleased to meet you, so sorry about what happened," as she wiped the tear from her eye and saw the blood.

It was nearly ten-thirty at **the little Mediterranean café** in Clapham was still technically owned by Gregor Nicolaescus but run by a friend of Lilly's after the murder trial. There were quite a few patrons enjoying brunch, Rhona had decided to take the small table for two at the back. Although Gregor was Romanian, he and his wife thought Mediterranean based menu would be the most popular way to go with predominantly Italian, some Greek meze and Spanish tapas. They had been right and it was one of the most popular cafes. Lilly had explained on the phone she would be too busy for breakfast.

"Have breakfast before I get there, as I will only have time for coffee myself."

Rhona looked through the nicely laid out men. "Can I get eggs benedict please with orange juice and skinny cappuccino?"

The waiter spoke, "You do not look like you need a skinny."

Rhona laughed. How men could not help flirt with attractive women? She found women were less obvious, although the reason men flirted more than women was yet to be agreed on by scientists.

"I do if I want to eat eggs, Benedict."

Rhona was still mopping up the last of egg yolk and hollandaise sauce with soda bread when the tall lady walked into the café. Rhona looked up from her finished plate, barring lifting the plate up and licking it clean like a dog; the breakfast had been demolished.

The tall lady was facing away from her at the till, ordering a coffee. She had long brunette hair coming out from under her baseball cap, her denims shoed how lovely the woman's legs were. It was when she turned around Rhona started to shake. "Aunty, what you did with your hair?"

The women came over to the table and Rhona stepped up, the lady put her arms around her began hugging and as their cheeks touched. "Why are you not wearing a channel but have Joe Malone? Sorry baby, I am Anna, your mum."

The woman squeezed her tightly. Rhona could almost not breath.

It was the first time Rhona really cried in her life. Seeing her father had caused some emotion but this was different; how and why was her mother that the world believed to be dead?

The killer was sobbing uncontrollably as the tall woman crouched over her to hug her, so Rhona's head was on her shoulder and Anna could feel the salty tears on her shoulders and neck and her cheeks. Maybe it had been a mistake to have left her but it was what she thought was the best for her little princess.

This would be very complicated to explain and longer than one quick meeting and need her daughter to stay quiet about this, not that anyone would believe her, apart from Gregor, who was desperate to get out of prison.

"But, but, how?" spluttered Rhona.

"There is a lot to explain and we need to sit down and have long talks," said Anna.

Rhona looked pale. "Please excuse me," and she rushed to the bathrooms. As Rhona held herself over the toilet under the fluorescent, the breakfast painfully retched out of her stomach. She was happy there was nothing more left to come up, she held her as she put her mouth under sink to wash the remaining vomit from her mouth and face.

She emerged from the bathroom to find the tall women had disappeared. In a cold panic, she ran out of the café looking both ways but the woman was nowhere to be seen. The Romanian waiter was calling her, "Lady, you haven't paid."

She took a deep breath to regain her composure. The last time she was this flustered was the escape of Chester. "Sorry, did you notice which way the woman went?" He looked at her blankly. "Sorry, I didn't. She gave me some cash and took a bottle of water."

Chapter 174

Rhona needed answers from her aunt and to see her father again.

News today, Boris Johnston was on the TV addressing the nation. Today a national lockdown was to start and only essential travel. "From this evening, I must give the British people a simple instruction—you must stay at home."

Rhona rang the governor, he confirmed she would not be allowed to visit because of this crisis.

Rhona's grand project would have to go on hold but right now all she could think about was finding out what had happened to her mum and using her big brain to get to the bottom of all of this. Her university lessons were difficult, all the practical stuff was suspended, only the research element via video conference.

She finally got through to her aunt. "Did you know?" said Rhona, her voice shaky.

There was a long pause. "I only just found out myself recently but thought it would be more detrimental for you to know," said the policewoman.

"Surely that was not your decision." Rhona hung up on her aunt; she was angry. *What the fuck gives her the right to keep such important information from me?* She needed a kill but wait, killing in this mindset was not the way to go. She got home and knew what to do and gave herself the very sedatives she used on her victims; it should let her sleep for a good few hours.

Lilly sat with her head in her hands; should she break lockdown rules, as this was not for a phone call and go tell her the truth or even some of it. She would sleep on it. She took the book out of her safe. Where did she start? There was so much to tell.